Shadow

A Novel

Rhonda Tibbs

For my faithful readers

Shadow

Daniel Coulter
Shadow, Oklahoma
Spring 1962

ONE

The third storm in eight days darkened the southern sky and thunder rattled the old iron bridge beneath his bare feet. Danny hovered above the rain-swollen river on the outside rail and peered up at the threatening clouds. The storm was almost upon him and he had to make a decision.

"Come on, Danny Boy! Don't chicken out now," his cousin Elliot called from below.

Danny ignored the goading. He had been building his courage toward this moment over the last week and wasn't stopping now.

Seven days ago he got the notion to jump from the bridge to the water and developed a plan of action, first climbing over the rail and standing on the outside edge of the bridge facing in toward the road then, with his back to the river and holding on, he closed his eyes and counted to twenty-five. For three days straight, he repeated this step until his knees stopped shaking. On days four and five, he once again climbed over the rail, but this time turned and faced outward with his hands gripping the rail behind his back then closed his eyes and counted again. On day six, he stood on the outside edge without holding on until he managed to stay five full minutes, then climbed back over the rail to the road and repeated this routine ten times while the other kids swam below. Today was day seven and the jump would be the coup de grâce.

The distance from the side of the bridge to the river was around twenty feet. The Kiamichi River was deeper here than mostly anywhere in the county, especially this year with the extra rain they were having.

Convinced he could make the leap unharmed, he lifted his arms and the warm wind slid over his body.

"Let go," he whispered.

Springing forward, he fell through the air for only moments before plunging into the cool water. He kicked hard and popped up a little down river. There were several young bystanders scattered around the river bank and bridge. When he surfaced, some of the kids yelled and applauded, but his sister Denise wore a familiar look on her face and he knew she would spare no time in informing their mother of his violation of the rules.

He climbed up the river bank, wondering if he had time to jump again as thunder rumbled louder. While the other kids scattered toward their respective homes, he tossed on his T-shirt, slipped on his battered Keds, snatched up his beloved sketchbook then hurried up the path to the blacktop. He was small for eleven, but his legs were strong and carried him swiftly over the bridge as lightening snaked vertically across the sky.

"One one-thousand, two one-thousand..." he counted off.

Thunder rolled across the pastures and bounced off the mountain ridge that bordered the back of his family's fifteen-hundred acre ranch. Home was a mile and a half from the bridge if one used the roads, half that distance if you cut across the hay field. Danny passed the long gravel road leading to home, angled to the right, scrambled down the embankment of the blacktop, and jumped the split-rail fence.

Having been duly informed of his violation of the rules by Denise, their mother waited on the wraparound porch of their two-story farmhouse with her hands on her hips, directing her most ferocious scowl his way. She cupped her hands in front of her mouth and called to him just as lightening struck the ground. Danny jumped and lost his grip on the sketchbook and the loose drawings scattered in a whirlwind. He turned and chased them, catching all but two. He took the time to carefully place them back into the sketchbook before resuming his trek toward home.

There seemed to be no preliminary drops of rain. The dark clouds opened up and started dumping water on the earth. He tucked the sketchbook under his shirt in an attempt to protect his current collection of work. Instantly, little muddy rivers flowed across the already saturated ground. He angled left and was within a few yards of the house when he spotted his grandmother's old hound standing in a little gully. The water was already up to her belly, yet Old Gal just stood there squinting in the rain. Danny turned back for the dog.

His mother threw her arms up in disbelief. "Daniel! Come here now!"

Mud sucked the shoes from his feet, but he didn't stop until he reached the fat old dog. He pulled her along by the collar through the pounding rain, finally reaching the porch in the worst of the storm.

The dog followed him onto the porch then slipped away to safety under one of the rockers. Danny's mother grabbed him by the shoulders and gave him a good shake. She was a strong woman and shaking his undersized body was no problem.

"Ow, Mama!"

"Denise said you jumped off that bridge," she said.

He looked up, trying to hide the pride he felt in his accomplishment. "Yes, ma'am."

She shook her head and nudged him toward the front door, giving him a little swat on the butt. "I swear that river will be the death of you yet."

She had been singing this song as far back as he could remember. Nearly twelve years ago, she stood in the middle of the river and came within minutes of delivering him right there in the smooth current, weeks ahead of schedule. Always a believer in 'signs,' his usually practical mother feared the river would someday claim him.

The gloomy prophecy didn't frighten Danny. He would be twelve in a few months and had been swimming in that river for years with no incidents. The river felt like a second home. The quiet, grassy bank under the bridge was his favorite place to escape all the commotion at home and explore his passion for drawing uninterrupted.

"Get upstairs and take a bath," his mother said.

There were three bedrooms on the second floor. His sister Denise had a private room at the top of the stairs. His older brothers, Dwight and Darren, shared the bedroom facing the front of the house. Danny shared the back bedroom with David, the youngest of his siblings.

His parents' bedroom was on the first floor and they had a private bath. All five children shared the upstairs bath. Now that they were getting older, use of the single bath sometimes led to arguments, but this afternoon the bathroom was all his. After bathing, he dressed in clean clothes then spread his damp drawings on the floor of his bedroom to dry.

At ten minutes after five, Danny took a seat on the top step of the front porch and watched the road for his father's truck with growing dread. Old Gal waddled over, dropped next to his hip with a big sigh, and promptly began to snore. Danny knew no such peace. His immediate future wasn't looking too bright.

His father ran the post office in Shadow and closed the doors at five every afternoon before driving the seven miles to home. As long as there was no slow-moving farm equipment on the road, his father arrived at their front door by five-fifteen, give or take a minute.

At five-fourteen, his father brought his truck to a halt in front of the house. He opened the truck door, eyed Danny, and sighed wearily. "What did you do now?"

His father came by this expectation from experience. Of all his siblings, Danny was the one who climbed the highest trees, jumped from the hayloft using a sheet for a parachute, tied a rope to a tree on the ridge and rappelled down the steepest cliff. He rode the fastest horses and walked the top rail of the corral when the orneriest bull was feet away pawing the ground and warning him to back off.

Last summer, after reading the book Tom Sawyer, he and his brother Darren built a raft with the notion of having an adventure downriver. When Darren assessed the finished product as questionable and backed out, Danny stubbornly jumped on, floating downstream until the raft broke apart and he had to swim to shore then hike five miles back home.

Confessing today's offense was self-destructive, but Danny looked directly at his father and answered his question. "I jumped off the bridge."

His father's eyebrows shot up in surprise. "You did what?"

"I jumped off Purser's Bridge."

His father whistled, long and slow. Typically, his father was a calm man who used words sparingly. The whistle spoke for him. They had been here before.

Although his brothers took risks, Danny knew he stood out. He didn't really believe he was reckless. He had a yearning to push himself, to ride a good horse like the wind or shimmy up to the highest branch of the tallest tree, and jump off the bridge to feel the drop and plunge into the water from that height.

When the screen door slammed behind his father, Danny began to fidget. He still had at least a half-hour before they took a walk behind the barn.

Unless it was an earthshaking matter, nothing interfered with his father's routine. For his first thirty minutes at home, interruptions were not permitted. His father would change out of his work clothes into a worn shirt and denim jeans then sit at the kitchen table with a cup of coffee and the newspaper, reading it front to back before tackling the problems of his brood of five children.

For Danny, the waiting was almost worse than the whipping.

Danny followed his father out the back door for the hike to the barn, which sat a good distance downhill from the house. Behind the barn, a wide creek meandered through his father's section of the ranch, winding for half a mile to the blacktop where it passed under single-lane bridge, and eventually fed into the river.

Near the barn, a wooden bridge over the creek led to a rough dirt road that ran up into the forested hills to one of the highest points in the county, a place Danny loved almost as much as the river. Right now, he tried to imagine sitting up there among the trees instead of on this march to certain pain, but that didn't work.

Lost in their individual concerns, neither of them spoke. Some of the horses in the pasture looked up in idle concern as Danny and his father rounded the end of the barn.

In hopes of getting to the point quickly, Danny bent forward, placing his hands on his knees. A veteran of these events, he knew the drill. His responsibility was to be ready when his father got around to striking him with a well-worn strap. Waiting for the first smack of leather was always the worst, and his father liked to draw the tension to its maximum height.

He looked over his shoulder and found his father studying the rushing water in the creek. The passive expression offered no hint that he was about to raise a hand against one of his four sons. Finally, his father turned and the serene look melded into grim lines.

"How many licks do you think you've earned?" his father asked.

"I don't know, Daddy." Danny sighed. "Please, just do it."

His father stepped closer, the strap dangling from his hand. "How many times have we told you not to jump off that bridge?"

Danny tensed, "About a hundred."

"Then that's how many licks I should give you, don't you think?"

"No, sir. I think you'll probably want to leave something on my bones for next time."

The strap whistled through the air and struck him so hard Danny stumbled forward upon contact.

"Tell me there won't be a next time," his father said.

Danny couldn't respond. The blow had driven the air from his lungs. He sucked in another breath as the strap whistled again. This time he braced himself for the impact. This blow overlapped the previous spot and he gasped.

"I'm waiting," his father said.

"There won't be a next time," he managed to say.

"Good."

Danny groaned when leather smacked his bottom again. Tears filled his eyes and his knees threatened to give out.

"Look me in the eye and tell me what I want to hear," his father said.

Danny looked over his shoulder, trying to keep his voice steady. "I promise to obey the rules."

"Then I guess we're done with this episode."

Danny straightened his back and willed his trembling legs to hold him upright.

His father patted his shoulder. "You know having to do this hurts me, don't you?"

Right then, his father's attack of conscience seemed irrelevant, but Danny didn't wish to test his father's patience, so he nodded his head.

His father reached out and gently wiped a tear from Danny's face with the pad of his thumb. "I truly wish you'd learn to tone it down a bit. You have to stop giving your mama these jolts to the heart."

Danny could have explained about how careful he was with the jump, but didn't want to appear unrepentant and risk a new whipping.

His father folded the strap in two and nodded toward home. "Go on."

At the top of the hill, he looked back to see if his father was following, but found him staring at the creek again, as if the answer to some troubling problem lay in the rolling water.

The screen door slammed behind him and he wandered from the back of the house to the living room where his brothers, fifteen-year-old Dwight, twelve-year-old Darren, and seven-year-old David, were watching television.

He eased down onto the couch next to Darren. From his birthday in late July until Darren's in September, they were the same age. However, no one would ever mistake them for twins. Like, Dwight, Darren was tall and showing promise of the strong Coulter physique. Of course there were other differences between Danny and his siblings. His older brothers participated in the local rodeo and all of his siblings belonged to the local 4-H club. Danny had little interest in either activity, which led his parents to fear he was a bit of a lazybones. Danny figured he had all the contact he needed with animals right there on the ranch. Any spare time he had was devoted to his love of art or an occasional book. The only apparent commonalities he and his older brothers shared were dark brown eyes and hair.

Darren glanced at him then right back to an episode of Mr. Ed on the television.

"How many licks this time?" Darren asked.

Danny held up three fingers.

Darren shook his head. "It's a wonder you have any butt left."

Danny leaned back against the softness of the worn couch and watched TV for a minute then grunted.

"A talking horse," he said. "What a stupid show."

Fifteen-year-old Dwight, shot him an irritated look. "Leave if you don't like it."

Since entering puberty, the once amiable Dwight had morphed into a full-time jerk and seemed contemptuous of anyone except his friends. Despite the disparity in their age and size, Danny normally loved to spar with this particular brother, but the whipping had taken that from him for the moment. Instead, he drifted into the kitchen to see what his mother was preparing for supper.

His sister Denise, the informer, stood near the sink mixing a pitcher of orange Kool-Aid. Like him, Denise was fine-boned and petite, but in her case the reason was thought to be strictly genetic, since she apparently took her DNA directly from tiny Grandma Coulter, instead of their parents' stouter lineage; while his small size was always believed to be due with his premature birth.

Despite her pint-sized body, Denise was a feisty, tomboyish girl who held her own in a house full of brothers.

Their mother called Darren, Danny, and Denise her bing-bang-booms, referring to their tight birth order. Darren came first in 1949, Danny ten months later in 1950, and Denise followed within thirteen months in 1951.

His mother added pieces of floured chicken to hot grease in a cast-iron skillet and let loose with a favorite hymn. Though she couldn't carry a tune, Caroline Coulter always sang with enthusiasm. Denise looked at Danny and rolled her eyes.

Danny grinned and swiped a slice of cucumber off the cutting board.

"Stop it. Those are for supper," Denise said with authority.

His mother turned, her joyful song abruptly cut off. Her expression shifted to worry when her gaze fell on him. Danny hated these moments. Due to the fact that his body refused to grow at the same rate as his older brothers, his mother seemed to expect great illness to present itself at any moment. When she looked at him the way she was doing right now, all squinty eyed with her forehead wrinkled in concern, all she seemed to see was weakness. She left the stove and came at him.

"You're awfully flushed." She wiped her hands on a dishtowel and pressed a hand to his forehead, evidently forgetting the fact that his father had just given him three licks which might just account for his face being red.

He backed away from her touch. "I'm fine, Mama. Do I have time to take Old Gal back to Grandma's before supper?"

His mother returned to her frying pan. "As long as you come right back," she said.

Danny bounced down the front steps of his parents' house and whistled for Old Gal to follow him. His grandparents' house was nearly one-quarter mile down the gravel road.

To date, five generations of Coulters had lived on this ranch. Danny's great-great-grandfather, an immigrant Scotsman who worked as a trapper and soldier, settled the bit of land where Danny's grandparents' house now stood back in the late 1880's. White women were scarce in the territory at the time and he married a Choctaw woman. Through the years, the Coulters had grown their ranch to the 1,500-acre spread it was today.

Danny's grandfather inherited the land from his parents and managed to hang on to the property through the Great Depression and Dust Bowl years that devastated so many others, sometimes even hauling water from the river to keep things going.

Danny's father, Cecil, was the second of three sons. Cecil's older brother, Robert, married and, like Cecil, settled down on the same plot of land as their parents. The third son, Hal, was what everyone called a "change of life baby," coming along twenty years after Cecil. Throughout high school, Hal's wild ways of drag racing on blacktop roads, drinking, and carrying on with girls were notorious. Three years ago, Hal finished high school and joined the Army. On the day he boarded the bus for basic training, Hal mailed a letter to his parents saying he was through with their Bible-thumping, tee-totaling, work, work, work lifestyle. Everyone prayed the Army could work miracles with the wayward Hal and he would come back to them a changed man.

Danny ambled along, thinking of the current drawing he was working on. A week ago, he discovered a book in the school library with a lithograph of Mark Twain straddling Halley's Comet shooting through the night like a rocket. School would be over in a week and he needed to finish the drawing so he could return the book.

He found Grandma Coulter sitting on the front porch with her worn Bible open on her lap. She removed her glasses and smiled as she spotted Old Gal following him up the stone walk. Old Gal climbed the porch steps with considerable effort, waddled over to Grandma Coulter, gave her knee a lick then plopped down on the porch completely exhausted from her efforts.

"I wondered where she was," Grandma said patting the old dog's head. "Thank you for bringing her home, Danny."

He sat next to her in his grandfather's wooden rocker and cringed. One spot where the strap had landed on the back of his thigh felt like it was on fire. He kicked back and the old wooden rocker creaked.

Grandma looked across the wide expanse of property and sighed. "This land God made is so beautiful, especially after a good rain."

Danny had to agree. The property stretched before them to the blacktop for a little over half a mile with most of the fifteen-hundred-acres of pastureland running south and a little east of the family homes, corrals, barns, and outbuildings. The late-day sun shining down on the plane infused a golden hue to the rolling terrain dotted with ponds and an occasional tree or two. Even the nearby cluster of cattle and small goat herd seemed to glimmer in the ethereal light.

He and his grandmother rocked together, admiring the view as the sound of the evening news drifted out the open window of his grandparents' living room. His grandfather swore loudly at the television and Danny smiled.

Grandma, on the other hand, shook her head in disgust. "He's in there watching that stupid box again," she said. "I keep telling him that thing is a waste of time."

His father's whistle rolled across the ground, calling him home. Danny rose without hesitation. He bent to kiss his grandmother's soft cheek and noted that she always smelled like roses.

"I'll see you tomorrow, Grandma."

"Wait a minute, Danny." She went inside and returned with a quart jar of homemade bread and butter pickles. "Stop by Uncle Robert's and give him this for me."

Grandpa Coulter still oversaw the ranch, but was handing Danny's Uncle Robert more and more responsibility. In addition to the cattle, there were horses, numerous goats, two mules, working dogs, and chickens to be cared for. Along with a full-time ranch hand and Uncle Robert's son Elliot, Danny and his older brothers worked every day and their father helped on weekends.

Uncle Robert's wife, Violet, was a court reporter at the county courthouse and they managed to keep their brood of children to three. With their smaller family and Aunt Violet's added income, they could afford a more expensive lifestyle. Their home was nicer, as were their car and clothes. Despite their financial advantages, Danny noticed they seemed less content than his own family.

Uncle Robert's house sat almost dead center between Danny's grandparents' home and his own. His father had already notified him to come home, so he ran to deliver the pickles and get home before more trouble came his way.

He knocked on the front door of Uncle Robert's house and waited impatiently. Finally, his cousin Elliot appeared behind the screen door. Elliot was

Uncle Robert and Aunt Violet's only son and the baby in his family. He was one month younger than Danny, and, in the opinion of most, three times as dumb. Elliot, on the other hand, was under the impression he was a cut above nearly everyone in the county, especially his cousins. Danny's mother commented more than once that the arrogance stemmed from Aunt Violet's side of the family. No one disagreed.

Elliot sneered at him through the screen door. "Get your licks yet?"

Danny opened the door and shoved the jar of pickles at him. "Grandma said to give these to your dad."

Elliot snorted. "Doesn't she know they've got these in the store now?"

"Your dad asked for them."

Elliot shook his head. "You all have to eat this homemade stuff, not us."

Danny's father's whistle cut through the air for a second time, shorter and with a shrill edge. When his father whistled like that, it was a last warning and none of Cecil Coulter's children dared test his patience twice in one day.

Elliot grinned widely. "Better hurry before he gets the strap again."

Danny flipped Elliott the bird then whistled loudly in response to his father as he ran for home.

TWO

Danny found a seat near the back of the school bus where he pulled out a favorite comic book to entertain himself with on the ride home. He was studying the drawings, lost in thought, when he realized the kids around him were in an excited state. Looking up, he saw the Adams girls exiting the front of the bus, but everyone's attention was focused out the windows to his right where old George Beckett stood in a clump of rose bushes without so much as a sock on. His thin body gleamed white in the afternoon sun. Though completely alone, George was gesturing and talking loudly.

Danny gathered his things and ran to the front of the bus before they started moving again.

Seeing his approach in her mirror, the bus driver shook her head. "No, no, no. Your mother will give me a fit if I let you off this bus again."

Several times throughout the school year, she had allowed him to get off the bus to help the old man. The last time, his mother had cornered her after church, telling her in no uncertain terms to keep him on the bus for home. His mother had also explained to Danny if he saw a problem with George, he was to stay on the bus and tell her once he got home, she would then see to Mr. Beckett's needs. This of course was an excellent plan, but Danny couldn't stand all the kids laughing at the naked old man.

"Please, Mrs. Dixon, you know Mr. Beckett doesn't have anybody."

They argued another hundred feet. Finally, the driver sighed loudly and stopped the bus. "Fine, since this is the last week of school and all."

Danny walked back to where old George still stood among the roses. He dropped his books on the porch then approached George quietly, careful not to startle him.

"Come inside, Mr. Beckett," he said, laying his hand gently on George's arm.

George patted him on the head and smiled. "I'll be with you just as soon as I'm done helping Josie with these flowers."

Danny took his hand. "Josie wants you to come inside with me."

He managed to get George inside, found some clothes, and helped the old man dress. He then guided him to the kitchen and into a chair.

"Did you eat today Mr. Beckett?"

"Oh, I don't know." George lifted a hand then let it drop to his lap. "I don't seem to get hungry anymore."

There was no edible food in the refrigerator, but a chicken had laid a few eggs out back so Danny scrambled them and made some toast. While George ate, Danny took out the trash and washed a sink full of dirty dishes.

After the food settled, George seemed to come back to himself. "What was I doing this time, Danny?"

"You were standing in the front yard talking to the roses."

George lifted his head and looked past him, sorrowful and lonely, his old eyes watery. "Josie's favorite."

"You don't have any food in the house Mr. Beckett."

"The truck's not running. I can't get into town."

Danny knew there was a 1954 Chevy collecting dust in the garage. The car had belonged to George's wife and was most likely in better condition than George's old truck.

"You could take the car…"

George shook his head. "That car was Josie's pride and joy. I don't touch it."

Danny glanced at the wall clock which read four-fifteen. His father would be home in one hour. Even using the shortcuts, home was a long walk. If he didn't get started on his chores there was sure to be punishment in his future.

He patted the old man on the shoulder. "Why don't you walk home with me and have supper at my house? Maybe Daddy will take a look at your truck."

"You're Mama might not like having an uninvited guest."

"One more mouth at the table won't matter to my mother."

Danny helped George over the fence and they skirted the edge of the hayfield. His little dog Patience spotted them and ran at full speed, jumping into his arms. As Patience licked his face, he looked toward home and saw his mother sitting on the front porch reading the county paper. With her uncanny mother's intuition, she lifted her head and zeroed in on him as he and George drew closer.

George removed his hat. "Afternoon, Caroline."

"You're looking thin George."

George twisted his hat in his hands, "Yes, ma'am, I suppose I am."

"You're welcome to stay for supper."

Danny smiled at his mother and she almost smiled back, but caught herself and wagged a finger at him. "You get your work done. George can sit here and visit with me until supper."

After supper, Danny dumped the paper trash into the burn barrel and dropped in a lit match. He spread the Sunday comics on the grass, turning the pages until he found Prince Valiant. The stories didn't interest him as much as the drawings. Just then one of

Patience's little pups trotted over and squatted on the paper for a tinkle. Danny sat back, rolled the paper into a ball and threw it into the fire. The little puppy jumped at him and barked for attention. Danny gave the puppy's little head a quick rub.

His father came around the corner of the house and whistled for him. "I'm going over to look at George's truck. Want to ride along?"

Danny picked up the puppy and stood, "Yes sir."

"Leave the dog here."

"Don't you think Mr. Beckett would like one of these puppies, Daddy? He could use the company."

Cecil smiled. "Let's ask George if he wants a dog."

After that day, Danny was allowed to visit old George twice a week. Since George had one of Patience's pups, he usually took her along for a visit.

At George's house, he dusted, swept floors, vacuumed the threadbare carpet in the living room, washed laundry, dishes, and windows. He mowed the grass, pulled weeds, fed George's handful of chickens, gathered eggs, and mended the coop. After finishing whatever tasks he could find, he sat with George on the front porch, with the puppy and Patience lying at their feet. Usually George did all the talking, always about days gone by, happier times, especially those with his wife and only child, a son who lived in Phoenix.

Danny's mother always prepared food for him to take along, like a container of chicken and dumplings with green beans and blackberry cobbler or meatloaf with mashed potatoes and homemade gingersnap cookies.

On Sunday morning his parents began stopping by George's house to take him to church. The old man seemed to enjoy being crowded in the back of the station wagon with the five Coulter children. After church, he joined the family at the ranch for the big dinner of the day.

Some kids, like his cousin Elliot, teased Danny about spending time with the old man, never understanding how much he gained from the relationship. He truly enjoyed listening to George's stories and helping out. He wasn't particularly worried what other kids thought anyway. Spending time with George felt right and that was all that mattered.

Shadow

Shadow, Oklahoma
Summer 1962

THREE

On a warm Saturday afternoon in the middle of June, Danny sat high in the bleachers watching his brother, Dwight, play baseball. Baseball had become a passion he shared with his father and brothers. While he didn't much care for Dwight these days, he was a good athlete and a terrific second baseman.

As usual, his seven-year-old brother, David, had followed him up to the top of the bleachers where the wind blew steady and cooled them in the afternoon sun.

Danny leaned back, resting his elbows on the rail behind him. David shifted his position so they were pressed together, thigh to thigh.

Danny pushed his brother away. "Do you have to sit so close?"

"I'm scared up here," David complained. "It's too high."

"Well, go on down with Mama then."

David's face puckered and his chin quivered. "She said I should stay with you."

This of course was a half truth. David had asked permission to follow him and their mother said yes.

For reasons that escaped Danny, his little brother always wanted to be right by his side. David climbed into bed with him with every thunder storm that struck in the middle of the night or when they stayed up on Saturday night and watched old black and white horror movies on the TV, like Frankenstein or The Mummy. He also sat by Danny's side in church every Sunday, at the dinner table, and in the car. And, without fail, David always wanted to tag along wherever he went.

Unlike him, David was a quiet, timid boy and sometimes got overlooked at home. Most of the time, Danny honestly didn't mind his brother's constant presence except when he was engrossed in his drawing, but David had learned to respect that time to some degree and usually left him alone.

Seeing David struggling with his fear, guilt got the best of Danny. "We'll go down in a little bit."

He turned his attention back to the game in time to see their father marching across the infield straight for Dwight at second base. Dwight actually took a step back and seemed to be turning paler with each step their father took.

Danny stood and started down the stairs. "Come on."

At the bottom of the bleachers, Danny found his mother standing with her arms folded over her chest, her forehead wrinkled in concern.

"What's going on, Mama?" Danny asked.

"See that boy over there?" She pointed to a slender boy from the opposing team whose foot rested on the bag at third base. "Your brother called him an ugly word."

His father grabbed Dwight by the arm and marched him across the field, right up to the boy on third base. While Dwight apologized, Danny studied his father's face and saw his brother's immediate future written in the grim lines. His mother heaved a big sigh.

After supper that evening, his mother filled two grocery sacks with buttered popcorn and a large thermos with cherry Kool-Aid then the whole family loaded into the station wagon and headed to the drive-in theater for the double feature.

In the summer months, a trip to the local drive-in was a family tradition. Usually, Cecil's brother Robert would join them with his family. The adults had devised a seating system for their brood: Robert's two daughters and Denise were assigned the interior of the station wagon and all four of Cecil's sons were relegated to a quilt thrown over a tarp on the hard ground in front of the station wagon. Sometimes cousin Elliott would lower his standards and sit with

Danny and his brothers, but most of the time, he stayed in his parents' car, at least until he finished all of the treats he was allowed to purchase at the snack bar.

When the lights went down and the movie previews began, Caroline lined up her sons and poured mosquito repellant into their palms, ordering them to rub it on any exposed skin except their faces. Danny joined his brothers on the quilt and his little brother squeezed between him and Darren, the girls climbed inside the station wagon, and their parents joined Uncle Robert and Aunt Violet in lawn chairs in front of Uncle Robert's late model Ford.

After his humiliation over his foul language at the ball game earlier in the day, Dwight was in a particularly foul mood and was looking for any excuse to vent his anger. As the end of the movie, Old Yeller, drew near and the boy shot his beloved dog, tears rolled openly down Danny's face, providing his big brother with just the outlet he was looking for.

Dwight punched him in the arm. "Knock it off, you big crybaby. You want the whole world to see what an idiot you are?"

"Leave him alone," Darren said. "It's sad."

Dwight ignored Darren and gave Danny a knuckle punch. "Now you've got something to cry about."

Danny rubbed the knot in his upper arm and kept a wary eye on his oldest brother.

Fearing he was next in line for torment, David scooted closer to Danny and started whining. "I'm going to tell Mama."

Dwight shoved David and he immediately began to wail.

Danny, in turn, shoved Dwight. "Leave him alone, you jerk."

"You'd better keep your hands off me Danny!" Dwight hollered.

Denise stuck her head out the car window. "Stop it! We can't hear."

Their father jumped to his feet and peered through the darkness at them. "Don't make me come over there boys!"

"Your puny body isn't the only thing that's not developing right," Dwight said. He leaned closer to Danny, lowering his voice. "Doc Forbes told Mama and Daddy your brain is only about the size of a pea." He held up a thumb and forefinger millimeters apart to demonstrate just how miniscule Danny's brain truly was.

"After your next birthday," Dwight continued, "they're going to take you up to Tulsa to this lab where they do research on mutants. They would've locked you up sooner, but they have to wait until you turn twelve." He grinned and poked Danny in the chest. "It won't be long now."

Danny didn't want to believe Dwight, but he was indeed a runt, so there might be some truth in what he said.

Dwight smiled and waved at him, "Bye-Bye, Danny."

Out of the corner of his eye, Danny saw Darren roll his eyes. The reaction told Danny all he needed to know.

"You're a liar Dwight," he said.

"And you're dead." Dwight grabbed a handful of Danny's shirt. "Don't think about going to sleep tonight, I'm coming for you."

Dwight released him with a toss. Danny immediately rolled to his side and kicked Dwight in the stomach with his heel. The ensuing melee brought their father upon them as the lights came up for intermission before the next movie began.

FOUR

The ball left his hand and sailed toward the plate. The best hitter on the other team swung and missed the slider by inches. Danny's team exploded with joy. They had just whipped the first place team.

Danny grinned and removed his cap, wiping the sweat from his forehead. The game was over. Since this was the last game of the season and they were down four runs in the sixth inning, the coach finally gave in to his repeated requests to leave his shortstop position for the pitcher's mound. This win was Danny's victory.

He looked toward the stands to see if his father was watching, but his father was deep in a conversation with the owner of the John Deere dealership. This seemed to be the burden of being a third son, all the big moments had already happened with Dwight and Darren.

Darren had finished his own game earlier and watched Danny pitch with his fingers intertwined in the fence. Darren stuck two fingers in his mouth and whistled louder than anyone.

Since Darren rode in the front seat on the way to town, it was Danny's turn to ride shotgun on the way home. He jumped onto the front seat of the old station wagon and turned around, grinning at Darren. "Did you see my slider?"

"Yeah, it actually wasn't too bad."

"Not bad? They couldn't hit it. That's all that counts, isn't it?"

"That's not the way I taught you to throw it." Darren said. He sighed dramatically. "They don't do it that way in the majors."

Danny laughed. "Gee, I guess that's why I'm still in little league."

Darren gave him the finger. Danny turned back around and realized they were headed to the other side of town instead of toward home.

"Where are we going, Daddy?"

"Over to pick up Uncle Hal. Do you remember him?"

Danny grunted. "I remember the poke in the eye he gave me before he went away."

"Now, Danny, don't hold on to that grudge. Uncle Hal said it was an accident."

"It wasn't an accident. It was his elbow."

Danny remembered the incident perfectly. Uncle Hal enjoyed antagonizing his nieces and nephews. Because Danny was small, he became a favorite target. Hal was forever grabbing him and giving his head a knuckle rub, then would rap on his forehead as if it was a piece of wood. The last time Danny had struggled, catching Hal's elbow in the eye. In his opinion, Uncle Hal's three-year absence hadn't been long enough.

"He had me, Daddy," he said. "He didn't need to poke me in the eye."

"Well, be nice anyway or I'll tan your butt."

Hal was in front of the drug store, pacing back and forth in front of the building. From the pile of discarded cigarette butts on the ground, it appeared he must have been waiting a while.

After greeting Cecil, Hal reached for Danny's head. "Hey, Runt, how you been?"

Danny dodged his uncle's big hands and pulled his ball cap down tighter, "Fine."

"How old are you now, eight or nine?"

Danny glared at him. "I'm almost twelve."

Hal made a "tsk-tsk" sound. "Boy, you need to join the Army. Maybe they could make you grow. Look what it did for me."

Hal had a point. He definitely wasn't the gangly eighteen-year-old who ran away three years ago. Danny planned to avoid him whenever possible. If Hal got a grip on him now, he would be in major trouble.

He climbed in back with Darren and they argued about baseball all the way home. Their arguments were never serious. Most of the time, Darren was too easygoing for anyone to rile.

Even though Hal hadn't given much notice of his impending arrival, Grandma and Grandpa were hosting a family get together to honor his homecoming. When they arrived, the women were inside the house getting the food together. The men gathered on the porch, discussing Hal's travels and the ranch. Bored with the conversation, Darren and Danny moved out to the edge of their grandparent's yard with their ball and gloves to practice Danny's slider.

Darren crouched and held up a catcher's mitt. "All right, bring it."

Danny loosened his shoulder and let one fly. The ball snapped in the glove and Darren smiled.

"Not bad, but you're letting go a little early. Try it again."

He brought his arm back and as he came forward to release the ball Denise ran between them chasing her cat. Danny dropped his arm just in time.

"Hey, Denise!" he called, "I almost nailed you in the head."

"Sorry," she called, running through again.

Their mother came out to the porch and frowned at them. "You boys go home and clean up before we eat."

They ambled along, talking about the upcoming baseball playoffs, always comfortable with each other's company. At the house, they flipped a coin to see who would bathe first and Darren won. While Darren went upstairs, Danny headed to the kitchen for a glass of water. When he pushed through the swinging door, he discovered Uncle Hal perched on the kitchen table with is back to the door and talking on the phone.

"Honest Baby, I'll come get you next week," Hal was saying. As he listened for a moment to the person on the other end, he took a long drag on a cigarette and a swig from a pint bottle of whiskey.

"I promise," Hal said. "I just have to get them used to the idea of me getting married and all. Of course, I love you. Didn't I give you a ring and everything? Well, all right then. I don't want to hear anymore about me not keeping my word. I can't wait to touch you again." He dropped his voice to a whisper. "I need you so bad, I'll probably explode."

Danny coughed loudly to announce his presence. Hal glanced at him and pointed at the door indicating he should leave, but Danny filled a glass with water and sipped it leisurely while his uncle concluded his call. Of course, the polite thing to do would be to leave Hal to talk in private, but this was just too interesting.

"Okay Sugar, I'll see you on Friday," Hal said. "You be packed and ready to go. I don't want to spend any more time with your Daddy than I have to."

Hal tossed the receiver into the cradle and took a long pull from his pint. He pointed his cigarette at Danny.

"Keep your mouth shut, Runt."

Danny cocked his head to the side, "About what? Sitting on our table smoking cigarettes and drinking whiskey or talking dirty on the telephone to a girl nobody knows about? Which part, Uncle Hal?"

Hal took a puff of his cigarette and squinted at him through the haze. "Quite the little smart ass, aren't you?"

"Yeah," Danny said nodding his head solemnly. He placed his glass in the sink and turned back to Hal with a big smile. "But I think that maybe, if I try real hard, one day I'll be as sophisticated as you."

Before he could escape, Hal grabbed him and gave the top of his head a knuckle rub he wouldn't soon forget.

"Say uncle," Hal said.

"Uncle," Danny managed.

Hal tossed him away. "Remember that."

Danny pushed the swinging door open, but after two steps turned back and poked his head inside the kitchen again. Hal looked over at him and Danny grinned.

"Oh Baby, I'm gonna explode," he said then ran for the stairs.

Hal chased him to the bottom of the steps, but was grinning. "You'd better run!"

Two weeks after Hal's homecoming, Danny was helping his grandmother in her garden one morning when a strange car flew down their private road with the radio blaring Wake Up Little Susie and kicking up dust.

His grandmother straightened up and squinted at the car. "Do you know who this might be Danny?"

"No, ma'am," he said.

Danny followed his grandmother from the garden to the front of the house near the porch steps. They watched in silence as a red-haired girl emerged and approached them. Grandma Coulter stared at the girl with an open mouth.

This girl had the strangest style Danny had ever seen. Even though it was summer, she wore a fluffy pink sweater with a poodle appliqué on one side. The tightness of her straight-line gray skirt accented the distinct pooch of her abdomen, which on such a slim girl could only mean one thing. She teetered on skinny high heels as she came up the stone walk, looking as if she might turn her ankle at any moment. Plastic colorful hoops dangled from her earlobes, making little clacking sounds when she moved her head. Her hair was piled high on her head in some kind of a big-haired, twisted thing and she had on more eye makeup than any female Danny ever saw, even in the movie star magazines cousin Elliot's sisters read.

Grandma shook off her trance. "Can I help you?"

"I'm looking for Hal Coulter," the girl said.

Grandma wiped her hands on her apron. "Hal's not here at the moment."

The girl pulled her shoulders back, standing rigid as Grandma and Danny studied her with bewildered expressions.

Danny wondered if this was the girl he overheard Uncle Hal talking to over the phone a few weeks back. If so, Uncle Hal was overdue in keeping his promise.

The girl glanced around with a pinched expression, her plastic earrings clacking.

"I'm Rosalie Spencer," she said. She reached up to pat her pile of hair. "Hal's my fiancé."

Grandma was gripping her apron so tight her hand had turned white. "Well, come on in. I'll see if we can track him down for you."

Danny shuffled back to allow the women up the stairs. Rosalie glanced at him before entering the house.

"Danny," Grandma said, keeping her eyes on the strange girl.

"Yes, ma'am?"

"Go find your uncle."

Danny found Hal near his grandparents' barn working on the engine of an ancient tractor. He was talking to himself and didn't notice Danny approach.

"Uncle Hal?"

Hal looked up from the engine his face pinched in displeasure, obviously annoyed at being interrupted.

"Someone named Rosalie is looking for you," Danny said.

Hal threw a socket wrench into the toolbox and let loose a string of colorful words Danny never heard before.

"Where is she?"

"With Grandma."

Hal wiped the grease from his hands and looked toward the house with a sour expression. "Well, that's just terrific."

Hal started towards the house and Danny tagged along. After a few feet, his uncle turned and scowled at him. "This isn't any of your business, Runt. Go home."

He watched his uncle disappear inside his grandparents' house before turning toward home.

Due to pressure applied by Danny's grandparents to do the right thing by the pregnant girl, a less than enthusiastic Hal married Rosalie the next week in a small ceremony at their church.

Hal and Rosalie settled into Grandpa and Grandma's home while the Coulter men built a house for the newlyweds on the hill behind Danny's parents' home.

Although Hal and Rosalie's marriage was not the happiest of unions, it appeared they had enough affection for each other to settle into married life. Unfortunately, Uncle Hal's commitment wasn't as long lasting as his new wife's.

Since returning from his military service, Hal did help some around the ranch, but spent the bulk of his time running with his old crowd drinking and generally living it up. There was a brief hiatus in these activities after the wedding, but he soon resumed his carousing ways. This in turn brought about some fierce battles with Rosalie, both private and public. These fiery moments were quickly followed by a period of highly demonstrative, overly-affectionate behavior. Danny's mother called this make-up period their "pink cloud," adding the whole affair was a vicious cycle.

While Hal promised to walk the straight and narrow path as a husband and soon-to-be father, family confidence ran on the low side.

FIVE

Though they were on summer break from school, there was no such thing as sleeping in on the Coulter ranch. Danny and his brothers were up by six and already working before their father left for the post office. The work was an endless rotation of jobs, but fortunately there were a few hours of leisure in the middle of the day.

After tackling the last of their morning chores, Danny and his brothers ate a quick lunch of bologna and cheese sandwiches then were free for awhile. Danny grabbed his sketch book and newly acquired colored pencils, placing them in a canvas knapsack before accompanying Darren and David to their clubhouse high in the hills above the ranch.

The clubhouse was Dwight's brainchild a few years ago and the brothers gathered any discarded wood they could salvage and pieced together a nice little hideaway. These days, grumpy Dwight preferred the company of his friends over family and spent very little time in the clubhouse, leaving Darren, Danny, and David in peace.

While Darren and David made themselves comfortable inside, Danny climbed onto the roof to sketch out the spectacular vista before him. The day was hot and humid, but the tall trees provided plenty of shade. He closed his eyes and enjoyed the steady breeze, relaxing for a moment before opening the sketchbook.

Down below, Darren and David lounged on the floor of the clubhouse with their collection of comic books. Their occasional soft chatter drifted out the open door and windows of the rough structure. Unfortunately, Elliot soon joined them and lent his loud-mouth to what had been a pleasant afternoon. Danny did his best to tune out the irritating racket and immersed himself in his drawing.

Half an hour after Elliot's arrival, Darren poked his head above the edge of the roof. "Want to go up to the cave with us?"

"No thanks."

He didn't bother looking up from the sketch book. He was at an interesting point and really wanted to continue. Besides, he had been in the cave once and that was enough for him. The damp confinement didn't suit him in the least.

Elliot pulled himself up beside Darren and grinned at Danny. "Are you chicken to go in the cave Danny Boy?"

He sighed loudly and finally looked at the two of them. "I just want to sit here and draw."

He turned his attention back to the sketchbook, hoping they would go on and leave him in peace.

"All right, suit yourself," Darren said. "Just don't tell Mama, okay?"

When Danny didn't respond, Darren reached into his pocket and withdrew a marble. With Darren's customary deadly aim, the marble struck Danny square in the forehead, prompting Elliot to chortle in his hee-haw donkey way.

Danny glared at them. "Knock it off!"

"Don't tell Mama we're going in the cave, okay?"

He shrugged and went back to his drawing.

Several drops of rain plopped onto his head, pulling Danny out of deep concentration. He looked around, reorienting himself. Apparently, he had been lost in his drawing for quite some time.

He popped everything back into the knapsack and swung down through the open doorway of the empty clubhouse. His brothers' comic books were scattered on the floor where they left them.

Because the sky was dark, he had no idea how much time had elapsed. If he was late, hurrying now was of little use, but he ran anyway, hoping he still had time to get his chores done before his father arrived.

His mother greeted him on the back porch with hands on her hips and a scowl on her face. "It's about time. Where are your brothers?"

He hadn't given much thought to Darren, David, or Elliot. He had assumed they were already home.

"I don't know Mama."

"Weren't you boys together?"

"They left a while back to go exploring."

He really hoped she didn't ask where they were exploring or he would be in a real bind. Luckily, his mother held out her hand for his knapsack and didn't press the issue.

"Give me that and get your work done."

His small size made no difference in the assignment of chores. He was expected to do everything his older, larger brothers did, but he couldn't lift half of what they managed, so each task took longer. Halfway through feeding the horses, a hard, steady rain started falling, but he was too stubborn to go back to the house for a slicker. He finished his work and was closing the barn door when his father approached.

"Where are Darren and David?"

"I don't know for sure."

"What do you mean for sure? Weren't y'all together up there?"

Danny shifted his weight, stalling on breaking his word. "Yes sir, for a while…"

"What?" Cecil asked impatiently.

"They went in the cave with Elliot."

His father swore under his breath. "How long ago was that?"

"A couple of hours, I guess."

His father peered through the rain, toward the hill. "Go back to the house and get Dwight and some flashlights. And have Mama call Uncle Robert."

Dwight entered the shallow cave entrance first and their father followed. Danny was usually eager for an adventure, but not this. He truly dreaded the cave. Pushing aside the fear surging through him, he stepped inside.

His father shined his light off the damp walls and found a tunnel. Bending down, he called into the hole. "Darren! David! Elliot!"

Darren's voice echoed from a distance. "Down here Daddy!"

Cecil hunched down, shining his light inside, he considered the passageway for a moment then stood straight again, shaking his head. "Danny, you'll have to go it alone. This space gets too small for Dwight and me."

Danny eyed the tunnel, panic rising in his chest. Before fear took complete control, he moved forward. Ten feet inside, he had to stoop to continue.

The floor of the tunnel was damp and slippery. The narrow tunnel gradually sloped downhill and mud covered the bottom. He pushed on until he came to a split where the walls opened up a bit. A shuffling sound came from his left. Danny swung his flashlight in a slow arc and found another downward-slanted shaft just as Darren emerged, crawling forward on his hands and knees. Water flowed down the tube, swirling around Darren's arms and legs.

Danny helped him out of the hole. "Are you all right?"

"I'm fine, but David's stuck down there. The water's getting deep." He paused for a breath and looked back down the slope. "He's really scared."

Danny directed his light down the passageway and heard David's muffled cry.

"He found this little space and crawled inside and got his foot stuck," Darren said.

"Why didn't you get him out?"

"The only way in is too narrow for me." Darren gave him a hesitant look. "I think you're the only one small enough to get to him."

Danny sighed loudly, "How could you let him go so far back?"

Darren looked sheepish. "He followed Elliot."

At the mention of his cousin's name, Danny realized he hadn't considered Elliot's whereabouts. "Where is Elliot?"

"He came out a while ago and told me David was stuck." Darren took a breath and looked back to the tunnel where their little brother was trapped. "Then he left."

Danny shined his flashlight down the tunnel. There was no way he could crawl and keep the flashlight out of the water. After tucking his shirt into his waistband, he stuffed the larger flashlight inside his shirt, pulled out the pocket flashlight he brought as a backup, and placed the light between his teeth. Despite the fear clanging in his head and the nearly overwhelming desire to run the other way, he took a deep breath and crawled into the tunnel.

The passage seemed to narrow with every inch he gained. He had to crawl along through water and muck. Water splashed up his nose. He gasped and cursed when the light fell out of his mouth. David heard and started calling frantically.

Danny spit out the bad taste in his mouth. The little flashlight illuminated the shallow water. He plucked the light from the water and addressed his hysterical brother calmly. "I'm coming David, hang on."

"Danny! I knew you would come."

Nearly five years separated them and since the day they started sharing a bedroom, David seemed to look up to him with near hero worship, starting with his fear of the dark then branching out in all directions. Danny didn't bear the weight of David's adoration well. He was willing to help his shy, fearful brother, but knew his fall from grace was inevitable. He prayed this wasn't the day.

David's panicked voice rose to a high pitch. "I'm going to drown. Get me out!"

"I promise I won't let you drown."

Cold water was running over Danny's back now, trying to enter his nose and mouth from two directions. He stuck the light back in his mouth and started down the slope.

The passage curved to the right and about six feet ahead he finally saw the top of David's head. Seeing the light, David started screaming, whipping his head back and forth until he swallowed a mouth full of water and choked.

"Be still!" Danny said.

David's upper body partially plugged a hole in the rock. He reached toward Danny, grabbing at his face, pulling on his ears, poking him in the eye. Danny pushed his hands away.

"Stop it!"

"Get me out!"

His brother's panic nearly mirrored his own. Knowing he couldn't let David see how frightened he was, Danny took his brother's face in his hands. "You have to calm down," he said as evenly as he could.

The little chamber rose above his head to about eight feet. Danny sat up, braced his heels against the sides of the rock, put his hands under David's arms, and pulled. David came forward a couple of inches then screamed in pain. Danny dropped his hands immediately.

"Don't stop!" David cried.

"I don't want to hurt you."

"I don't care if you pull my foot off, Danny." His voice broke. "Get me out."

Danny sat back and shined the light up the rock wall to the top of the little chamber over his head.

"We've got to get your foot loose," he murmured.

David followed the beam of light. "Elliot said it goes all the way through up there."

"Did he try?"

"He thought about it, I guess, but he said there was no way he was going to get stuck too. He went back up and got Darren, but Darren is too big."

The rock curved inward, forming a little shelf. Danny pulled himself up into the narrow passage, but couldn't see the end.

"Are you sure this comes out on the other side?"

"That's what Elliot said."

Danny didn't allow himself the time to consider any reason for not attempting to crawl through the hole. He shifted the larger flashlight still resting inside his shirt to the side, lay on his belly, and pulled himself along. A sharp rock dug into his shoulder, so he pushed back, shifted left, started again. This time the sharp edge caught his back and cut him just below the lower part of his rib cage, digging, and ripping into his skin as he moved forward. He gritted his teeth and kept moving. The journey probably took no more than a minute, but felt like a lifetime. Finally, he reached the opening and crawled out into another smaller chamber.

At the bottom, David's body partly blocked the entrance. A steady stream flowing from a crack in the rock above their heads was filling the little room. The water was to Danny's knees.

He bent over, felt around for David's legs, discovering David's right foot wedged in a narrow crevice and turned at an odd angle. He tugged on the leg and heard his brothers' muffled cry of pain. He reached through the water and managed to blindly untie his brother's shoe and work the foot out. David immediately moved through the tunnel and water rushed from the room. Because this interior chamber was downhill from the outer one, the water sloshed right back in again.

Despite the rush of water coming through the tunnel, he decided to take his chances and follow David through the hole rather than brave the narrow overhead opening again. He took a deep breath, dropped, felt around for the opening, and pushed himself through. When he emerged on the other side, he drew in a mouthful of water and panicked before finding a pocket of air.

Upwards and around the bend, he found David struggling up the hill in the dark.

"Hurry up!" he said.

"I can't see. I'm going as fast as I can."

"Can you reach back and take this flashlight?"

After several attempts, David took the larger flashlight from Danny's hand and started forward again. The uphill journey seemed to go on forever, but they finally reached the larger tunnel. Up ahead, the others called encouragement as they navigated the last leg of the journey.

Cecil pulled David out of the opening and gathered him into his arms. Danny followed and Darren smiled at him. "I knew you could do it."

As they moved toward the cave entrance, Danny watched their father loop his arm around David's shoulders. The fact that his father said nothing to him personally stung a little, but mostly he was relieved his brothers were okay, no thanks to their cousin.

Elliot was smaller than Darren and could have managed to navigate the narrow overhead ledge. He could have saved David. Instead, he ran like a coward.

"Someone needs to kick Elliot's butt," Danny said.

Darren nodded in agreement. "Yep."

Danny took a bath then his mother cleaned his torn skin with peroxide and poured iodine into the raw flesh. After supper, Danny and his brothers, sat through their father's long-winded lecture about the dangers of caves.

After their father concluded his speech, Danny shuffled off to his bedroom. His body was tired and sore. Both hands and feet had cuts. His knees were bruised. His body had a thousand tiny nicks and a long gash that stretched all the way from his ribs to his left hip.

The bedroom he and David shared was the smallest in the house with each twin bed tucked into an alcove at opposite sides of the room. Danny had taped a number of his favorite drawings to the walls around his bed. Others were stacked in a loose pile on the surface of their desk.

He sat on his bed and opened his sketchbook to examine the drawing he had worked on all afternoon.

David joined him a few minutes later. After changing into his pajamas, he lay down on his bed with a sigh. "I'm never going in another cave as long as I live."

"Good."

Their father entered and eyed the loose drawings on the desk, the sketchbook in Danny's hands, and the drawings taped to the wall. He held out his hand for the sketchbook. "Give me that."

Danny looked up at him in surprise. "What? Why, Daddy?"

"I need to teach you a lesson about putting family first, before any personal interest."

"Crawling into a hole and nearly drowning wasn't enough?"

David gasped. In two quick steps, their father put only inches between he and Danny. "Give me those drawings."

Danny kept a wary eye on his father as he handed over the sketchbook.

"And you best save the sarcastic talk for your friends," his father said. He pointed to the drawings on the desk. "I'll take those too."

He had to struggle to keep his voice level as he gathered up the stack. "Why am I responsible for what Darren and David did? Why aren't you taking something away from them?"

"Because your brothers could have died while you sat there, scribbling your pretty drawings, thinking of no one but yourself."

"Daddy, please..." He blinked back sudden tears and looked around the room. "Take something else... Give me a whipping."

"I'm taking these drawings to teach you a lesson about what's important. I'm tired of you wasting time with this foolishness anyway." He held up Danny's drawings and shook them in the air. "In the morning, they go in the burn barrel."

The injustice of the punishment struck Danny hard. He turned to his bed, ripped down the drawings taped to the wall, picked up the box of drawing pencils he saved six months to buy, and shoved the whole lot at his father.

"Throw those in while you're at it," he said.

His father tossed everything onto Danny's bed and unbuckled his belt, keeping a level gaze on Danny. "David?"

David watched from his bed, his eyes wide with fear, "Yes sir?"

"Shut the door on your way out."

David scurried out of the room. Their father folded his belt in half and sighed tiredly. "Do you want me to do this?"

"No, sir," Danny replied quietly.

"Then apologize to me."

His father could wait until he was six feet under. He had no intention of apologizing. Though his heart was pounding in fear, he met his father's gaze head on. After a few beats, his father intuitively recognized his resolve. His father shook his head in disbelief and raised the belt.

Danny's mother threw the door open, grabbed the belt out of his father's hand, and pushed him backward toward the door.

"No, sir," she said quietly. "You will not do this."

His father stared wide eyed then blinked a few times, as if recovering his senses. When his father stepped over to Danny's bed, his mother laid a protective hand on Danny's shoulder. His father gathered a handful of the scattered drawings into his fist with a single swift motion and left the room without another word to either of them.

His mother pulled him into her arms and held him close. Not even the comfort of her embrace stilled his shaking.

His body hurt so much sleep was impossible. Near eleven that night, Danny slipped down the stairs and headed for the kitchen. When he pushed open the swinging door, he found his father sitting at the table with a glass of milk, the confiscated drawings spread on the table before him. Danny hesitated, unsure whether to enter.

His father looked up and considered him for a moment. "I'm glad it's you," he said finally. "Have a seat."

Danny eased his battered body into a chair and waited.

"I lost my temper up there in your room," his father said.

Danny kept his eyes on the tablecloth. "I did my part."

"No," his father said shaking his head. "I was wrong. Your brothers made the decision to go in that cave, not you. I just...I need for you to understand how important family is."

Once again, his father laid the weight of his brothers' decisions to go in that cave on him. He could only imagine the lifelong burden he would have carried had some terrible fate befallen his brothers.

He had to try one more time to confront the injustice of his father's thinking.

"I know how important family is," he responded stiffly, looking his father in the eye.

His father absorbed the unspoken challenge, took a sip of milk, and sorted through a few of his drawings. "I guess these are pretty good. I just don't know what can ever come of such a hobby." He paused, exhaling wearily. "I just wish you would apply yourself to something more useful."

Danny wanted to respond, but saw that his father wasn't finished speaking.

"I may never understand why you spend so much of your time drawing pictures, but that doesn't make me right about taking these from you."

Danny fingered the blue and white checkered tablecloth, tracing a design with his index finger. He never gave any thought to what compelled him to draw. The need came naturally. He needed art the way he needed to eat, sleep, run, laugh... breathe.

His father slid the stack of drawings, sketchbook, and pencils across the table to him. "You can take those back to your room."

"Thank you," Danny said.

"Mama says you got hurt pretty bad in that cave today."

Danny shrugged. He didn't want to talk about the pain of this day anymore.

His father tapped his hand. "Look at me."

He raised his head and looked directly at his father.

"I'm sorry," his father said.

Danny's eyes watered. "Me too."

Two days after the cave incident, the usually even-tempered, good-natured Darren caught Elliot alone and taught him a lesson their cousin wouldn't soon forget. When Elliot's parents questioned him about his black eye and bruises, he insisted they were the result of messing with the wrong horse, a fitting metaphor that left Danny smiling.

SIX

Steeped in self pity, Danny rounded the corner of the barn with the wheelbarrow, grumbling about the mountain of work facing him today, all because he made a small noose and hung Denise's favorite doll from the guttering outside her bedroom window. She hadn't even missed the stupid doll until she went to bed. Of course, when she looked through the window and spotted the beloved doll hanging there, she started screaming her head off like some drama queen, bringing everyone in the house running to see what the ruckus was all about.

He supposed the grin on his face and his little brother's giggling didn't help the situation. His parents decided an appropriate punishment for torturing his sister would be to stay home and work today instead of attending the livestock auction in

Stigler as planned. Since his brothers were allowed to go, he had been assigned some of their chores along with his own. The long list would keep him busy for hours.

He parked the wheelbarrow outside a two-room outbuilding and stepped over the entry board to retrieve a 50-pound bag of chicken feed. As he reached for the bag, he heard strange grunting sounds and a woman's voice moaning "Oh, Hal" coming from the other room.

A peek around the dividing wall provided quite an eyeful. Perched on a workbench with her skirt hiked up around her waist was Vera, Uncle Hal's sister-in-law. Hal stood before her with his pants down around his ankles and was moving frantically between Vera's long white legs. Vera wrapped those long legs around Hal's waist and braced herself on the bench, tossing her head back with her mouth wide open.

Aunt Rosalie's older sister had swept into their lives a few weeks ago like a bleached-blonde bomb dropped in their midst. Vera had a loud, careless laugh and a freewheeling lifestyle that didn't mesh with their small town life. Like Rosalie, she favored tight clothing. However, Vera was a few years older than Rosalie and her body was filled out in all the right places. The snug garments accentuated her generous curves in every possible way. Her big, jiggly breasts pushing out of her too-small blouses had every man around giving her more than a passing glance, including Danny's own father. Dwight called her "Vera Va-Va-Voom," and, due to full-blown hormonal influx, often stared at certain of Vera's more robust features to the point of drooling.

With the exception of Rosalie, the women in the family wanted Vera gone.

Vera's recent divorce left her footloose and in transition. The supposed purpose for her visit was to help her younger sister as she advanced in her pregnancy and after the arrival of the new baby. Yet, after a mere three weeks, she and Hal were betraying Rosalie in the worst possible way.

Danny knew enough about sex to know what they were up to. What he didn't understand was why they would choose his grandparents' storage shed for their escapade. Apparently any spot would do when the mood struck, or perhaps the thrill of discovery was an added bonus.

Uncle Hal and Rosalie's marriage was a consistent roller coaster of heartache and good times. Without a doubt, Uncle Hal was a difficult man to live with; his bouts with the bottle, gambling, and disappearing for hours on end made Rosalie's life very difficult. Of course, after a downhill slide, he was sincerely apologetic, seemingly humbled, and so far Rosalie forgave him. Danny doubted this particular twist with Vera would blow over so easily.

He backed out of the storage shed quietly and hurried home, hoping to stall until Hal and Vera finished their business so he could get back to work.

His mother and Denise were making apple pies and looked up when he came through the back door of the kitchen. He took a glass from the cupboard and filled it with water, gulping it down before filling it again.

"My goodness Danny, your face is fire-engine red," his mother said.

He shook his head and told a half lie. "I'm just hot."

She wiped her hands on a dishtowel and waved him over. "Let me see if you have a fever."

Though the temperature outside hovered in the nineties, her cool hand did indeed detect a fever in his flushed face, so she reached for her favorite cure-all, a big bottle of castor oil. Danny's stomach lurched at the sight of the bottle. He shook his head and held up a hand.

"No, Mama, honest I'm just hot," he said.

His mother filled a tablespoon and came at him. Danny backed away, knowing full well there was no escape.

"Open your mouth," she said.

Danny immediately gagged and shook all over, provoking giggling out of his sister until their mother threatened to give her a dose, which stopped her humor cold. She insisted he take another spoonful, her exact dose for a fever. He gave thought to complaining of not feeling well to see if he could get out of the long list of chores his father had given him, but decided against the lie.

"Go on and finish your work," his mother said. "I'll check on you in a little while."

Danny cautiously approached the storeroom, listening carefully before entering. Once his eyes adjusted to the dim light and he determined he was alone, he crossed the threshold to retrieve the bag of feed. Since he couldn't lift the fifty-pound bag, his only option was to drag it to the door, roll it over the threshold, tilt the wheelbarrow on its side, roll the bag into the wheelbarrow then right the wheelbarrow again. As he struggled to roll the bag, grunting and grumbling, Hal came along.

"How come you didn't go to Stigler with the rest of them, Runt?"

He stood upright and wiped the sweat from his brow with his hand. "I'm being punished."

Hal bent forward, picked up the feed bag, and tossed it into the wheelbarrow. "Never say I didn't help."

Still embarrassed at the mental image of Hal and Vera going at it, Danny couldn't look at him directly. "Thanks."

Hal stepped in front of the wheelbarrow, blocking his path. "Vera says you might have seen something…"

Danny wanted no part of this conversation. He grasped the handles of the wheelbarrow. "I have to get my work done."

"If you did see something, I'd appreciate it if you kept it to yourself."

Danny squinted up at him now, the sun behind Hal making it impossible to see anything but his outline.

"I didn't see anything," he said flatly.

Hal patted him on the head. "Good boy."

Danny jerked away. "Stop patting me on the head like I'm some dog."

"Well, aren't we in a sour mood?"

"You would be too if you ever actually did any work around here."

He turned back to the wheelbarrow, lifted the handles, and set off for the hen house. Hal followed.

"I'll make you a deal, Runt. You tell me what you have to do and I'll help. Then we'll go down to the river and cool off."

"What's my part in this deal?"

"Just keep your mouth shut."

As it happened, Uncle Hal did indeed know how to work when he put his mind to it. The long list of chores was accomplished in no time.

Danny stopped by the well, pumping cold water over his head to cool down then went home to let his mother know he had finished all of his work. Since her quick hand detected no fever this time, he received permission to go swimming with Uncle Hal's little group.

He started toward Hal's place, but met Hal's car coming down the hill. The car skidded to a stop with Hall allowing him just enough time to jump in the backseat next to Vera and they were off again. He did his best not to make eye contact with Vera as the four of them headed for the river.

Rosalie's tight bathing suit accentuated every bit of her pregnant belly. Her enlarging breasts filled out the top and then some. She spread a blanket on the grass, turned on a transistor radio then lay back on the blanket with a magazine.

Vera shed her short robe, revealing a crimson swimming suit that appeared one size too small. She fluffed her hair and stretched her arms over her head striking a sexy pose.

A few yards away, Danny kicked off his shoes and pulled his T-shirt over his head. Uncle Hal stood next to him, seemingly mesmerized by his sister-in-law.

"You're such a jerk," Danny muttered.

Hal snapped out of his reverie and grinned like the fool he was. "Someday you'll understand Runt."

Vera joined Rosalie on the blanket, lying back on her elbows, striking another pose. She looked over at the two of them and smiled.

Hal shook his head and headed for the water. "I'd better cool off before I get in trouble."

Danny jumped for the rope attached to the underside of the bridge, caught it then swung back to the bank where he backed up and ran hard, swinging out over the middle of the river before dropping. Hal caught the rope as it swung back again and followed suit.

Hal quickly tired of swimming and joined the women on the blanket, sucking down the ice-cold beer Vera handed him from a cooler. He gave Rosalie a kiss on the lips and her belly a gentle rub. Vera watched him with a sly smile then looked away.

Hal stretched out on his back and placed a pair of sunglasses on his face, lying there basking in the late afternoon sun like a contented cat. Danny decided this was his cue to move on. He pulled on his shoes and T-shirt and passed by the three on the blanket.

"Remember our bargain Runt," Hal reminded him.

As Danny turned for the path that would take him to the road, Vera puckered her ruby-red lips in a kiss and winked.

Isabelle Long
Tulsa, Oklahoma
Spring 1962

SEVEN

Amateur night at this old tavern had attracted a capacity crowd willing to venture out on an early spring night to purchase a cheap pitcher of beer and have their say about the local talent. Isabelle's mother drew an early number and was the third person to try her luck before the rowdy crowd.

Isabelle looked on with pride as her mother stepped onto the stage. She smiled up at her father to share the moment, but his attention was focused on the bartender from whom he had just asked permission to watch his wife's performance.

The bartender's bloodshot blue eyes narrowed, as if he were viewing a pile of garbage left on his doorstep. When his cold gaze slipped down to Isabelle, she stepped behind her father. She was tiny for ten years old and felt safe there.

"Y'all can stand by the back door while she's singing," the bartender said, his ugly mouth curling into a tight grin. "Hell, as dark as you are, nobody will see anything but the whites of your eyes anyway."

Isabelle felt her father's body tense, but "thanks" was all he said.

His quiet assent surprised Isabelle. She didn't understand why he would stand there and thank the ugly man for telling him where he could or couldn't go. Given his job with the rodeo of protecting bull riders from being stomped or gored to death, no one ever accused her father, Marshall Long, of being short on courage.

She tugged on his hand. "I don't like that man, Daddy…"

"Hush." He reached down and lifted her to his shoulder so she could better see the stage. "Mama is about to sing."

Isabelle's mother smoothed her best dress over her small, shapely frame and straightened her back. Isabelle knew, without seeing, that her mother's long, thick braid lay neatly against the curve of her spine halfway down her back.

The MC stepped up to the microphone and looked at the card in his hand. "Alright now, y'all give a big welcome to a little gal with a big voice, Miss Carrie Long."

The audience fell quiet as her mother treated them to an emotional rendition of a popular Patsy

Cline song then all those beer-swilling folks burst into rowdy applause.

Isabelle smiled widely, her little hands smarting from enthusiastic applause. She looked down to see her father's reaction. A smile lit his handsome face and he gently set her back on the floor.

The bartender nudged her father's shoulder with a yardstick. "Go on now, show's over."

Marshall eyed him calmly. "I'd like to wait for my wife."

"She can stay to see if she won, but you and the kid wait outside."

Marshall guided Isabelle out the back door and down a set of rickety stairs. Two steps toward the parking lot, she dug in her heels.

"I want to wait inside," she said.

"You can't Sugar. Come on now, let's see if we can find us a Coke somewhere."

Marshall purchased a soda and a bag of peanuts for Isabelle from a gas station on the corner. Isabelle sat on the bench seat of their old truck and carefully dropped her peanuts into the bottle one by one.

Her father shivered and turned the key in the ignition. He revved the engine a bit and turned up the blower on the heater.

"I don't understand why we had to leave, Daddy."

He lit a cigarette and rolled down his window, keeping his eyes on the bar. "Drink your Coke."

Isabelle stuck a straw in the bottle and took a long pull of soda into her mouth, swallowing the sweet liquid in a gulp then belched loudly.

Her father shook his head. "You need to stop doing that. People will think you don't have any manners."

Even from this distance, she could hear music and was pretty sure she heard her mother's laughter.

"Why doesn't Mama wait out here with us?"

"She has to see if she won."

Isabelle stuck out her lower lip and eyed the bar. "I don't like being told to wait out here. I ain't a dog."

"Don't say ain't."

"Okay, I'm not a dog."

He sighed. "Hush."

Giving up easily wasn't in her nature. "How come you let that smelly man treat us this way? I want to go back inside."

Marshall slumped against the steering wheel and put his head on his hands. Isabelle had never seen him so miserable.

"What's wrong, Daddy?"

He sat back with a sigh. "It's better for your mama if we don't push our luck."

She thought over his quiet response. "I don't understand."

Marshall drew in a long breath then exhaled loudly. "We're the wrong color."

Isabelle chewed on that for a moment, "Color?"

He looked over at her. "I'm a mixed up mess and your mama's Cherokee. That puts us at the bottom of the pile around here."

Isabelle knew her father had a family history of mixed races. She heard him talk about a great great-grandfather who was Cherokee slipping off with an African slave owned by his family to Michigan before the civil war. Although their union was never legally recognized, Marshall's great great-grandparents had nine children, one being Marshall's great-grandfather who in turn married an Irish woman, and their eldest son married a Cherokee woman. So the history went, including Marshall himself who married her Cherokee mother.

All this talk of color just made Isabelle angry all over again. "So why did Mama stay?"

"They'll hurt her soon enough. Right now," he said, looking back to the bar, "she's seeing her dream through."

"Well, I think it's a stinky dream."

"Oh, Isabelle, leave me be."

Isabelle sighed. "You must love Mama a whole bunch."

Her father nodded solemnly. "Always have."

A while after she had finished the Coke and ate the peanuts, her father rolled up his window and opened the door. "Stay inside the truck until I get back. Lock the doors and do not open them for anybody. Understand?"

"I want to go with you, Daddy. Don't leave me out here by myself."

He forced a smile and kissed her forehead. "I'll be right back."

He closed the door and waited until she pushed down the lock before going back to the bar. Isabelle sat on the edge of the seat, watching him walk across the gravel lot to the back door. She didn't yet comprehend the full extent of the courage it took to face a room full of drunken white men, but after the look in that bartender's eyes she understood more than ever just how brave her father was.

After what felt like an eternity, the back door opened and her mother stepped into the night. Her father closed the door behind him just as she tottered and nearly fell. He gripped her elbow to steady her, but she jerked away.

"Leave me alone!"

Isabelle unlocked the doors of the truck and waited quietly. Her mother slid in beside her and gave her a wet kiss on the cheek. She reeked of cigarette smoke and beer.

"Your mama won first prize Issy-Belle," her mother said with a lopsided grin.

~ 73 ~

Isabelle didn't care that she won some stupid contest. She moved away from her mother and crossed her arms over her chest.

"They wouldn't let Daddy and me stay inside," she said.

Her mother smiled. "Honey, we've got fifteen dollars to spend. I'll buy you a new dress."

Her father climbed in the driver's side and started the old truck. He turned onto the highway and rolled his window down. Isabelle was grateful for the fresh air. She leaned against her father and soon fell asleep.

Later that night, her parents' voices rose in argument. Isabelle slipped out of bed and crept to the kitchen door, peeking in at them.

Her mother was at the table smoking a cigarette, her bare feet propped up on a chair. Her father leaned against the sink, staring out the back door.

"You can't expect me to keep on this way," her mother said. "I've been stuck here for years with nothing to look forward to while you're out chasing after that damned rodeo."

"That's how I make a living Carrie."

Her mother lifted her head and glared at him. "I'm taking the job and that's that."

Her father turned his head slowly, looking down at her. "You'll hurt our family," he said.

She glared at him. "At least I'd have more than one dress."

"I do the best I can."

"Well, your best isn't good enough. I'm sick of being poor, of never having a thing for myself." She slammed her hand on the table. "Why do you have to be so selfish?"

Her father crossed his arms over his chest and looked away from her.

"You better listen to me this time," she continued. "I'm not the stupid teenager you married anymore. I finally have the chance to be somebody. Winning this prize has opened new doors for me and I'm moving through before they slam in my face."

"And what happens to Isabelle while I'm on the road and you're living out your dream?"

"She can stay with my mother."

He shook his head. "She's our child."

Isabelle's mother rose and pushed her chair under the table with deliberate care. "I'm doing this." She stood straighter, her voice hard. "I don't care what you think anymore."

Her father's eyes glistened as he watched her push past Isabelle, the hurt of that moment forever etched into his face. Isabelle ran to him and wrapped her arms around his waist. He stroked the top of her head.

"I hate it when you and Mama fight," she said.

"I know," he said, then gently. "I know."

He scooped her up in his arms and carried her back to her room. After covering her, he sat on the edge of the bed, but stared out the door to the hallway.

"I love you, Daddy."

"I love you too." He smiled tiredly and kissed her cheek. "It's late. You need to go to sleep."

"Will you be here in the morning?"

He inhaled deeply then released the breath with a little sigh. "I will."

Sunday morning the sun shined brightly through her bedroom window, chasing away any lingering gloom. She recognized the smell of French toast, her father's specialty. She stretched her arms and studied the smooth coppery brown of her skin, thinking of her father's comment about them being the wrong color. People always told her how pretty she was, there had been no mention of color, ever.

She studied her appearance in the mirror as she brushed her teeth, turning her head this way and that. She had her father's gray-green eyes and small nose. Her long black hair was more like her mother's with nice soft waves. She decided people like that stupid bartender could just go on and think what they wanted. Who cared what any of them thought?

She spit out the toothpaste. "Pooh on you, Stinky Man."

She dressed quickly then hurried to the kitchen. Her mother was still in her nightgown sipping coffee at the kitchen table. The radio on the kitchen counter blasted out the song Jambalaya. Her father sang along as he flipped the egg-soaked bread in the pan.

She approached her mother first, and was greeted with a customary embrace, as genuine and loving as ever. Thankfully, the smell of cigarettes and booze was gone.

"Morning, Issy-Belle," her mother said with a big smile.

Her father glanced her way, wiggled his hips, and sang his song a little louder, making her giggle.

They ate breakfast, talking lightly about nothing important. Isabelle tried to ignore the fact that their focus was on her. Her parents never once looked at or spoke one word to each other.

That afternoon, while her father packed for another road trip, her mother went to the front porch with a favorite magazine. Isabelle sat on her parents' bed watching her father pack.

"When will you be back?" she asked.

"In a few weeks."

"I don't want you to go."

He tossed pairs of socks into the suitcase. "I'm sorry, Baby, but I have to."

Isabelle stood on the front porch next to her mother and watched her parents kiss goodbye. All the outward signs were comfortingly familiar, but she sensed their lives had shifted in a very bad direction.

EIGHT

Isabelle opened the back door of their house and set her school books on the kitchen table. Usually when she returned from school her mother would be watching her favorite soap opera on the television in the living room. Today the house was strangely quiet. She drifted through the living room and down the hall to her parents' bedroom. The door was partially closed and Isabelle heard her mother laughing. Peeking around the edge of the door, she saw her mother sitting on her bed with the phone receiver pressed to her ear. Her mother crossed her legs, tossing her long hair over her shoulder and pursing her lips like she was posing for some girly picture.

Isabelle pushed the door open all the way. "Is that Daddy?"

Her mother jerked upright, frowning at her. She covered the phone with her hand. "Go on out to the kitchen and have your snack."

Isabelle knew by her tone that there would be no negotiation. When she balked at the command, Carrie rose and gave her a little push into the hallway then shut the door in her face. Hurt and angry, Isabelle began kicking the door.

"I want to talk to Daddy!"

Her mother yanked the door open and spun her around, giving her a couple of whacks on the bottom. "Go to your room, right now!"

Isabelle slammed her bedroom door and flung herself onto her bed. For the most part, her mother had always been soft spoken and gentle with her, but lately her patience ran short all the time.

Her father had been gone for weeks and she longed for the stability he brought to their home. Her mother seemed to be changing into someone Isabelle didn't know anymore. She needed her father to right her world again.

When her tears ran dry, she rolled to her back and wiped her face, listening to the sound of her mother's voice in the next room. Minutes later, her mother's footsteps approached her door. After tapping softly, her mother opened the door and sat next to her on the bed. Isabelle rolled to her side, facing the wall. Her mother rubbed her back in small, comforting circles.

"Issy-Belle you know I love you," she said.

Isabelle began to cry again and her mother lifted her, hugging her softly. "Shh, I'm sorry I hurt your feelings, but that call was very important."

"I wanted to talk to Daddy."

"I wasn't talking to your Daddy."

Isabelle pulled back and looked at her mother. Remembering the way her mother perched on the edge of the bed tossing her hair and the strange, lilting sound of her voice brought a sense of prickly discomfort for the second time in half an hour.

Her mother smiled widely and her eyes twinkled. "They're going to pay me to sing, Issy-Belle."

"I don't like that smelly bar," Isabelle said, pouting.

Her mother's smile slipped and she frowned. "What bar?"

"The one where you won the prize."

Her mother laughed and waved her hand in the air. "Oh my goodness, I'm not going back there. We're going to Kansas City."

The notion of a trip, maybe even a stay in a hotel thrilled Isabelle. "When are we going, Mama?"

Her mother's happy expression disappeared again. "You can't go Honey. You have to stay here and go to school."

Isabelle's mother parked their old Buick at the curb in front of her grandmother's small duplex. The place wasn't much, but Grandma Sarah owned the home outright, renting out one side and living in the other.

Grandma Sarah and Isabelle's grandfather had divorced when her mother was just a small child. Sarah had married a second time to a man twenty years her senior and lost him to cancer a few years ago. Now she lived in the small duplex alone. She didn't have much in the way of worldly possessions or money. She got by on a small pension from her second husband, rent from the duplex, and a housecleaning job for some rich people in the better part of town a few days each week. Still, she always seemed content and happy.

Her grandmother's legal name was Sarah Smith, but most people called her Sarah Two-Fingers. Isabelle assumed people called her that because of the missing pinky and third fingers of her left hand.

Grandma Sarah hadn't cut her hair for the last forty years. Most of the time, her waist-length hair was confined in two neat braids, but if she was going out or feeling festive, she combed her hair out and clipped a brightly colored bow on top of her head, never bothering to look in a mirror to see if the bow was centered or standing straight. She shaved her eyebrows and painted them in with an eyebrow pencil. She also believed in the liberal use of blue eye shadow, rouge, and a mix of bangle bracelets, some pure silver, one was gold, and a few plastic ones she had purchased at the Ben Franklin five and dime.

With the exception of Sundays when she wore a dress for church, her usual wardrobe consisted of a pair of loose denim overalls and a man's T-shirt tie-dyed in a variety of pastel colors. In the winter months, Grandma might slip a flannel shirt over her thin arms and put on brightly-colored socks before donning her favorite type of shoe wear…high-top Keds.

Grandma Sarah's house was only five blocks away from Isabelle's house and Isabelle frequently walked over to visit, spending hours enjoying her grandmother's company, but today she was filled with dread. Her mother was leaving to sing with a band, "taking her shot," as she put it. Isabelle's stay at her grandmother's was supposed to last a week, but she had the sinking feeling life was turning in a new and uncertain direction.

The screen door opened and her grandmother headed toward them with a big smile. This morning she had on pink overalls, purple shirt, and black Keds. Her long hair hung around her like a black cape. Straight bangs lay across her forehead and a pink and white polka dot bow rested slightly off kilter on the top of her head. Her lips were smeared with bright red lipstick. Her cheeks were tinged with burgundy rouge, and her eyes streaked with the much-favored blue shadow.

Isabelle's mother groaned as Sarah approached their car. "Here comes the clown."

Sarah yanked open Isabelle's door and planted a loud kiss on her cheek. "Hey-O, it's good to see you Little One."

Isabelle wrapped her arms around her grandmother's thin waist and gave her a big hug.

Isabelle's mother jerked a large suitcase from the backseat and slammed the car door.

Sarah considered the suitcase for a moment. "Just what are you up to Carrie? There's got to be enough in that suitcase for the whole summer."

"You said she could stay Mama," Carrie said, using the particularly peevish tone she saved exclusively for her mother.

Sarah's eyes narrowed considerably. She stepped closer, peering at her daughter. "How long you gonna be gone?"

"It should only be a week."

Sarah wagged a finger in Carrie's face. "This is all wrong."

"Don't start criticizing me again!" Carrie said her voice rising. "If I'm going to be somebody, I can't do it here."

Sarah reached out to touch her face, but Carrie ran for the driver's side of the car.

"I'll be back in a week."

As the Buick disappeared around the corner, Isabelle realized her mother hadn't bothered to say good-bye. Stunned, she did her best not to cry.

Sarah smiled gently and took her hand. "Let's have cake."

Every room of Sarah's house brimmed with odd treasures collected over her lifetime. After having their cake, Grandma Sarah started a load of laundry and Isabelle poked around in the living room, idly inspecting the artifacts. Based on her mother's behavior today, Isabelle feared she might have plenty of days ahead to explore her grandmother's collections.

A small wooden chest contained a collection of handmade wooden toys, but Mason jars seemed to be the most popular containers for Sarah's treasures. One jar held old coins, another arrow heads. Three more jars were stuffed full of Cracker Jack charms like plastic frogs and spiders, tiny baby dolls, whistles, a metal car, and more. On the coffee table was an old coffee grinder, a pink pillbox hat (a replica of the one Jackie Kennedy wore) still in its hat box, and antique penny banks. Isabelle spied a jar full of buttons resting on a bookshelf near the television.

"How come you save all these buttons, Grandma?"

"Bring that jar here. I'll show you."

Sarah placed a cookie sheet on the kitchen table and dumped the contents of the jar onto it. The buttons tinkled and rolled to the edges. Some had rhinestones and glittered like diamonds. Some were yellow or silver metal with imprints of birds and other symbols. Others were smooth pearls. Isabelle picked up a yellowed, oblong object.

"This is a button?"

Sarah nodded. "It belonged to my father. He made a whole set from the horns of his favorite bull when the old beast died. My mother sewed them onto a shirt she made for him. They buried him in that shirt." She picked up the button and smiled. "I got this one before they shut the lid on him."

Isabelle's eyes widened in horror, "You took this from your dead father's shirt?"

A little smile softened her features. "I loved him."

Isabelle tried to imagine the man she never knew and his beloved bull. Sarah picked up another button and it glittered in the afternoon sunlight filtering in through the window.

"This button belonged to your mother," Sarah said. "I made her a real nice gypsy costume for Halloween when she was a little bit older than you." Sarah ran a fingertip over the surface of the button. "One of the few times she wasn't ashamed to be my daughter."

Sarah slumped a little and placed the button back on the pile. Isabelle desperately wanted to erase the sadness from her grandmother's face. She picked up a metal button and prayed she had made a good choice for a bit of distraction.

"Whose button was this?"

"My great-grandfather took it off a confederate soldier's uniform."

"And the man let him?"

Sarah chuckled. "He didn't have a say in the matter. Grandfather caught him stealing chickens and popped him upside the head with a shovel."

"Why did he take the button?"

"He wanted to impress my grandmother. This started out as her collection. Since he was a poor man, he seized the moment."

Isabelle grinned and took a closer look at the button. "I guess it worked."

"They were married seventy-four years."

"Seventy-four? How old were they when they got married?"

"Grandfather was sixteen. Grandmother had just seen her fourteenth birthday."

Isabelle looked down at her hands, thinking of her parents' disintegrating marriage. "I wish Daddy would come home."

Sarah studied her for minute. "He'll be around soon I expect."

"When he finds out what Mama's doing he's going to be mad."

"Well," Sarah said with a sigh. "I don't expect he'll put up with much more of these shenanigans."

Isabelle had already come to the same conclusion. Her father probably wouldn't go on pretending everything was okay much longer.

She dropped the button back in the empty jar and watched it rolled around the bottom. "Do you think he'll move on without me?"

Sarah smiled at her. "Your daddy is a good man. He will always take care of you."

Isabelle wiped away the tears spilling from her eyes with her fingers.

Sarah stood and held out her hand. "Let's play some music."

Isabelle followed her grandmother to the living room where Sarah sorted through a stack of records. "Ah, this one would be perfect."

She placed a record on the spindle, set the needle down, and turned up the volume to Jerry Lee Lewis pounding piano keys and singing Whole Lotta Shakin' Goin' On. Sarah took her hand and twirled her around. Soon they were dancing, silly and free. Sarah whooped and whistled, calling out encouragement to Isabelle as she bopped around, twisted, leaped in the air, and twirled a crocheted afghan around her as she gyrated to the music.

Afterwards, she gave Isabelle a warm embrace. "I love you, Little One."

"I love you too Grandma."

Sarah's face spread into a warm smile that Isabelle just knew came all the way from heaven.

That evening, she joined her grandmother in the living room as Sarah strummed a battered ukulele and sang hymns. Sarah's voice was truly beautiful, even more than Isabelle's mother's. The sound of her voice was sweet and smooth, with a natural vibrato. Isabelle closed her eyes and let her grandmother's songs lift her above the troubles of her young life.

Sarah never had much of worldly value, but she had heart. Isabelle didn't care what people thought of her spirited grandmother. Like her father always said, if they couldn't see beyond the physical, they were missing the point.

The first week at Sarah's flew by easy enough. Sarah walked her to school, met her afterwards, and walked her home. After finishing her homework, Isabelle joined her grandmother in the kitchen for an adventure in cooking. One of Sarah's pastimes was reinventing recipes. Currently, she was experimenting with chicken. They had roasted chicken coated with peanut butter and honey (not good), chicken simmered with root vegetables and root beer (okay, except for the turnips), fried chicken coated with cornmeal and flour, various herbs, and a too-generous amount of cayenne pepper (singing along to Blue Moon, Sarah had closed her eyes while adding the spice). The pièce de resistance was roasted chicken pizza, which turned out excellent.

After school on Friday, Isabelle listened for her mother's car with heightened anticipation, running to the window every time she thought she heard a car stop outside her grandmother's house. As daylight faded into night, so did the hope that her mother would come. She lay in bed that night and pleaded with God to send her mother home soon.

She was picking at her chocolate chip pancakes Saturday morning when the phone rang. Sarah answered before the first ring was complete. She smiled at Isabelle and covered the receiver with her hand.

"It's your daddy," she whispered.

Sarah's smile slipped as she listened. "Oh, goodness, I'm so sorry Marshall. Isabelle's just fine. She's been here with me."

She listened, shifting her gaze away from Isabelle to the wall behind the stove. "Well, she was supposed to be back yesterday."

Sarah listened a little more, nodding her head. "Of course."

Sarah held the receiver out to Isabelle. She rose from the table and accepted the receiver with a heavy heart.

"Daddy?"

"Hey Baby. Are you getting by okay at Grandma's?"

"Mama didn't come home," she said, her voice cracking.

"Now Baby, you cheer up, everything's going to be just fine," he said gently.

Tears came to Isabelle's eyes and she swallowed hard as they talked a bit more. Sarah moved closer and patted her on the back. At the conclusion of the call, Isabelle replaced the receiver and wrapped her arms around her grandmother's waist.

NINE

In the following weeks, she remained with her grandmother. Her father came home when he could, sometimes driving hundreds of miles just to see her for a few hours. Occasionally, he spent the night on Sarah's sofa, but he never took Isabelle back to their house. When out traveling with the rodeo, he called every Sunday without fail. He also regularly sent money to her grandmother to cover expenses.

Her mother was an entirely different story. After weeks of silence, she called on a Friday night and announced she would be there around noon on Saturday.

Isabelle finished lunch and hurried to the porch to wait for her mother. Around four that afternoon, an unfamiliar car pulled to the curb and the passenger door swung open. Isabelle watched as her mother leaned over and gave the driver a quick kiss on the lips. Her mother swung her legs out and swayed up the sidewalk on spiky high heels. Even though the weather was warm, she had a fur wrap slung over one shoulder. She had on a form-fitted red dress and on her head was the ugliest little hat Isabelle had ever seen. The dome-shaped black hat had foot-long purple feathers stuck in the band and a short black veil falling just below her mother's nose. Isabelle thought her mother had a lot of nerve criticizing Grandma Sarah for her fashion choices.

Her mother paused, holding out her arms. "Hey Issy-Belle, come give Mama some sugar."

Isabelle obeyed, but her heart wasn't in the act. Her mother smelled like stinky perfume and whiskey. Isabelle wrinkled her nose in disgust and backed away from her mother.

Sarah appeared at the screen door, "Shame on you for keeping this child waiting all day…"

As Sarah continued to scold her daughter, she switched to native Cherokee. Isabelle's mother didn't listen anymore than she ever had. She knelt in front of Isabelle and pulled a folded piece of paper from her purse, handing it to Isabelle. It was a flyer announcing the appearance of Bob Taylor and the Troubadours featuring vocalist Carrie Long at the Crystal Lounge in Dallas, Texas.

"See Issy-Belle? Mama's a real singer now." She looked over Isabelle's shoulder to Sarah. "It's all working out for me."

Her mother rose slowly and pulled a roll of bills from her purse as she approached Sarah, who remained behind the screen door. "I brought some money for you, Mama."

Sarah ignored the money. Looking past her daughter, she pointed at the car parked curbside. "Who's that man?"

"My boss, Bob Taylor."

"Does he know you're a married woman?"

"Yes, ma'am," her mother responded with a toss of her head, "and he doesn't mind at all."

Sarah grunted and pushed the screen door open. "Get inside, Isabelle."

After Isabelle stepped over the threshold, Sarah shut the inner door blocking her out, but Isabelle ran to the open window where she could see and hear their conversation perfectly.

"What you're doing is all wrong and you know it," Sarah said.

Carrie thrust the bills at Sarah once more. "Take it, Mama. Buy Isabelle some clothes."

Sarah folded her arms over her thin chest and shook her head. "That money's tainted."

"Do what you want with it." Carrie tossed the money at Sarah's feet and turned back to the car. Isabelle flung the door open and ran after her.

"Mama wait!"

Carrie didn't look back. She opened the car door and before Isabelle reached the sidewalk her mother was on her way again.

Isabelle grabbed a handful of rocks from the gutter and threw them at the car. Sarah sidestepped the roll of money, came straight to Isabelle, and handed her more rocks.

Shadow

TEN

On Sunday, Isabelle attended church with her grandmother. While the pastor said a prayer, Isabelle bowed her head, begging God to please bring her mother home and for her life to return to normal. In exchange for giving her back her family, she promised to make her bed and brush her teeth without being told, and to never, ever be sassy again. She would be a good girl from here on out. Amen.

As they strolled home from church, Sarah sang the last hymn, and Isabelle reached for her hand. Sarah squeezed gently and kept singing.

They turned the corner and, like an answer to her prayer, there was her father leaning against his truck in front of Sarah's duplex.

Isabelle ran to him. "Daddy!"

He knelt on the sidewalk and wrapped his arms around her.

"I've missed you so much, Baby," he said.

"How long can you stay?"

He stood, took a breath then smiled thinly. "I won't be leaving you anymore."

"Good for you Marshall," Sarah said.

He nodded at Sarah then looked down at Isabelle. "We're going to be just fine, you and me."

After lunch her father told her to get her things together, they were going home. Isabelle obediently went to her bedroom, but instead of packing she spied on her father and grandmother through a crack in the door. Though they spoke in quiet tones, she heard the conversation taking place in the kitchen perfectly.

"I went to the house this morning," her father said. "Carrie's things are gone."

He reached into his coat pocket and pulled out an envelope then placed it on the table. "Divorce papers," he said bitterly.

Isabelle gasped. Her best friend at school said divorce meant your parents fought all the time and didn't live in the same house anymore. She tried to calm down and listen as her father continued.

"She left them on the kitchen table with a note saying she wants me to sign them and mail them to her at a post office box in Dallas," he said.

"I'm not surprised," Sarah said.

Sarah went on to explain the recent visit from Carrie in less emotional terms than Isabelle would have used. Still, the account of events hurt all over again.

Marshall lowered his head and Isabelle couldn't see his face or gage his reaction to the news.

When Sarah finished the brief narrative, she patted his knee. I'm sorry."

He inhaled then released the breath slowly. "My cousin Derby caught up with me in Albuquerque. He's been checking the mail for me and found an overdue notice from the bank on the house."

He kicked his feet out in front of him and sighed tiredly. "So, I called the bank about the house payment. They said there wasn't enough money in our account. There should have been over five-hundred dollars in the there." He paused for a moment then continued in an even softer voice. "I can't believe she'd do this."

Sarah rose and retrieved an old coffee can from the cabinet above the stove. She pulled out the roll of bills Isabelle's mother threw at her feet and held the roll out to Marshall.

"Carrie left this."

Her father stared at the money, but didn't reach for the roll. He looked beat down and tired. Finally, he shook his head. "I just didn't see this coming."

Sarah placed the money on the table before him and patted his shoulder. "Well, it's here."

All the longing, disappointment, and fear of losing her mother swelled in Isabelle's chest. She backed away from the door, sank to the floor, covered her face with a pillow, and released her heartbreak.

Isabelle stepped inside their house and looked around the living room. Though this was the only home she knew, she felt like a trespasser in her former life. Like in some science fiction movie, she expected to see another Isabelle, a happy, contented girl with the confidence that her mother still loved her. They would play games at the kitchen table, laugh, and tell silly jokes just like before.

The family photos still rested on a shelf above the console television. There they were smiling, cherished, contented, before the impossible yearning her mother hid so well rose like a demon and swallowed their happiness whole.

"She didn't take the pictures," Isabelle murmured.

Her father seemed just as struck down as she. He was still standing just five steps from the front door, nearly mid stride, holding her suitcase, as if they were playing a game of statue and someone had yelled freeze! When she spoke, he turned to look at her, blinked a couple of times then inhaled sharply as if reminded to breathe. He turned toward the hallway leading to the bedrooms and she followed. He placed her suitcase on her bed and walked back toward the hall.

With the exception of dust, everything in her room was exactly as she had left it. The quiet of the house added to the weight of sorrow blanketing her.

She looked over at her father who remained half in/half out of the room, seemingly lost. Anger stirred in her and she crossed to the window, yanking it open with force.

"We need some air in here," she announced, mimicking Grandma Sarah.

Her father focused on the window then looked to her, his face relaxing a bit. "Yes," he said. "Let's air the house out."

ELEVEN

Marshall's new job working with horses at a local ranch barely covered the bills, but they got by. If he was unhappy about leaving the rodeo, he never let on. In the evening, he prepared supper while Isabelle did her homework at the kitchen table. After a bath, she settled on the couch next to her father and they watched TV until her bedtime.

Isabelle did whatever she could to help around the house. She tried her hand at laundry, mostly by trial and error. School let out at three-thirty, so she was home an hour before her father. She swept the floors, made the beds, dusted furniture, and started attempting a little cooking with Grandma Sarah's guidance. One night, after a second helping of a chicken and rice casserole, Marshall pushed his plate away and patted his mouth with his napkin.

"That was very good, Isabelle."

"I got the recipe out of a magazine," she said proudly, rising to start the dishes.

Her father caught her hand. "I want you to stop."

She looked at him in surprise. "Stop what, Daddy?"

"I appreciate everything you're doing, but I want you to be a little girl again."

She laughed. "I'm still a little girl."

He held up a hand, stopping her. "I mean it. Stop all this housework and cooking."

"I just wanted to help," she said, tears forming in her eyes.

"And you do a great job, but this isn't what I want for you. Let me be the daddy. Your job is to be the child."

"I want to do my part."

He considered her for a minute. "And that's fine. You can still help around the house by making your bed, doing your homework every day, picking up after yourself, and helping me clean the house on weekends."

"I like to cook," she said stubbornly.

"Fine," he said, holding up two fingers, "Twice a week, but only if Grandma or I are here to supervise."

Though his church attendance in the past had been spotty at best, Marshall now rose every Sunday morning and took Isabelle to the Baptist church his cousin Derby and his family attended. Every other week, they picked up Grandma Sarah and took her to lunch after church. On the other Sundays, Isabelle wandered over to spend the afternoon with Sarah while her father sat in his favorite easy chair reading the Sunday paper or watching a ballgame on television, both of which eventually led to a nap.

For the church's annual chicken and dumpling dinner, her father decided to donate a cake. He and Isabelle got out the recipe book and chose pineapple upside down cake. On Friday evening they shopped for all the ingredients and set to work. Due to an unlevel oven, the cake turned out uneven and nearly burnt on the thinner end, but they took the cake to the church anyway.

At the dessert table, a short, stout woman accepted the cake from Marshall's hands.

"We made it ourselves," Isabelle told her proudly.

The woman peeled back the aluminum foil covering the cake and inhaled, closing her eyes and smiling. "Um-um, this smells good!"

"It's more done on one end," Marshall said, pointing to the darkened part.

The woman looked him in the eye. "I'm sure the cake is just fine." She held out her hand to him. "I don't believe I've had the pleasure of meeting you before. I'm Rose Dix."

He took her hand and shook it lightly. "Marshall Long. And this is my daughter Isabelle."

Rose held out her hand to Isabelle and smiled even wider. "It's a pleasure to meet you Isabelle."

"You too, ma'am."

They purchased two chicken and dumpling dinners and found space at a table with Marshall's cousin Derby and his family. Halfway through the meal Rose Dix approached with a glass of iced tea in hand and another pretty smile.

"How's everybody doing?" Rose asked.

Marshall and his cousin both stood, but she waved them back to their seats. "Don't let me disturb your meal."

The knowing look exchanged between cousin Derby's wife and Rose Dix did not escape Isabelle's notice.

"Would you like to join us Rose?" Derby's wife asked.

Rose smiled even wider, "Don't mind if I do."

The only empty chair was conveniently located next to Marshall. As Rose settled in, Isabelle felt a stab of discomfort at the sight of another woman sitting next to her father. She watched with curiosity as her father and Rose chatted and laughed easily.

When her father and Rose Dix began dating, Isabelle knew the last hope of her little family coming back together again was gone, but she was happy to see that after months of grieving her father seemed to be coming back to life.

By eavesdropping on adult conversations, Isabelle learned that Rose Dix had lost a husband in some war and never married again. She had no children. She was a devoted Christian who loved gospel music. If she had any fault, it would be that she had a fondness for cats, in fact had three cats in her home and two neighborhood strays she fed routinely. Isabelle feared this could be a negative for her father, since his dislike of cats was great, but he passed right on by this information with no notice whatsoever.

Rose had a kind of inner joy that put people at ease and made everyone want to be in her company, cats or no cats. Isabelle was no exception. The woman was so kind, generous, and genuinely affectionate, Isabelle accepted her without reservation.

Tulsa, Oklahoma

Summer 1962

TWELVE

As spring turned to summer and the school year ended, Isabelle was still checking the mail for any news from her mother. She jumped to answer the phone every time it rang, hoping to hear her mother's voice. Her father had moved on, which was fine for him, but she hadn't given up the hope that her mother would return, or at least call, send a postcard, anything.

Her father took down all the pictures of her mother from the shelf over the console TV, wrapped them in paper and stored them away. Isabelle still had the photo of her and her mother sitting on the dresser in her bedroom. Sometimes she kissed the image of her mother. Other times, she stuck her tongue out and turned the frame face down.

In her haste to exit their lives, her mother overlooked a pair of worn red high heels in a corner of the closet. Isabelle took the shoes to her room before her father had a chance to throw them out. She placed the shoes in a shoe box, along with the flyer her mother had given her announcing the appearance of Bob Taylor and the Troubadours featuring vocalist Carrie Long at the Crystal Lounge in Dallas, Texas. Sometimes she closed her bedroom door, slipped the red shoes on, stood in front of the mirror, and sang along to the radio using her hairbrush as a microphone.

One evening, while her father and Rose sat on the front porch after supper, she closed her bedroom door, slipped on the shoes, turned on her radio and belted out a popular tune with abandon, forgetting the windows were open. She closed her eyes and imagined a crowd of fans listening to her every note. When the song wound down, she opened her eyes and discovered her father and Rose standing in the open doorway.

Embarrassed, she switched the radio off. "I'm sorry," she said.

"No, no," her father said coming into the room. "Honey, it's just… we didn't know you could sing like that."

"Beautiful!" Rose said. "I'm going to see to it that you join the choir!"

Her father's attention was drawn to the red shoes on Isabelle's feet. He looked back to her face, his eyes twinkling and sadness skittering around the corners of his eyes. He came closer and kissed her forehead.

"I love you Sweetheart," he said softly, brushing his hand over the top of her head.

On the last day of June, her father married Rose at their church in a quiet little ceremony. Rose moved into their little house with her cats, which Isabelle didn't mind one little bit. The cats took to her immediately and began sleeping with her with their soft fur, purring noises, and gentle paws.

Isabelle was truly happy for her father, and even a bit for herself. The big-hearted, joyful Rose loved her so unconditionally she found it impossible not to love her back. Still, she mourned the loss of her mother and the life she would not have again.

THIRTEEN

Isabelle's birthday fell on the Fourth of July and for every birthday she could remember, her father had been on the road with the rodeo. Her mother always took her on an outing, somewhere special, like a museum or the Tulsa Zoo. After their outing, she and her mother would go to Grandma Sarah's for cake and ice cream then Isabelle would spend the night watching fireworks from Grandma Sarah's little front porch and sleep over.

This year Rose planned a little party with Isabelle's closest friends. She made a beautiful cake and bought ice cream. There were games and lots of presents. For Isabelle, the best part was that her father would be there.

Before the party, Isabelle took a bath then went to her room to dress. There on her bed were two presents wrapped with pretty paper and big bows. She touched one of the bows tentatively.

"I got you a little something," Rose said from the doorway.

Isabelle glanced at her smiling face. "Thank you, Miss Rose."

Rose nodded at the packages. "Open the big one first."

Rose didn't need to tell her a second time. Isabelle was more than ready to rip into those pretty packages.

The first box contained a beautiful pink dress handmade in secret by Rose. Isabelle slipped the dress over her head and Rose buttoned it up the back then tied the waist bow. Isabelle smoothed the front of the frilly skirt with her hands wondering if her worn Sunday shoes would be fancy enough for such a fine dress.

"It's so pretty," she said.

Rose turned her around and smiled widely. "Baby you are such a beautiful child." Rose nudged her gently. "Go on, open the other box."

The second box contained a pair of black, patent leather dress shoes and fancy socks with lace and little pink flowers embroidered around the top. Isabelle squealed with delight. A few weeks ago, on a shopping trip downtown, she had admired these very shoes, but her father had insisted they were too expensive.

Rose wove her long hair into two braids and tied pretty bows that matched her dress at the end of each one. Normally, Isabelle avoided such pretties, as Rose called them, but when she looked at the bows she thought of her grandmother. The tribute made her smile.

"Thank you, Miss Rose," she said.

Miss Rose seemed on the verge of tears. "I'd like to ask a favor," she said in a strange, quiet voice.

Isabelle looked up from her braids and bows to the sweet face of her stepmother.

"Would you please consider calling me Mama Rose?" Rose asked quietly.

Isabelle smiled and gave her a hug. "I'd like that very much."

After the party, she went to Grandma Sarah's to spend the night, as was their tradition. Grandma Sarah presented her with the gift of a portable record player and a stack of 45 rpm records.

"This is wonderful!" Isabelle said as she sorted through the new records.

They played music, sang, and danced with abandon before settling on the front porch to watch the neighborhood fireworks. No one in this section of town could afford much, but Sarah gazed at the display of bottle rockets and a few bigger bursts of color with childlike delight. She clapped with delight drawing Isabelle's attention to her hand and prompting her to ask Sarah how she came to lose her fingers.

"Hey-O, you picked a good night for a story," Sarah said. "Let's get some ice cream and I'll tell you."

Eating at Sarah's was nearly always an adventure. Sarah took a carton of Neapolitan ice cream from the freezer and canned whipped cream from the refrigerator.

"Get us the ice cream scoop, two big bowls, and a couple of spoons," she told Isabelle.

From the pantry, Sarah gathered chopped nuts, a jar of maraschino cherries, two bananas, a jar of marshmallow cream, chocolate, strawberry, and caramel toppings and placed all of it on the kitchen table.

Once the ice cream was scooped into the bowls and toppings were added, Sarah launched into the story of how she lost her fingers.

"I met your grandfather, old Good-For-Nothing, when I was barely sixteen. He was twenty-two and I thought he was a grown man. When we were falling in love, he lied about everything. He said his family had this great big farm and led me to believe they had money. After we married, he took me home to live with his parents and I learned they weren't any better off than my folks."

She paused and pointed her spoon at Isabelle. "Don't ever fall for wooden nickels, Little One."

Isabelle had no idea what she meant. "There are wooden nickels?"

"It's just a saying. It means, be on your guard, don't fall for any lies or schemes just because the boy's a looker."

Sarah added a dollop of marshmallow cream to the scoop of chocolate ice cream in her bowl before continuing her story. "Good-For-Nothing was a mama's boy. His mama was mean, and jealous of me. Me and her never got along."

"Why not?" Isabelle asked.

"I expected her son to be a man. She wanted to keep him a baby."

Sarah swallowed some ice cream, smiled, and smacked her lips before continuing.

"One night, when your mama was almost two, Good-For-Nothing's mother and I were making supper when your mama strayed too close to the wood stove. Good-For-Nothing's mother popped her on the shoulder with the butt of a skinning knife. I was always just as skinny as I am now and the old cow was much too big for me to take on, but nobody was going to hurt my baby. Before I knew it, I had cut that mean old woman with my own knife and the fight was on. That's when she whacked off my fingers."

Sarah picked up a can of Hershey's syrup and poured a generous amount onto her ice cream then sprinkled chopped walnuts over it. Stunned about the knife fight, Isabelle handed her the can of whipped cream and waited for her to continue.

"When my hand healed," Sarah said, "I took my baby and left Good-For-Nothing to suck his mama's tit. I heard that mean old woman kept my fingers in a pouch around her neck and they buried her with them."

Sarah stuck a spoonful of ice cream in her mouth and smacked her lips again. Isabelle was flabbergasted at the thought of someone cutting off her grandmother's fingers and then keeping them in a pouch.

"That must have hurt something terrible!"

Sarah nodded. "Bled a lot too, but as you can see, I lived to tell the tale."

"Is that why they call you Sarah Two-Fingers?"

Sarah swallowed another spoonful and shook her head. "None of that has anything to do with my nickname. My mother gave me the name because I have a talent for seeing with my fingers."

She picked up Isabelle's hand, rubbing it lightly with her right thumb, index, and forefinger. "Like this."

"What do you see, Grandma?"

Sarah sighed and looked out the window as a rocket exploded then burst into colors right over their street. "The night you were born, I sat right out there on my porch and watched the most glorious fireworks." Sarah released her grip and gave Isabelle's hand a little pat. "I knew you were going to be special."

"I'm serious, Grandma. I want to know what you see."

Sarah smiled widely. "I see ice cream melting."

"Grandma, please?"

Sarah sighed, picking up her hand again. "One hint then."

Isabelle sat forward a bit, ready for her destiny to be revealed.

Sarah winked at her. "Don't burn bridges."

Isabelle rolled her eyes and sat back in her chair. "That's just an old saying Grandma."

"Maybe, but for you, it's perfect."

FOURTEEN

Sarah sniffed the hot bubbly strawberry goo in the big pot on the stove and smiled. "These preserves will be our best yet," she said to Isabelle.

Isabelle placed the last clean Mason jar on the table at the end of a neat line. Yesterday they picked strawberries at a nearby farm then brought them back to Sarah's. Surprisingly, Sarah did very little experimenting with this particular batch.

"It sure smells good," Isabelle said.

Sarah glanced into a smaller pot on the back burner. "Looks like the paraffin is ready. Just a few more minutes and…"

The wall phone rang and Sarah put the receiver to her ear, dragging the long cord back to the stove to stir her preserves.

"Sure thing," Sarah said. "These preserves are just about ready to go in the jars then we'll be right there."

She replaced the receiver and hurried to turn off the burner beneath the strawberry preserves. "That was your Daddy. He wants us to come over as soon as we finish. He's got some news."

Isabelle, along with Grandma Sarah, joined her father and Mama Rose at the kitchen table. Mama Rose had set out a coffee cake and a pitcher of lemonade. Isabelle's first impression was they were having a celebration, but one look at her father's solemn expression told her otherwise. As was his style, he wasted no time in getting to the point.

"I've taken another job," he said.

Isabelle said nothing, wondering with a sinking feeling if this meant he was going back to the rodeo.

"I'll be foreman on a horse ranch a few hours south of here," Marshall said.

Sarah blew out, kind of like someone just jabbed her in the belly with an elbow.

This was too much for Isabelle, too many changes. She shook her head, tears in her eyes. "I don't want you to go away again, Daddy."

"No, no, Baby, we'll all be moving," Marshall said.

She looked at her grandmother whose sweet face was drawn down in sad lines.

"Grandma too?" Isabelle asked. She knew the answer was most likely no, but hoped her father might just consider the option.

"My place is here," Sarah said turning to her. "This will be good for you, Little One, an adventure."

"We won't be that far," Marshall said. "I'll bring you up to see Grandma as much as possible."

In no time at all, their little house was sold, their belongings boxed and tucked away in the U-Haul trailer attached to Marshall's truck. Isabelle left the only home she ever knew with a heavy heart to spend one last night with her grandmother.

At nine the next morning, Isabelle stood on the sidewalk in front of her grandmother's house clinging to her waist as her father and Mama Rose waited at the curb. Today Sarah wore no makeup. No bow. No brightly colored shirts.

"Time to go," Sarah said softly.

Isabelle looked up at her. "I don't want to leave you."

Sarah reached down and gently wiped the tears from her cheeks. "I love you, Little One. You have to go now."

Isabelle walked toward Mama Rose's car. Mama Rose patted her back and opened the passenger door for her. As they drove away, Isabelle leaned out the car window, waving to her grandmother who blew her kisses from the curb until they turned the corner.

She laid her head on Mama Rose's lap and cried quietly for all she was leaving behind. Grandma Sarah was a big part of her sorrow, but the hope that she would see her mother materializing around some corner ended today.

Hours later, Mama Rose gently nudged her awake. "Time to wake up, Sugar. We're almost there."

Isabelle sat up and rubbed the sleep from her eyes, yawning widely as she took in the pretty town. There were flowers on every corner and dotting the town square. People strolled along the sidewalks, some stood talking and laughing. There was a movie theater, a small diner, and numerous other shops along the street.

"Where are we?" Isabelle asked.

Mama Rose smiled. "Our new home. Welcome to Shadow."

Shadow, Oklahoma

Summer 1962

FIFTEEN

A few miles outside the town of Shadow they came to a single lane bridge. Mama Rose slowed the car then stopped completely. After slipping the gear into park, she lifted her hands from the steering wheel and flexed her fingers.

"I just hate these old bridges," Mama Rose said, grimacing as Marshall drove across ahead of them.

By now, the sun was high in the sky and the temperature was rising. Isabelle rolled her window down, eyeing the land to her right. A packed dirt and gravel path, plenty wide enough for cars, sloped gently away from the blacktop toward the river. Isabelle got on her knees and poked her head out the window for a better look. She spotted a few kids milling about down by the river bank, their happy voices echoing under the bridge.

Hearing the children, Rose inhaled sharply. "My goodness! Are those children? Are they swimming in this river?"

"I'm pretty sure I heard a splash."

Mama Rose gasped and stabbed the air with an index finger, "Snakes!" She nodded for emphasis, apparently satisfied the single word was all that was required by way of an explanation.

Marshall had crossed the bridge and was now out of his truck waiting for them. He walked behind the U-Haul trailer, his brow wrinkled in confusion, and began waving them on impatiently. With a deep breath, Mama Rose shifted the car back into drive, depressed the gas pedal ever so gently, and gripped the steering wheel with both hands. As they began to move forward, she hummed the Battle Hymn of the Republic. Once she finally had all four tires on the bridge, she lifted her foot from the gas pedal, allowing the car to idle across. Confounded, Marshall tipped his hat back and shook his head. As he waited, he glanced at his watch several times, but never said a word to his new wife.

Once they reached the other side and were back on solid ground, Mama Rose once again brought the car to a stop, heaved a big sigh, and wiped the perspiration from her forehead with the dainty handkerchief she always kept in the pocket of her dress.

"I sure hope we find another way into town," she said.

A short distance from the bridge, they reached a fork in the road and turned to their left passing by a lot of pasture land. A few homes in the distance sat at the base of a ridge of hills rising high into the sky.

After a short bit they turned off the blacktop and passed through a fancy double-gated entrance onto a gravel road leading to the Wagner ranch and their new home. A white rail fence bordered each side of the nearly half-mile drive to the ranch.

Isabelle took in the high hills and the pasture land where horses grazed contentedly. "This place is big, Mama Rose."

"Daddy says they have about five-hundred acres."

They came to a stop in front of the main house where the ranch owners resided. Isabelle was happy to be out of the car after the long ride. She stretched and had another look around while her father mounted the front steps and knocked on the door.

The main house was a sturdy stone structure. Five steps led up to colored stone columns and an expansive concrete porch. The gravel road continued ahead until it split in two directions. Isabelle could see several stables, corrals, and outbuildings.

A woman appeared and pushed open the screen door of the main house. She smiled at Marshall like they were old friends.

"Welcome, welcome! How was your drive?"

"Just fine, Mrs. Wagner."

Mrs. Wagner caught sight of Mama Rose and Isabelle standing by the car and crossed the porch past Marshall then down the steps in a hurry. She held out her hand to Mama Rose.

"I'm Nora Wagner. It is a pleasure to meet you Mrs. Long."

Mama Rose, now recovered from her panic attack, smiled and took Nora's hand. "Please call me Rose."

Nora turned her energetic focus to Isabelle. "And who is this beautiful child?"

"This is our Isabelle," Mama Rose said.

Nora once again extended her hand. "How do you do Isabelle?"

"Just fine, ma'am, thank you."

Nora gave her hand a little shake then straightened up and turned to Marshall who had followed her down the stairs. She pointed toward the gravel road.

"See that fork in the road?"

They all turned, staring into the distance with her.

"Go to your left and you'll find your house down there on the right. I took the liberty of stocking the fridge with a few things."

"I should probably let Mr. Wagner know I'm here…" Marshall began, but she stopped his words with a wave of her hand.

"Tom's down at the stables. Y'all just go on to your house now and get settled in. I'll call down and let him know you've arrived."

"Thank you, Mrs. Wagner," Marshall said.

She shook her head. "We're just not the formal type around here. Call me Nora." She smiled, tossed her hands in the air then swooped back up the steps. "Gotta run before I burn the cake."

Rhonda Tibbs

Their new home was a roomy stone house some distance from the main house. Privacy would not be an issue. The yard around their house was expansive, loaded with flowers and a few shade trees front and back. The closest structure was a long stable some distance down the road.

Rose emerged from the car and smiled. "My goodness, isn't this pretty?"

Marshall whistled. "I never expected all this."

They entered the house and roamed around, inspecting each room in a kind of awe.

Isabelle spent the next few hours helping unload the vehicles then turned her attention to her new room. Before anything else was unpacked, she took the shoebox with mother's shoes and the flyer for the show in Dallas out of her suitcase and placed them in a dark corner of her closet.

She truly liked their new home, but that didn't stop the homesickness from eating at her. Every time the longing for what had been crept up on her, she did her best to push it from her mind.

Supper that evening was provided by the Wagner's on their expansive patio. Mama Rose's personality fit right in with Nora Wagner's friendly style. While the women discussed children, shopping, and churches, the men got to know each other better.

Isabelle grew bored listening to their conversation and asked to be excused. She wandered back to their new house and to her room where she opened her closet door and sat on the floor. She pulled her mother's red shoes from their box and slipped them on her feet. Tears came again and she allowed herself another good cry, vowing this would be her last, a vow she hoped to keep.

She woke sometime later when her father lifted her. The red shoes slipped from her feet to the floor with a soft thud. He sat on her bed and held her, rocking back and forth.

"It's going to be all right, Baby," he said, repeating the phrase over and over.

Sunday morning she woke to the sound of Mama Rose singing a hymn in the kitchen. Her bedroom window was open and the fragrance of flowers comingled with the scent of fresh air and horses.

She stretched her arms over her head and threw back the covers, determined to make this a day without tears.

Isabelle made her way to the kitchen and took a seat at the table. Mama rose placed a bowl of sausage gravy on the table next to a plate of biscuits.

"That Nora left us all kinds of food," Mama Rose said.

"This looks so good. I'm hungry."

"We're running late for church. Go ahead and fill your plate. I'll go get your daddy from the corral across the way."

"Church?"

"Nora gave me directions to a nice Baptist church in town."

"Are you ready to cross that bridge again so soon, Mama Rose?"

Mama Rose sighed loudly. "I'd better be, unless I want to drive 20 miles out of my way to get into town."

Marshall came through the back door and gave Mama Rose a kiss. "Smells wonderful in here."

He winked at Isabelle and headed for the sink to wash his hands. "Morning."

"Morning, Daddy."

Since her father drove them to church, the trip across the bridge was less dramatic this time. Mama Rose merely held her breath and squeezed her eyes closed while she hummed. They found the church easily. Isabelle was enraptured by the choir. After the service, friendly people welcomed them with honest warmth. Mama Rose wasted no time telling the pastor about her stepdaughter's beautiful voice.

"She would be a fine asset to your choir," Mama Rose said.

The pastor smiled kindly. "I'm sorry, but we don't have a children's choir."

"What? A children's choir? No, sir, I'm talking about the choir I heard today."

"Well, I…"

"When does the choir rehearse? I'll bring her by and she can try out. You'll see what I'm talking about."

The pastor seemed trapped by Mama Rose's enthusiasm. "Wednesday, six-thirty."

The pastor glanced at the line forming behind them then at Marshall who nudged Mama Rose along. "We need to get going."

Mama Rose shook the pastor's hand for a second time. "We'll see you on Wednesday."

After a nice meal at Ruby's Diner and a drive around the small town, they headed back to the ranch. As they neared Purser's Bridge they encountered a group of boys ranging from younger than Isabelle to teenagers standing or sitting on the side rails. Marshall stopped the car and waited for the group to clear the bridge.

"There sure seems to be a lot of kids around here," Marshall said as they started across.

"They swim in that river," Mama Rose said with a shake of her head.

From the backseat, Isabelle leaned forward so that her head was poking between her father and Mama Rose. "Could we come down here sometime and go swimming?"

Mama Rose's eyes widened in horror. "There are snakes down there."

"Now Rose, they're probably more snakes around the ranch," Marshall said.

Mama Rose shuddered. "Don't remind me."

Marshall met Isabelle's eyes in the rearview mirror, a little smile playing at the corners of his mouth and he winked.

On Wednesday evening, as promised, Mama Rose drove her to the church for choir rehearsal. The music director reluctantly agreed to allow Isabelle to try out. He sat in front of the piano and began playing "In the Sweet By and By." Since this was one of Grandma Sarah's favorite hymns, Isabelle knew the song well. And, though she never sang a solo before, she performed the song with enthusiasm as a tribute to her grandmother. Mama Rose couldn't have been prouder when she finished. The music director and choir members applauded.

"We don't have any children in our choir, but we could make an exception for this child here and there," the director said.

Every one of the adults in the choir agreed and with that, Isabelle took another step forward in joining her new community and one more step away from her old life in Tulsa.

SIXTEEN

Nora Wagner told Isabelle she was welcome to swim in their pool anytime she wanted, but the solitude of the quiet ranch pool wasn't what she was looking for. Every time they crossed the bridge she saw lots of kids enjoying themselves at the river. While the water of the Wagner pool looked cool and inviting, she was lonely and wanted friends more than anything.

One afternoon, while Mama Rose was in town attending a Bible study class and Marshall was busy with the horses, Isabelle rode her bike down to the river. Her spirits fell when she didn't hear any voices and didn't see any kids.

She walked her bike down the worn path leading from the road to the edge of the river and stepped into the shade under the bridge. Sitting on the grassy bank, she removed her shoes and dangled her feet over the water, humming a tune. Fascinated by the way her voice resonated off the water, concrete, and metal, she opened her mouth and sang without holding back. Finished, she leaned back on her elbows feeling better for her adventure. Behind her, someone whistled.

Turning, she locked eyes with a wide-eyed boy sitting cross-legged with a book on his lap. He smiled and gave her a short wave.

She jumped to her feet and shoved her fists on her hips. "Have you been spying on me this whole time?"

He shrugged nonchalantly. "I was here first."

He considered her for a minute, as if her face was something to be studied. "I like the way you sing," he said finally.

He probably had the most angelic face she ever saw. He seemed so guileless and sweet, she couldn't help but smile.

"Thanks," she said.

She walked over and looked down at a drawing on top of a sketchbook on his lap. Apparently, he had sketched her as she sat with her back to him, singing her song.

"That's me," she said softly.

"Want it?"

She shook her head. "If I take that home, they'll know I was here."

He pointed his pencil at the towel in her bicycle basket. "Were you going to swim, or did you just come to check the acoustics?"

"I wanted to swim, but not by myself."

He put the book aside and stood. "You're not by yourself."

Isabelle wasn't a reserved person, but this boy was fearless. He did back flips and jumps off the side of the river bank without a second thought. He grabbed the rope swing tied under the bridge, ran hard, then brought his knees up and swung way out, over the center of the river, before dropping.

Isabelle tried to keep up with his energy, but finally gave up. She spread her towel on the grassy bank and he joined her.

"Do you have any more drawings?" she asked.

He handed over the sketch pad, sat down, and slipped on his shoes. "You'll have to hurry, I have to get going."

Isabelle marveled at page after page of people, animals, and landscapes then took a closer look at him. He seemed to sense her stare and met her gaze. The sun glanced off the surface of the water and his big brown eyes sparkled.

"I never heard anybody sing like you before," he said. "Your voice gave me goose bumps."

"Thank you," she said, feeling suddenly shy.

She turned back to the drawings to hide her embarrassment. She held up one of a man riding a comet. "Who's this?"

"Mark Twain. Halley's Comet came through the year he was born and again right after he died. I copied that picture from a book at the library."

A vehicle rumbled over the bridge and he jumped to his feet. "I have to go."

He gathered his drawings and ran up the path toward the road then paused at the top, offering her a quick smile.

"I'm Danny," he said.

He ran away so quickly, she didn't have a chance to give him her name.

On the following Saturday, her father had business at a neighboring ranch and asked Isabelle and Mama Rose to ride along to meet the neighbors who lived just a few miles down the blacktop.

He smiled at Isabelle. "I hear they've got a lot of kids over there. Maybe you could make some friends."

Isabelle sat in her father's truck between him and Mama Rose for the short ride. When they turned off the blacktop onto a gravel road her father slowed for a cattle guard. Isabelle leaned forward trying to see the end of the rail fence that ran on either side of the road, but this ranch seemed to go on forever.

"Are these people rich Daddy?"

"Nope, they're ordinary, like us," her father said.

Isabelle smiled at his description. "Ordinary?"

Marshall chuckled. "I meant they work real hard to keep their heads above water just like me. This man I'm going to talk to has five kids to feed."

Marshall parked the truck in front of a wide, two-story frame house with a porch that wrapped around the front and one side. The windows were open and piano music drifted out.

Marshall knocked on the front door and a tall woman appeared behind the screen door. She wiped her hands on an apron and smiled as if pleased to see strangers on her porch.

"Good-morning, can I help you folks?"

"I'm Marshall Long. I'm the new foreman over at the Wagner ranch. I'm here to see Cecil Coulter."

The tall woman opened the screen door and held out her hand. "I'm Caroline. Cecil's my husband. Please, come in. Cecil's over at his Dad's. I'll just give him a call."

Once they stepped inside, Isabelle's father first introduced Mama Rose then her. Caroline's friendly face softened when she smiled at Isabelle.

"My goodness you're a very pretty girl, Isabelle."

"Thank you, ma'am."

Caroline leaned through the open doorway to the right where the piano music came from. "Denise?"

Denise hooked an arm through Isabelle's and led her away from the house. "Want to see some baby rabbits?"

They walked along a worn path toward the barn, with Denise chatting easily. Isabelle learned they were nearly the same age and would be in the same grade at school in the fall.

Just as they topped a little hill that sloped toward the barn, a boy flew out the door of the barn and landed on his back with a thump. He scrambled to his feet and charged right back inside.

"My brothers are at it again," Denise said breaking into a run. "Come on."

Fighting always scared Isabelle, so she dawdled along, hoping the boys would be finished before she reached them. She took a tentative peek inside the barn and had a pleasant surprise. The boy named Danny stood to the side watching two bigger boys rolling around on the hard, earthen floor. A younger boy hovered close to Danny's side, giving Isabelle the impression he felt safe there.

Denise had stopped just inside the doorway. "Get him Darren!"

Danny spotted Isabelle and sauntered over. The younger boy stuck by his side like a shadow.

"Hey, Isabelle," Danny said. "Did you come to check the acoustics in our barn?"

Hearing the sound of a fist hitting flesh distracted her from the surprise of Danny knowing her name. She looked to the others just in time to see one boy punch the other in the face. She shuddered and took a step backward.

Danny glanced from her to the fighting boys. "My brothers don't have any manners," he said, then turned toward the door. "Come on."

Danny's shadow tugged on his shirt, "Are you coming back?"

"You can come too, David."

The largest boy straddled his opponent's chest and grabbed a handful of T-shirt, but paused in mid assault to glare at Danny. "Where do you think you're going?"

"I'm walking this girl outside," Danny said. "Your fighting scares her."

"She can find her own way out. Get back to work."

"If you and Darren can take a break, so can I."

They walked out into the daylight and as they started up the hill Denise pulled Isabelle aside just as the biggest brother cut Danny's feet from beneath him with a sweeping kick.

Danny fell face first into the dirt, swiftly rolled to his back, and glared up at the much bigger boy. "We have company, Dwight."

Dwight turned to Denise. "Get out of here. If you tell Dad I'm down here kicking Danny's ass, you'll be next."

Isabelle didn't see Danny move, she felt it. He was on his feet and on his much larger brother in an instant.

A man charged down the hill with Isabelle's father a few paces behind.

"Stop this immediately!" the man hollered.

Dwight pushed Danny away and wiped blood from the split lip Danny just gave him with a swift upper cut.

Isabelle figured the angry man was their father. He addressed the biggest boy. "Do you intend to fight all day, Dwight?"

"No, sir."

"Then leave your brothers alone or I'll find you a job that will keep you busy for the rest of the weekend. Do we understand each other?"

"Yes, Daddy."

Dwight turned back toward the barn.

Danny's father looked to him, "How about you?"

Danny nodded. "I understand."

"Go on then, get your work done, and stop this foolishness."

Danny's father and Marshall continued to the corral at the other end of the barn. Denise started back to the house, but Isabelle hesitated, watching Danny walk away.

"Hey, Danny?" she called.

He turned, and grinned, lazy and sweet, walking backwards.

"How did you know my name?" She asked.

"Shadow's not exactly a metropolis, Issy-Belle. People talk."

No one but her mother had ever called her Issy-Belle. The reminder brought tears to her eyes. Danny's grin slipped and he started toward her when Dwight bellowed his name.

Danny looked toward the barn then back to her. "I'll talk to you later," he said softly.

Marshall concluded his business with Cecil and took Isabelle away before Danny finished his chores. Visiting with Denise had been fun, but Isabelle was drawn to Danny. She understood exactly why his little brother stood so close to him. Something about his character made her feel safe too.

She climbed into the truck, disappointed they had to leave so soon.

"Wasn't that a nice visit?" Mama Rose said.

"Those are some good people," Marshall said. He nudged Isabelle. "Looks like you've got a new friend."

She knew he meant Denise. "She's a nice girl," she said.

"Then why do you have such a long face?"

"I wanted to stay longer," she said.

This was true of course. What she didn't say was that while she and Denise shared many interests, were the same age, and would be attending the same grade in school, she had hoped to spend more time with Danny. Uncertain how her father would take that news, she kept the knowledge to herself.

"Maybe Denise will invite you back," he said.

After lunch, Isabelle flopped down on her bed and kicked off her shoes. She was in the middle of a Nancy Drew mystery, but reading didn't appeal to her right now. She closed her eyes and drifted off to sleep.

A while later, Mama Rose knocked softly then opened the bedroom door. She smiled at Isabelle. "Danny Coulter is here to see you."

She found him standing at the edge of the yard talking to her father. Hearing her approach, he turned and smiled.

He held out a roll of papers. "I brought those drawings we talked about."

"Let's see them," Marshall said.

Isabelle unrolled the drawing of Mark Twain and the one of herself. Her father and Mama Rose stood behind her eyeing the drawings. Since they believed she had just met Danny this morning, she knew she might need to offer some explanation for the drawing of her sitting by the river.

"My goodness," Mama Rose exclaimed. "Who drew these?"

Isabelle nodded at Danny, "Him."

Marshall pointed at the one of Isabelle and addressed Danny. "You drew this today?"

"No, sir, I drew it last week. I've seen you all crossing Purser's Bridge on your way to town. I go there all the time to draw."

Isabelle held her breath hoping her father would buy Danny's half-truth. Marshall looked back at the drawing then to Danny again.

"You kids do a lot of swimming down there, don't you?"

"Yes sir."

"So, it's fairly safe?"

Danny shrugged, "Unless the river's up."

Mama Rose made a face. "Are there lots of snakes?"

Danny shook his head. "I've seen one or two further down, where we fish, but not by the bridge. Maybe Isabelle could go swimming with us some time."

Marshall eyed him levelly. "I was thinking she'd already been."

Isabelle bit her lip. She could never fool her father. He kept a steady gaze on Danny, a look that usually made her squirm, but this boy knew how to hold his ground. He looked right back at her father and waited for him to further the point.

"Isabelle's too short for a person to see her sitting between me and Rose," her father said.

Danny smiled, looking as innocent as an angel. "Not if you're standing on the side of the bridge."

"Is that where you draw?"

"No, sir, sometimes my friends and I sit or climb around on the bridge, and I did jump from there one time."

Her father's eyebrows shot up in surprise. "That's a pretty good drop."

"When the river is healthy, it's about twenty feet."

Her father whistled. "Maybe Isabelle's got no business down there after all."

"She can jump off the bank underneath the bridge or use the rope swing like everybody else."

Her father turned his attention to her. "Have you seen the rope swing?"

She felt a heated flush in her face. "Yes, Daddy."

"Think it could hold me?"

After a minute, Isabelle absorbed the fact that he was forgiving her. She smiled and he grinned back.

Isabelle stashed the drawings in her room and walked with Danny to the stables nearest their house where his horse was tied to a post.

"I like your father," he said.

Isabelle smiled. "Me too."

"Do you think he'd really try the rope swing?"

"Sure. Daddy's kind of crazy that way. He chased bulls at the rodeo for a long time. It doesn't get any crazier than that, I guess."

"He rode bulls?'"

She shook her head. "He was a bull fighter."

Danny's eyes widened with excitement. "Do you think he'd tell me about it sometime?"

"Sure. He loves to talk about the rodeo."

They paused at the corral. Danny climbed to the upper rail of the fence and stood there watching a couple of horses chase each other out in the pasture.

"The Wagner's have some great-looking quarter horses," he said.

"I wouldn't know a quarter horse from any other."

He looked down at her and grinned. "City girl."

She stuck her tongue out at him and he laughed.

"I want to learn to ride," she said.

"I can teach you, if you want."

"Do you promise not to make fun of me?"

His expression softened and he looked away. "I promise."

"Isabelle?" Mama Rose called from their back porch. "Supper in ten minutes!"

"Yes, Mama Rose!"

Danny's gaze drifted from Mama Rose to her. "How come you call your mother Mama Rose?"

Isabelle squirmed around a bit. She hated answering this question. "She's my stepmother."

He watched her for a moment then directed his attention toward the horses again. When he didn't appear to have anything else to say, Isabelle jumped in.

"How many brothers and sisters do you have?"

"One sister and three brothers, you met them all today."

"Do all of your names begin with a D?"

He turned back to her again. "Mama and Daddy are the Cs: Cecil and Caroline. We kids are the D's: Dwight, Darren," he paused, pointing to his chest, "Danny, Denise, and David."

"Are you one of the younger ones?"

His smile slipped. "I gave you the names in order. I'm in the middle."

"So, what grade will you be in this year?"

"Guess," he said levelly.

She sensed this was a sensitive topic and wasn't about to offend him by guessing him to be younger than he was.

She shook her head. "I'm not good at guessing people's ages."

"Coward," he said with a little smile.

She laughed, "Yep."

"I'll be in seventh grade," he said softly.

Try as she might, Isabelle couldn't keep her astonishment from showing. He wasn't much taller than she, and people considered her petite.

Danny slipped off the fence and dropped to the ground, not bothering to hide his annoyance. "It was nice talking to you."

As he reached to untie the reins of his horse, anger overtook Isabelle.

"I'm small too, you know. Don't come around me acting like you're the only one who's cursed."

He frowned at her. "Cursed?"

"You know what I mean. People can't even talk to you without mentioning how small you are, like you don't already know it."

"But you're a girl, so…"

"It's no easier for me than it is for you," she said.

Danny swung up into the saddle. "Boy, do you have a lot to learn."

"Why don't you stay for supper?"

"I'd like to, but if I don't get home my father will find six hundred ways to make me miserable."

Shadow, Oklahoma
Fall 1962

SEVENTEEN

In late September, the elementary school was holding its annual talent contest. Isabelle slipped the flyer for the contest into her notebook. Later, as she spread her homework on the kitchen table, she pushed the flyer aside.

"What's this?" Mama Rose asked picking up the bright yellow paper.

"A talent contest at school."

"You should enter, Isabelle. Let them hear you sing."

"I don't know…"

"Honey, don't be shy. Wait until those other kids hear you."

Isabelle let Mama Rose convince her to enter the contest, but secretly dreaded the whole event. The day before the contest, fear swelled so big she was ready to back out. Mama Rose wanted to invite

Denise over for supper as a distraction. Though Mama Rose didn't understand Isabelle's request to have a boy over, she extended an invitation to Danny as well. At suppertime, Danny arrived alone.

"Where's your sister?" Mama Rose asked.

"Denise came home from school with a fever. Mama gave her some castor oil then sent her to bed."

After a supper of pork chops, mashed potatoes with gravy, green beans, homemade rolls, and chocolate cream pie, Isabelle guided Danny away to the steps of the back porch.

Danny eased down to the steps carefully and groaned. "I ate way too much."

Isabelle poked his little belly. "Look at that."

He grimaced. "Don't. I might explode."

One of the ranch dogs trotted up with a stick in its mouth. Danny took the stick and tossed it out into the yard for the dog to chase.

"I'm really worried about tomorrow," Isabelle said.

He leaned back on his elbows and studied her for a minute. "Why's that?"

"All the kids look at me like I'm some kind of freak. I don't fit in."

He grinned. "You're probably the first female midget they've ever seen."

She took a gentle swipe at him. "This isn't funny."

"Don't get all worked up. They're just kids like you and me."

"With one major exception," she said quietly.

The dog returned with the stick and dropped it at Danny's feet. He threw it farther out into the yard. "What's the exception?"

"A lot of the kids are white."

He studied her for a minute. "You can't let that hold you back," he said quietly.

Her eyes teared in anger. "That's easy for you to say. You're not living it."

"Trust me, they'll love you," he said gently.

"I wish you could be there."

He shook his head. "I can't skip class."

Though they rode the same school bus, he attended junior high in another building several blocks from her school. She knew what she was asking was selfish, but having him there would give her the courage she needed.

"I know you can't come," she said, then sighed. "It would just help me so much to see you standing there."

As her turn to take the stage approached, Isabelle had the strong urge to throw up. She gulped air and swallowed hard. As a distraction, she peeked through the stage curtain, searching for a friendly face to focus on. She could sing to this person and ignore the others. She had hoped to see Denise Coulter, but Denise was at home with the flu. Neither could she find her other new friend, Holly Adams, in the crowd.

The announcer called her name. Isabelle took a deep breath and stepped before the crowd. The microphone was too high, so the emcee rushed to adjust it. Isabelle nodded to the fourth grade teacher who was playing piano for anyone who needed accompaniment. As the teacher played the introduction, Isabelle quickly scanned the crowd one last time for a face to connect with.

Finally, the first note rose from her throat, but her voice was weak and shaky. She stopped and looked around the room in a panic. The kids started shifting around, murmuring, some even laughed. She took a deep breath and wiped her sweaty palms across her skirt. She took another gulp of air just as Danny opened the back door of the auditorium.

He didn't stop walking until he stood at her feet below the stage and offered her a big smile. "Hi."

She tried to return his smile, but it just wouldn't come.

"Come on, Issy. Remember how you sang at the river?" he said above the noise of the crowd. "Just let it fly."

She closed her eyes, recalling the image of sunlight reflecting off that lazy river, lighting his sweet face.

"Show them," he said backing away.

The song came to her easier now, without the pianist ever touching a key. She conquered her audience a cappella.

There was a long, tense moment as the last note faded then Danny produced the loudest whistle she ever heard. Walking backward up the aisle, he began to applaud and others joined him. Isabelle curtsied to him. Danny smiled, made a fist with his right hand and tapped that fist on his chest, right over his heart, before pushing through the auditorium door and disappearing again.

School ended right after the talent contest winners were announced. Isabelle climbed on the school bus with her little trophy and took a seat. When they stopped to pick up the junior high kids, Danny's brother, Darren, got on and took the seat across the aisle. She watched the door, waiting anxiously for Danny to appear so she could share her good news of coming in first place. When the driver closed the doors and started to pull away, a sense of panic swept over Isabelle.

"We're leaving without Danny."

Darren looked over at her and shook his head. "He had to stay."

"Why?"

"He got caught skipping the first part of seventh hour."

Seventh hour was when he stood at her feet and encouraged her to sing. Isabelle found it difficult to breathe. "How's he supposed to get home?"

"Daddy will have to come get him and that is real, real bad news for Danny."

Isabelle covered her face with her hands. First place meant nothing.

Isabelle grabbed her bike and rode down the blacktop to the Coulter house, intent on talking to Danny's father the moment he and Danny arrived. She took a seat on the front steps and waited impatiently.

When Cecil parked the truck, Isabelle stood while he and Danny climbed out. Danny looked at her questioningly, but his father was the one who spoke.

"What are you doing here Isabelle?"

"I wanted to talk to you about Danny skipping class."

Confused, Cecil squinted at her. "This doesn't concern you, Sweetheart."

"Mr. Coulter, please listen. I'm the reason he broke the rules. I was afraid to sing in front of all those kids at the talent contest today." She paused for a breath. "It's been hard for me to fit in. Danny was there because I asked him to help me."

Cecil looked down at his son. "Why didn't you tell me this?"

"I thought all that mattered was that I broke the rules," Danny responded soberly.

Cecil seemed genuinely disappointed. "I'm sorry you don't know me better," he said then turned back to Isabelle. "Want to join us for supper?"

"No, sir, I have to get home, but thank you."

Cecil started for the front door. "Walk your friend home Danny," he said without turning.

Isabelle grabbed her bike and they started down the gravel road. "Thanks for coming today."

"I should be thanking you. Daddy was considering some pretty serious punishment."

"I got first prize," she admitted shyly.

"Of course you did. I've never heard anybody sing like you."

They reached a fork in the road and he pointed to the left. "I know a shortcut."

They passed the barn and crossed a small bridge over a creek to a gravel road that sloped upwards into the wooded hills.

A little house sat back from the road and Isabelle spotted a woman sitting on the porch holding a bottle of beer in one hand and a cigarette in the other. Though the day had cooled as the sunlight faded, her only article of clothing appeared to be a sheer silk robe draped carelessly about her body and tied loosely at the waist. Her strawberry-blonde hair was teased high and kind of wild. Her lips were ruby red.

Heavy eyeliner and mascara accentuated her sleepy-looking eyes.

"Hey Danny Boy," the woman sang.

He offered her a little wave and kept walking.

"Who's that?" Isabelle whispered.

"My aunt's sister, also known as the guest who never leaves."

"Does she always dress like that?"

"Yeah, pretty much."

When the incline of the road steepened, Danny took the bike from her. "Let me push it."

"I know what you did today was risky. I really do appreciate your help."

He shrugged his shoulders. "It was worth hearing you sing."

As they crested the hill she saw the Wagner ranch and her home below. "Wow, you were right, this is much shorter."

The sunset was peaking in radiant red and gold hues. They paused side by side, bathed in the glow, admiring the view. The moment felt like a gift for just them.

"Perfect," she said.

Danny smiled with the sunset lighting his dark eyes. Isabelle couldn't remember being this comfortable with anyone outside of her family before.

"Well, thanks," she said. "I can make it from here."

She reached for her bike, but he shook his head.

"I'll walk you all the way," he said.

Later that night, she stared at his drawing of Mark Twain tacked on her bedroom wall, right next to the drawing of her. The drawing of Twain embodied the very spirit of Danny Coulter. A comet streaking through space was the perfect parallel to the courage and spirit of her new friend.

EIGHTEEN

Over supper on Friday evening, her father announced he had business in Tulsa the next morning. Isabelle was desperate for a visit with her grandmother.

"Can I go along?"

He nodded and took a sip of his coffee. "We'll all go. Mama Rose wants to visit with her sister."

"Can I take Danny?"

Her father's smooth forehead wrinkled in confusion. "Danny Coulter?"

She smiled widely. "Yes."

Her father and Mama Rose exchanged surprised looks.

"Wouldn't you rather take little Denise?" Mama Rose asked.

Up until now, she hadn't mentioned her difficult situation at school, thinking she would work things out herself. They didn't know what Danny did for her at the talent contest. Their obvious concern over her asking if a boy could go along on the trip made her rethink her secrecy. She finally explained how hard moving to Shadow and starting a new school was for her and Danny's role in making the transition easier.

"I like Denise and all, but Danny is my best friend," she concluded.

Her father seemed to accept that news with ease. "I guess it would be okay for him to go along. I'll give his parents a call after we finish supper," Marshall said.

Grandma Sarah hurried out to meet the car before Marshall turned off the car. Marshall and Rose got out and made polite conversation curbside, but were soon on their way, leaving Isabelle and Danny with Sarah.

Sarah didn't wait for Isabelle to introduce Danny. She just stepped up to him and gave him a big kiss on the forehead, leaving a smear of red lipstick.

"Hey-O," she said, patting the top of his head. "Welcome, Boy."

Isabelle had been concerned of what he might think of her eccentric grandmother, but Danny smiled at her like they were old buddies.

"Thank you," he said.

"I call him Comet," Isabelle said.

Danny's smile slid into a frown, "Since when?"

"Since you gave me that drawing of the guy riding the comet."

"That isn't a picture of me."

She rolled her eyes and made a face. "Well, duh, I know that."

He sighed and gave her a pained look. "Please don't call me Comet."

Isabelle wasn't about to be swayed. "Everything about that drawing is just like you. I put it up on my wall to give me courage, the way you did at the talent contest."

Sarah looked at Isabelle. "Comet is a good name for this boy."

Danny followed them into the house shaking his head. "My mother uses Comet to clean the bathtub," he mumbled.

While Isabelle sat with her grandmother at the kitchen table, catching up on the news, Danny wandered around the living room, examining Sarah's unusual collections with curiosity. Finally, Sarah insisted he join them in the kitchen.

"I made us some sassafras tea," she said, pouring each of them a cup. "It's not so easy to find anymore. People use that store-ought stuff and forget this root. It goes to waste."

Danny lifted his cup and inhaled the aroma. "My grandmother made this tea before."

Sarah smiled at Isabelle. "I like your friend. There's magic in his eyes."

Isabelle looked to Danny who grinned at her and wiggled his eyebrows. He had no idea he still had the lipstick kiss on his forehead. She giggled and decided to let him wear the red imprint a bit longer before telling him.

Sarah took Danny's hand, rubbed each finger and then his palm between her thumb, index, and forefinger. Danny patiently allowed her to explore his hand and had no visible reaction.

Sarah rocked and nodded, making a little humming sound, "A girl, stars all around, a beautiful daughter." Sarah looked up at Danny and smiled. "Are you an artist, Comet?"

"I draw a little," Danny said.

Isabelle smiled. "Don't let him fool you Grandma. He's wonderful."

Sarah kept massaging his hand and nodding her head. "The ghosts around you say you have a deep heart."

Isabelle wasn't so sure Danny would be comfortable with Sarah's talent. She started to stop her grandmother, but changed her mind when she saw him smile.

"My Isabelle was given some challenges," Sarah said, "but her load is not as heavy as yours."

"Do you know what I'm supposed to do?"

She nodded solemnly. "It's very good you will have broad shoulders."

He laughed softly. "You mean I won't always be such a runt?"

Sarah shook her head. "No, not like that."

Danny's smile dissolved. "Oh."

"Do you know your Bible Comet?"

He grimaced at her use of his new nickname. "I go to church."

"Well, in Luke it says 'To him whom much is given, much is expected.' That's you, Boy. That's what I mean."

Danny seemed to be mulling over Sarah's prediction as she continued to massage his hand. Sarah took a sudden sharp breath. Even with all the make-up and her naturally dark complexion, her sudden lack of color was apparent.

"You be careful of that river," she said in a hushed tone.

Isabelle laughed nervously. "You're scaring me, Grandma."

Sarah shot her a hard look. "Drink your tea. Comet's here for a reason."

Isabelle turned her attention to Danny. His focus remained fixed on Sarah.

He took a deep breath. "What else do you see?"

A visible shudder rocked Sarah's thin frame. She dropped Danny's hand and looked him in the eye, seemingly mesmerized. "You...are a remarkable boy," she whispered.

Isabelle hated the suspense, "What is it Grandma?"

Sarah looked away from them, outside at the day, a wistful expression on her face. "A thousand stars, saying good-bye."

That evening, as they drove home, her father tuned the radio to the third game of the World Series and Mama Rose launched into a long story about how her sister's oldest boy had joined the Army and married some girl in Germany. Isabelle kicked off her shoes and curled her legs beneath her on the back seat next to Danny.

"So did Grandma's saying that about you and the river give you the heebie-jeebies?"

"Is she called Sarah Two-Fingers because of that thing she did with my hand?"

She poked him in the ribs and giggled. "Maybe you're not such a turnip-brain after all."

Danny grinned. "Don't get your hopes up."

"Didn't you feel strange when she was saying all that stuff to you?"

"Not exactly." He looked out at the dark night gliding by and shrugged. "Down deep, it felt like the truth."

Up front, Marshall slapped the steering wheel with his palm and grunted. Meanwhile, Mama Rose never skipped a beat in her story.

"I bet you were a cute preemie," Isabelle said to Danny. "You probably looked like a little doll."

"Mama says that's why I'm so much smaller than everybody else."

"Well, according to Grandma, you're going to grow."

"She ever wrong?"

Remembering the look of fear on her grandmother's face and the involuntary shiver that rocked her thin body, Isabelle took a deep breath. "I don't think so."

NINETEEN

Hal Coulter, Jr., was born in the wee hours of a Friday morning. Uncle Hal stopped by on his way back from the hospital to share the good news just as Danny's family was sitting down to a breakfast of buttermilk pancakes and crispy bacon.

"Sit down, Hal," Caroline said flipping a row of pancakes on the griddle. "Denise, get your uncle a plate."

Hal placed a box of cigars on the table, opened the top, and handed out cigars to Cecil and all four nephews with a proud grin.

"That's generous of you Hal, but no," Cecil said motioning for the boys to return the cigars.

"Aw, let them have a little fun."

"They'll have all the fun they can handle at school today."

"It isn't like a puff or two will stunt their growth," Hal drawled. "If that were true, it would appear Runt already had more than his share."

Danny glared at his uncle. "You're such a jerk."

His mother swung around from the stove waving her spatula at him. "Daniel!"

Hal grinned and smeared butter on a stack of pancakes. "Runt's just kidding around, aren't you?"

Danny ignored Hal and took a big bite of pancake. The bus would be coming soon and lately he couldn't seem to get enough to eat.

Cecil finished eating, pushed his plate away, and took a sip of coffee. "How's Rosalie doing?"

"She did a great job. Of course she's tired. It's a good thing Vera will be here to help her when she comes home."

Other than Caroline's very audible sigh, silence fell over the usually noisy group. Everyone knew Vera had overstayed her welcome, but Danny figured he was probably the only one aware of Hal's indiscretion.

After school that day Danny headed down to the barn for his evening chores, while Darren and Dwight were in the pasture filling the cattle troughs. There were several horses corralled near the barn and Danny needed to give them fresh water and hay. As he filled the galvanized water trough, he heard his uncle laughing. Looking up the hill, he spotted Hal and Vera sitting on the back steps of Hal's house. As was her custom, Vera wore only a thin robe. She leaned back with her bare legs splayed out, robe gapping, and one of Uncle Hal's fat cigars in her mouth and started blowing smoke rings.

Denise's gentle buckskin mare moseyed over to Danny, drawing his attention away from the show on the hill. The horse was nearly ready to drop her foal and her belly was wide and heavy. Danny offered her half an apple and rubbed her neck.

"How are you today, Candy?"

Vera's peal of laughter drew his attention away from the horse. This time he got a real eyeful. Up on the hill, Hal was chasing Vera in the backyard. Her robe was flapping in the wind and Danny could see nearly every inch of her naked body. Hal caught the robe and it slipped off Vera's shoulders. Vera didn't seem to mind running around naked one bit. She laughed loudly and the sound bounced around the hills. Hal rushed at her, catching her up in his arms, kissing her mouth with intensity. The scene embarrassed and infuriated Danny.

While he hadn't really bonded with Rosalie, the thought of her lying in the hospital after giving birth to Hal's child and the tiny baby depending on Hal to be a father got Danny's blood pumping. He grabbed Candy's halter to steady her and let loose the loudest, angriest whistle of his life. Praying he had the lovers' attention, but too embarrassed to look, he turned back to Candy and gave her the other half of the apple. In the short time it took for Candy to finish her treat, Hal and Vera were nowhere to be seen.

During the usual after-church meal in his grandparent's dining room, Vera slid into the chair next to him. Once the blessing was said and the food passed around, everyone began talking. Vera leaned in close to Danny's ear, using a voice that couldn't be heard by anyone except him in the din of a Coulter get-together.

"Did you enjoy our little show Danny Boy?"

"No, ma'am."

She pressed her index finger to his lips. "I hope we can count on you to keep our secret."

Repulsed, Danny swung his head away. "Don't touch me."

Vera smiled, but lowered her hand away from his lips. Whether by accident or intent, that same hand slipped across his upper thigh, brushing his most private area.

Stunned, Danny shoved his chair away from the table directly into the path of his mother who was on her way to the kitchen with an empty platter.

"My goodness, Danny, watch what you're doing!"

Vera grinned wickedly and gave him a wink.

Only moments earlier he had been so hungry he was certain he could devour every bit of food on the dining room table, including the bowl of collard greens he despised as a rule, but his encounter with Vera left him nauseated.

He announced he didn't feel well and excused himself from the table before his mother returned and determined he was once again in need of a dose of castor oil.

After changing out of his church clothes, he grabbed his sketchbook and wandered down to the river, hoping for a little peace and quiet. Even though the water was too cold for swimming, there were a few cars and people milling about by the bridge, so he followed the path along the riverbank toward a favorite fishing spot.

He opened the sketchbook and fiddled around with a drawing while he considered what, if anything, he should do about the situation with Vera and his uncle. He had just relaxed a little when he heard approaching footsteps. Looking up from the drawing, he was relieved to see Darren coming along the bank with a fishing pole and tackle box.

Darren dropped down to the soft grass next to him, bated a hook, and skillfully cast his line to the middle of the river before acknowledging Danny. "So what's the matter with you?"

Danny focused on the page in front of him, "Nothing."

"You're acting weird."

"I'm having a problem with Vera," he blurted out.

Darren stuck a cherry Tootsie Roll Pop in his mouth, keeping his eyes on the fishing line. "Like what?

He blushed crimson. "She touched me."

Darren laughed. "Oh, somebody help, she's touching me." He gave Danny a little shove. "Don't be such a baby."

"This isn't funny Darren. It was gross."

Darren's smile slipped. He shifted the sucker in his mouth. "Maybe you should explain touching."

Danny couldn't look at him and say the words. He faced the river and took a deep breath. "She put her hand on me, you know..." He couldn't say more. Just recounting the incident in vague terms brought a new flush to his face. "I don't know what I'm going to do."

"Stop your whining," Hal said.

Danny's eyes widened in fear. He and Darren turned to find Hal standing behind them.

Hal laughed heartily. "Shut your mouths, boys."

Hal dropped down beside Danny and laid a heavy hand on his shoulder. "Actually, you've given me just the excuse I've been looking for. I need to make some decisions now that the baby is here."

Danny shook off Hal's big hand. "Don't use me for an excuse. I haven't done anything."

"Lust is one of the big ones, Runt. When you wake up in the middle of the night with your little woody as stiff as a fence post, I know it is Vera's assets you're dreaming of. Don't deny it." To further his point, Uncle Hal held his cupped hands up to his chest, indicating breasts with a wicked grin.

"I think you're confusing him with Dwight," Darren muttered, referring to Dwight's obvious lust for Vera.

Danny squinted at his uncle. "My little woody?"

"Aw, come on Runt, don't you know all the cute nicknames for your itty-bitty pecker?"

Danny grunted. "Not as well as every female in three counties know yours."

Hal laughed and lay back in the grass, pulling his hat down over his eyes. "One of these days that mouth is going to get you in a lot of trouble, Danny Boy."

"I'd rather it was my mouth doing the talking instead of my little woody."

"Oh, your day is coming. You just wait and see. That little thing will be in charge and get you in all sorts of trouble."

The next day Hal brought Rosalie and his newborn son home. That evening there was a family gathering at Danny's parents' home to welcome the new baby and Hal behaved like the ideal proud father and devoted husband.

While everyone else seemed fooled by Hal's play acting, Danny caught the looks exchanged between his uncle and Vera when they thought no one else was looking. Their game sickened him, but he kept his mouth shut.

Danny was sleeping soundly near midnight when David shook him. "Wake up!"

Startled, Danny rolled over and squinted at his little brother who hovered over him. "What?"

David pointed to the open the window. "Listen!"

He didn't have to wait long to hear the very sound that had alarmed David. An eerie scream ripped through the quiet night. Danny threw the covers back and hurried to the window. Their bedroom was at the back of the house, facing the hills and Uncle Hal's place.

"Is it a mountain lion?" David whispered.

The scream came again, raising the little hairs on Danny's arms. He pulled on a pair of jeans and a T-shirt then slipped his feet into tennis shoes before heading for the door.

"Don't go out there Danny!"

Recognizing the utter panic in his brother's voice, Danny stopped cold and attempted to calm his brother.

"That was Rosalie screaming, David," he said, forcing himself to speak evenly. "I'm going up there. Go wake up Daddy and tell him there's trouble at Uncle Hal's."

Danny carefully picked his way up the hill through the moonless night to Hal and Rosalie's house, wishing he'd thought to grab a flashlight and a jacket. The journey got easier as he drew closer, since every light in the little house was burning brightly. Hal's clothes were scattered over the porch, down the steps, and littered the gravel drive. Inside, Rosalie's screaming had turned to a mournful wail. The sound set Danny's teeth on edge. There was a loud crash, the sound of glass breaking, and Hal bellowed a string of ugly words.

He mounted the steps quickly, but had to jump aside as Vera rushed out the door with a suitcase in her hand. She didn't bother to look his way and clomped down the steps in her high heels with her thin robe untied and flapping in the breeze.

He stepped inside and paused, his heart pounding, partly due to the exertion of climbing the hill, but mostly from fear. The living room was a mess of broken glass and overturned furniture. The baby wailed in a bassinette over in the corner, his tiny face angry and red, his body alternately rigid then shaking as he thrust his tiny fists in the air and pumped his thin little legs. Danny hurried to the infant and picked him up, cuddling the tiny body to his chest. He grabbed a small blanket from the bassinette, wrapping it as best he could around the baby's body, hoping to make it feel secure.

"What the hell do you think you're doing?" Hal asked.

Startled, Danny swung around. Eight feet away, his uncle swayed on his feet. Even with the distance separating them, Danny could smell liquor. Hal's hair stood on end in places and his eyes were glassy and wild.

Hal came toward him, reaching for the baby with his big hands. "Give him to me."

Danny turned his body sideways to Hal, cradling the infant closer to his chest. Hal closed the distance between them in two quick steps and slapped him across the face with such force Danny staggered into the wall. Cornered now, with his vision blurred and a clanging sound in his head, he and Hal engaged in a terrifying dance of wills as Hal attempted to pry the infant from his arms and Danny managed to stay out of reach.

"Damn it all! Give him to me, Runt!"

Screaming like a banshee, Rosalie rushed into the room, locked her hands together and hit Hal squarely between the shoulders. "Get away from him!"

Hal turned and pushed her to the floor. When he swung back toward Danny, Rosalie scrambled to her feet, pummeling him with her fists.

Hal grabbed a fistful of Rosalie's hair, jerking her away, and she fell against the wall with a solid thud. He drew back a big beefy fist to punch her just as Cecil burst into the room like a charging bull. Cecil knocked Hal off his feet then grabbed him by the front of his shirt and leaned in close.

"Here's what's going to happen," Cecil said tightly. "You're going to get in your car and leave, right now."

"This is none of your business!" Hal said.

Cecil hauled Hal to his feet and shoved him toward the door. "Get out of here!"

Hal slammed into the screen door and stumbled out of the house. Cecil followed as far as the porch. Rosalie collapsed on the couch and began sobbing. Danny eased to the window to see if there would be more trouble.

Outside, Hal teetered at the edge of the steps, eyeing the mess littering the porch and all around. He snatched up random items on his way to the car then tossed everything in the back seat. Climbing behind the wheel, he gunned the engine, and raced down the hill in a cloud of dust and gravel with Vera bouncing on the front seat next to him.

Danny watched the taillights of Hal's car disappear down the road and sagged against the window frame. Looking down at the tiny bundle in his arms, he saw that by some miracle the baby had fallen asleep. He carefully returned the child to the bassinette, ensuring the receiving blanket was tucked around him securely. As he bent forward, a sudden hammering in his head rocked him. Standing straight again, he gripped the edge of the bassinette and realized his nose was running. He put his hand to his nose and found blood.

His father stepped back inside, assessing first Rosalie's condition then turning his attention to Danny.

He stepped forward quickly, eyed Danny's swelling face, and handed him a handkerchief. "Are you all right?"

Danny wiped his nose and shrugged. "I think so."

Cecil patted his shoulder. "Go home and let Mama look at you."

Danny nodded solemnly. His father took an audible breath then went to Rosalie. Danny stepped out on the porch but his legs felt rubbery and he wasn't certain they were going to cooperate with the walk downhill. Thinking he just should wait a little while before tackling the uneven terrain, he leaned against a support post and listened as his father spoke soft, comforting words to Rosalie.

On the downhill slope, a narrow beam of light zigzagged across the road. When his mother emerged from the darkness, relief coursed through Danny. His parents were here and he could step back into childhood.

After surveying the chaos of clothing scattered about, Caroline directed her gaze up the steps to him. She studied him for a moment, her expression hardening as she moved closer. Raising the flashlight, she shined it on his face. She quickly mounted the three steps and came close, lifting his chin with her hand, turning his head this way and that, making his ears ring and head pound worse.

"Did Hal do this to you?"

"I'm okay, Mama."

"Well, he'd better not show his sorry face around here for a long, long time or I'll teach that miserable excuse for a man a thing or two about hitting women and children."

Danny shivered in the damp night air. He considered retrieving one of his uncle's shirts from the ground, but just as quickly shook off that notion. The thought of wrapping Hal's shirt around his own shoulders was repugnant, as if Hal's loutish essence lingered there in the cotton threads and could possibly leach into his skin.

His mother never seemed to miss a thing. She removed her jacket and placed it around his shoulders. She pressed the flashlight into his hands. "Go on back to the house and put some ice on your face."

As Danny made his way home, he attempted to sort through some of what had taken place. He didn't understand what would make a man behave so despicably, and was certainly grateful his father and Hal were so different in character. He was also thankful his father had arrived at the best possible moment and resolved the situation swiftly in his usual calm, no-nonsense style, leaving no room for debate.

Despite the difference in their ages, Cecil took the younger man down easily. As Danny considered what might have happened if Hal had challenged his father, his mother's statement about teaching Hal a lesson popped into Danny's head. Like his father, his mother was no nonsense. However, Danny had no doubt she wouldn't hesitate to whack a person…hard. He had to smile. Hal probably got off easy when his father came through the door first.

At home, he went to the little bathroom off the kitchen to examine his face. His upper lip was swollen and discolored. His cheek was turning a deep crimson with a tinge of purple. He thought there might even be the start of a black eye and despite the pain, he felt good about himself. He had protected the baby. A black eye was his badge of honor.

He wet a washcloth and cleaned the dried blood away. Opening the medicine cabinet for aspirin, he spied the castor oil. He really hoped his mother wouldn't consider castor oil to be a cure in this particular situation. For the second time in minutes, he smiled.

Back in the kitchen, he popped the aspirin in his mouth and downed a glass of water. After cracking an ice tray, he placed a handful of cubes in a kitchen towel, sat at the table, and pressed the bundle to his throbbing face. Hearing a shuffling sound, he looked up to see David coming through the swinging door.

David eyed his face and the blood on his shirt with wide eyes. "What happened?"

"Uncle Hal hit me," he said.

David cast a worried look toward the door. "Where's Mama?"

"She's still up there with Daddy and Rosalie."

Seeing the pinched, fearful look on David's face, he hurriedly added some reassurance. "Everything is fine now. Uncle Hal is gone. Mama and Daddy will be home in a little bit."

"Are you coming back to bed soon?"

Danny sighed tiredly and rose. "Let's go."

Sometime later, his mother tiptoed into their bedroom and sat on the edge of Danny's bed. He opened sleepy eyes and peered up at her silhouette. David had climbed into his bed and lay between him and the wall and she rearranged the covers over both of them.

"Is Rosalie okay?" he whispered.

"Rosalie's going to be just fine. How about you?"

He yawned widely. "I'm okay."

"I want you to promise me you'll never run into a situation like that again Danny. That was very dangerous."

"I heard Rosalie, and well, I just didn't think..."

"Shush now my little champion. I know what kind of heart you have and I love you for it, but you have to let Daddy and I handle things like this."

"Do you think Uncle Hal will come back?"

She sighed and pushed at her hair. "Yes, eventually, but I don't want you worrying about him, all right?"

"Yes, ma'am."

Shadow, Oklahoma
Spring 1963

TWENTY

In addition to raising their own line of top quality quarter horses, the Wagner ranch boarded horses. Within months of his arrival, Marshall Long's ability to change horses other people considered difficult into calm, willing partners was well known in the county.

Because the Coulters had about fifteen to twenty horses at any given time, Danny had a working knowledge, but Marshall's patient, gentle skills fascinated him. He convinced Isabelle's father to allow him to work with him for a few hours every weekend so he could learn firsthand.

One Saturday afternoon, he approached the stall of Marshall's most challenging boarder, a three-year-old Appaloosa gelding named Jessup. He climbed onto the side of the stall. Jessup stomped, snorted, reared his head and rolled his eyes back, exposing most of the white. Danny didn't flinch, but he did remain safely out of reach, calmly watching.

"You be careful around that one," Marshall cautioned as he passed through.

"He's a beautiful horse."

"He has no trust."

Danny figured if he was going to learn how to deal with difficult horses, Jessup would be the best lesson. "Could I help you work with him?"

Marshall considered his request. "The owner is an impatient sort and is paying for priority to get this horse turned around as quick as possible. Can you come by after school a few days a week?"

After a week of patient steps, Marshall had worked his magic and the horse allowed Marshall to approach him and ride him without a problem. To further the horses trust, Marshall had Danny release Jessup from his stall every afternoon for exercise. At the end of that week, the horse allowed Danny to rub his neck and back.

Isabelle joined him in the stable and climbed onto the side of the stall next to him. After watching him stroke the horse and talk quietly to him, she sighed loudly. Between her father and Danny, she was learning more than she cared to about horses.

"He looks like he wants to bite you," she said softly.

"He won't. He's just scared."

The horse tossed his head, stomped his right forefoot, and huffed, as if he understood.

"I don't see what good this is doing. You still haven't ridden him."

"I probably never will. That's not why I'm doing this."

Hearing voices, they turned in unison. Jessup's owner and Marshall approached, apparently in a heated argument.

"He's not ready yet," Marshall said.

The owner eyed Isabelle and Danny with irritation. "Excuse me."

They hopped down obediently.

When the man reached for the horses lead, Marshall put Isabelle and Danny behind him. "You kids go on."

Isabelle immediately started away, but Danny stood his ground. "What's going on Mr. Long?"

Marshall glanced down at him. "Go," he said firmly.

Isabelle knew that tone of voice and tugged on Danny's arm. "Come on."

Danny reluctantly collected his own horse and was about to call it a day when he heard a commotion behind him at the stable. Turning, he saw a cloud of dust, heard the pounding of a horse running, then Isabelle's scream. He quickly tied the reins of his bay to a post and ran back to the stable.

He rounded the corner of the exercise arena where he found Marshall cornered by the appaloosa.

Blood oozed from a gash in Marshall's forehead. The owner was standing with his back to the stable wall holding a short length of two by four in his hand.

Danny slowed to a walk and eased around the pen. The appaloosa spotted him and turned full circle, then swung back toward Marshall again, stomping his forefeet and snorting.

"Is there something I can do, Mr. Long?" Danny said quietly.

"Can you throw a lasso?"

"Yes sir."

"Swing it over his head, once it's around his neck, loop your end around a post as fast as you can."

Danny grabbed the lasso from the tack room, climbed the fence, and swung the lasso over his head in slow, hypnotic circles. He kept his attention on Jessup and started talking low and soft, the way he did every afternoon. Jessup turned his head, the ear closest to Danny came forward and the powerful horse stopped moving.

"That's it," Danny said softly. "You know I won't hurt you."

Out of the corner of his eye, Danny saw Marshall edging along the wall toward the owner. Jessup lowered his head and pawed the ground.

"Come on, Jessup," Danny continued softly. "Let's get this over with."

Marshall and the other man eased through the gate. The click of the gate latch caught Jessup's attention and he lifted his head. Before Jessup had time to charge, Danny threw the lasso with smooth precision and the rope slid down the horse's neck. He quickly wrapped his end of the rope around the post. The horse charged, stopping short of the fence to rear and show his teeth. Danny stepped off the fence and backed away.

The horse paced and danced back and forth, pulling the rope tight while Danny slowly approached, then returned to the top of the fence. Eventually, Jessup's breathing became ragged, and his coat was foamy with sweat. Through it all, Danny kept silent and stayed his ground.

Marshall had come around the outside of the pen and patted him on the back. "Good job, but it's getting late. You'd better go on home now."

Isabelle had been standing on the tailgate of Marshall's truck watching the episode unfold. She jumped down and followed Danny to his horse.

"What happened, Issy?"

"That man took Jessup out to the arena, but when Jessup wouldn't cooperate, he picked up that board and hit him right between the eyes. Daddy lost his temper and jumped in there with them."

Behind them at the fence, the owner raised his voice. "Dammit, Long, don't argue with me. Put him down today."

Danny turned, eyeing the man with contempt. Seeing the look on his face, Isabelle cringed.

"Don't get involved," she said quickly. "Daddy can handle this."

Danny led his horse back to the men and looked up at the owner. "Why don't you give him to me?"

The man laughed. "He's too dangerous for a little kid."

"You're the one that's dangerous. How could you hit an animal with a board?"

The man looked back to Marshall. "Put the horse down."

"Give him to me," Danny said again. "It will save you money."

Marshall eyed Danny for a minute then looked back to the owner. "If we can't turn this horse around then I'll put him down at my own expense."

The owner shrugged and threw up his hands. "Suit yourself, but I think you're all crazy."

After the man disappeared in his fancy car, Marshall turned to Danny again. "Get on home, before your daddy gets after you. We'll see you tomorrow."

"I'll put Jessup away first."

Before Marshall could stop him, Danny untied the rope holding Jessup from the post and dropped silently into the exercise yard. He approached the big horse slowly, talking softly, and the appaloosa stood quietly. Danny slowly lifted his hand, grasped the bridle then turned toward Jessup's stall and the horse followed calmly.

"Well, I'll be damned," Marshall said.

Danny closed the stall door and climbed back over the fence to where they stood. He picked up the reins of his horse and swung up into the saddle.

"I'll see you tomorrow."

And with that, he rode off toward the shortcut at a gallop.

Staring after him, Isabelle shook her head. "He really scares me."

"He should, a horse as big as Jessup can do a lot of damage."

"I was talking about Danny. Sometimes I think he has more courage than brains."

Her father turned to her. "It takes a strong mind to set fear aside and go against the grain. I never forgot to use my head when I stepped in with a bull. If I had, you wouldn't be talking to me right now."

"Yeah, but you didn't take chances the way Danny does."

He smiled slowly. "Honey, nobody in the rodeo takes more risks than the bull fighter."

Danny's whistle cut through the quiet of the afternoon. Isabelle looked toward the hills where Danny now sat on his horse. She answered back with the whistle he taught her.

"You have a fine friend in that boy," her father said softly.

While she agreed with her father, she also knew he had only witnessed the surface of their relationship. Danny was more than her friend. She was convinced he was the answer from God to all her many prayers to ease the pain of losing her mother.

Danny Coulter was her gift.

Three weeks after the incident with Jessup and the rude man, Danny arrived at the Wagner ranch to find Marshall saddling Jessup in the arena. Marshall waved him over.

"Time you rode him, don't you think?"

Danny climbed over the fence and approached slowly. "If you think he's ready."

He patted Jessup's neck and the horse lowered his head, nuzzling Danny's shirt pocket, where he kept a favorite treat, peppermint candy. Laughing, and knowing Jessup well by this time, he took a few steps back, reached into his pocket and removed the candy, hurrying to remove the cellophane wrapper as Jessup came at him. Jessup eagerly took the candy from his open hand.

"All right then, let's get you on board," Marshall said after Jessup devoured his treat in no time at all.

Jessup was a little over sixteen hands high and Marshall gave him a boost to get in the saddle. The horse didn't balk as Danny eased onto his back. While Marshall adjusted the stirrups, Danny lifted the reins and patted Jessup's neck. He rode without incident and climbed off, offering Jessup the second peppermint he brought along.

Marshall pulled some folded papers from his pocket and held them out. "Here's the bill of sale and registration."

Danny looked down at the papers in Marshall's hands, but did not reach for them. Marshall shook the papers at him and laughed softly. "Go on, take them, he's yours now."

TWENTY-ONE

On a particularly warm Sunday afternoon, after chores, church, and the usual family dinner, Danny met Isabelle at the peak of the shortcut between their homes then took her on a hike. They headed past the clubhouse, down a few hundred feet then up again to the highest point behind his family's home where the wooded hills merged with a steeper rocky terrain. From this height, the Coulter ranch houses and buildings seemed small and the ranch spread out in the distance.

He made a soft bed of pine needles and spread an old quilt over them to sit on. Down below the air was heavy with humidity. Up here, a steady southern wind and the shade of tall pines cooled them both after the exertion of their climb.

Isabelle spread her arms wide, tilted her head back, and smiled. Sunlight filtering through the trees warmed her face. With a sigh, she dropped her arms and took in the vast expanse of land before them. "I bet you can see a hundred miles from here."

She looked to Danny to see if he agreed and found him watching her with a strange, nearly tender expression.

"Something wrong?" she asked.

A little smile tugged at the corners of his mouth. "Not a darn thing."

He sat on the quilt and leaned back on his elbows, watching a red-tailed hawk gliding gracefully on the air currents. "It must feel great to leave the ground and soar through the air."

Isabelle joined him on the quilt. "Maybe you'll be a pilot someday. Daddy took me to this air show once and they had these really fast jets. You could join the Air Force and fly one of those, your own personal comet."

Danny shook his head. "I think I'm too small."

"Oh, for heaven's sake, that's all you talk about!"

He thought for a minute then shrugged, "Just stating a fact."

She nudged him with her elbow. "You make up for it in heart."

He laughed softly, "Whoopee."

Isabelle lay on her back and watched the hawk swoop over the hill. "On days like this, I'm glad we moved here."

"Do you think you'll always want to stay in Shadow?"

She was certain that what she dreamed of could not be obtained in this small town. "No way. What about you?"

"I'd like to travel some, but I won't live anywhere else."

Isabelle squinted at him. "You can't decide a thing like that when you're a kid."

"Why not?"

"You don't know enough yet."

Danny returned his attention to the sky. "I know where home is."

Isabelle sat up and hugged her knees to her chest. "Well...if I'm going to be somebody I can't do it here."

Danny chewed on that statement for a moment. "I guess it depends on what you mean by being somebody."

The special emphasis he placed on the word "somebody" stung. Of course, Danny had no way of knowing she had unintentionally mimicked her mother's exact words. The fact that they had tumbled out of her mouth so easily took her by surprise. And just like that, the whirlwind of hurt was back, nicking at her insides, seizing the peace she had found lately and squashing it like a bug.

Danny nodded at the southern sky. "A storm's brewing."

The dark clouds gathering on the horizon mirrored the thoughts running through her head. *Let it rain*, she thought. *I hope it pours down on my head and soaks me to the bone. Come on rain! Wash away all this misery that just won't leave me alone.*

She realized Danny was now sitting up and staring at her intently, perhaps he had even spoken.

"Did you say something?"

"We should go before that storm gets here," he said.

He was right of course. The storm appeared to be advancing quickly and they had quite a walk to reach safety. She just wasn't ready.

"Issy?"

With the exception of Grandma Sarah, she never talked to anyone about her mother anymore. She thought she knew Danny well enough to finally trust him with her deepest hurt.

"My mother did things all backwards," she blurted out with much more force than she intended. She looked at the far southern sky, calming herself. "First, she married Daddy when she was just sixteen, then she had me. The whole time all she wanted to do was stand on a stage and sing. When the chance came to chase that dream, she ran off and left us."

Her throat tightened and she swallowed hard. "I want to get my life right," she said after a moment.

She paused for a breath and whispered. "I don't ever want to hurt anybody the way Mama did."

Tears spilled down her cheeks. Danny hadn't taken his eyes off her. Embarrassed, she brushed the tears away. A strong burst of wind swept over the hill stirring up dust, pine needles, and whipping through the trees.

"She just up and left me Danny," she finished softly, her words carried away on a second burst of wild wind.

When she fell silent, he leaned over and kissed her cheek. "I'm sorry."

That was the first moment she knew she loved Danny Coulter.

In the near distance, heavy rain was falling in sheets. The wind struck them in increasingly powerful bursts. In his short life, Danny had witnessed enough turbulent skies to know the approaching storm was dangerous.

Exercising considerable patience, he allowed her tears to subside before attempting to urge her to leave. There was no way they could make it down the hill in time to reach shelter. Though he dreaded the idea, the cave wasn't that far and that was their safest choice.

He got to his feet and held out his hand. "Issy," he said calmly, "we have to get off this hill."

When she looked up at him, her face so full of trust and vulnerability, he wished he was strong enough to carry her to safety where no one or anything could ever hurt her again. Right now, all he had to offer was his hand. She put her hand in his and rose. He grabbed the old quilt with his free hand and pulled her behind him.

Unfortunately, Isabelle ran as if she had no sense of the impending danger. On a particularly steep angle, she released his hand and began to daintily pick her way through a cluster of bushes.

Danny hurried back and grabbed her hand again, pulling her more forcefully now. "Come on!"

He kept dragging her downward to the lowest point between the two hills then swung right, deeper into the woods toward the cave. All the while, she yelled that he was hurting her and attempted to pull her hand free. The entrance to the cave was within sight as the front edge of the storm reached them. Pounding rain and dime-sized hail pummeled the thick forest of trees, reducing the impact on Isabelle and Danny, but still pelting them enough to raise a few welts. A gust of wind brought a large tree limb crashing to the ground only feet away and Isabelle screamed.

Danny tugged her into the cave where he finally released her. He dropped the quilt, put his hands on his knees and tried to catch his breath just as an earthshaking roar rolled toward them, louder, and louder still. He recalled hearing people say a tornado sounded like a freight train. At this moment, he believed they had greatly underrated the description. The sound was deafening.

The cave entrance offered minimal protection, but there was no time to reach one of the tunnels. Isabelle stood frozen, covering her ears with her hands. He leaped toward her, backed her into the deepest corner, wrapped his arms around her, and held on. The wind swept through the cave opening like a tidal wave, alternately pushing then pulling at them, making his ears pop, pummeling his back with rocks, pinecones, twigs, all of the shredded debris the forest had to offer. Isabelle buried her face in his shoulder and clung to him.

He wanted to pray, but in his terror all he could manage was: "Please, please, please."

When finally the uproar lessened then faded into complete silence, Danny released his hold on Isabelle. Stepping away to the edge of the cave, he took a deep breath, closed his eyes, and whispered. "Thank you."

"Was that a tornado?" Isabelle asked in a small voice.

"I think so."

He glanced back at her and found that she was still standing where he left her. She was shaking as if she were cold.

"Are you okay?" he asked.

She nodded but her eyes filled with tears. Oddly, the quilt he dropped earlier lay in a tight ball near the opening of the largest tunnel. After giving the quilt a good shake, he wrapped it around her shoulders.

"We'd better get home," he said gently.

Outside the southern sky was clear blue and rain dripped on their heads from the trees. The storm had moved on to the northeast. All that was visible in that direction were dark clouds and heavy rain. Danny wondered if the tornado was still on the ground.

"My legs are kind of wobbly," Isabelle said.

He looked to her again. "Can you walk?"

She studied him for a moment, her forehead wrinkled in a frown. "You have sticks and stuff in your hair."

Her long hair probably was probably twice the mess as his own, but he already knew enough about girls not to mention that fact. He bent forward, running his fingers through his tangled hair as best he could, shaking the debris loose.

"Better?" he asked.

She nodded solemnly.

"Good. Let's get off this hill."

He walked her home, knowing his family would be concerned about his whereabouts, but couldn't leave her now. He planned to phone them from Isabelle's house, but as they descended the hill toward the Wagner ranch that notion faded away.

The tornado had apparently come down on this side and struck the Wagner ranch a glancing blow.

Full-grown trees were toppled in a swath of land to their right. The mighty force had driven a tree, bigger around than Danny's body, into the rocky earth. Stripped clean of all leaves, limbs, and bark, the tree stood erect like a totem pole waiting to be carved.

Part of the Wagner's smaller stable was missing half of the roof. An ancient oak had toppled over onto the adjacent corral, crushing the fence. Isabelle's father stood near the stable assessing the damage with the Wagner's. Danny put two fingers in his mouth and whistled loudly.

Marshall ran to them and grabbed Isabelle, hugging her tightly. "Where have you been?"

"Danny and I were on the big hill. He took me to a cave."

Marshall kissed the top of her head then hugged her again. "Thank God you're safe."

Danny started to turn away. "I'd better get home."

"Give me just a minute to check a few things and I'll run you home," Marshall said.

Danny followed Isabelle down the road to her house where they discovered a tree had fallen through the roof and into Isabelle's room. Her bedroom window was shattered and the curtains fluttered against the side of the house.

Isabelle's hand flew to her mouth. "Oh my gosh!"

Inside the Long house, Danny immediately went to the phone, but there was no dial tone. He followed

Isabelle down the hall to her room where Mama Rose was attempting to pick through the debris, trying to salvage Isabelle's belongings. Isabelle had stopped in the doorway, surveying the mess that was her room.

Mama Rose set a broken lamp on the floor and embraced her. "Daddy and I were so worried about you!"

"I was on the hill with Danny. We hid in a cave," Isabelle repeated.

Mama Rose gave her a second hug. "I'm so glad you're alright."

Mama Rose stepped over a pile of bedding and hugged Danny as well. "You too, Sweetheart. Does your family know you're okay?"

"The phone is down. Mr. Long said he would drive me home in a minute."

Isabelle picked up one of her broken records and looked around at the mess. Mama Rose waved her hands in the air.

"Don't get upset now Sugar. The important thing is everybody is just fine. All this stuff can be replaced."

The top of the fallen tree divided Isabelle's bedroom in half diagonally. Other than the roof of course, the worst damage was to her closet. The sliding closet doors had popped off the track and were lying on the floor. A limb had snapped the closet pole in half and all of the hanging clothes were lying in a heap.

Isabelle began frantically digging through the clothes, throwing things out left and right. Mama Rose stood nearby, looking helpless and close to tears. Finally, Isabelle cried out and sank down on her knees.

Danny knelt next to her. "What are you looking for?"

She swiped at the tears on her face. "Mama's shoes."

Danny immediately understood that she didn't mean Mama Rose's shoes and how very important the shoes must be to her. "Let me try."

He began removing piles of clothes and carrying them to her bed. When the closet was half empty, Isabelle spotted one of the red shoes. Unfortunately a small branch had speared the shoe and driven it into the floor.

Isabelle started pushing at the branch, but Danny realized there was no way to remove it without a saw.

"We'll get that shoe later," he said. "Let's find the other one."

After more digging, he found the other shoe inside a crushed shoebox. Isabelle hugged the shoe to her chest as if she had just discovered gold.

Danny turned to Mama Rose. "Do you have a saw I can use?"

Mama Rose nodded. "Be right back."

After a few minutes of sawing the branch was free and Danny handed Isabelle the pieces of the red shoe.

Marshall appeared in the doorway. "Let's get you home Danny."

"Yes sir," he replied, standing. "I'll talk to you later Issy."

She looked up at him clutching the red shoes. "Thank you."

Her dirty face was streaked with tears. Her clothes were muddy and wet. Her hair was tangled, twisted, and standing out at all angles like Medusa's snakes.

All he saw was her smile.

His parents were relieved to see him climb out of Marshall's truck and his mother hugged him like they hadn't seen each other in years.

The Coulter ranch had sustained minor damage, nothing at all like the Wagner's. Still, there was cleanup to be done. After supper, Danny accompanied his father and brothers to Isabelle's house to help them deal with the tree in Isabelle's room.

As Danny watched his father and Marshall discuss how they were going to remove the tree and the necessary repairs to the roof, Isabelle smiled at Danny and nodded to the undamaged wall near her bed.

"I still have your drawings," she said.

Discovering she had tacked his drawings to the wall was eye opening. Knowing she prized those drawings second to her mother's red shoes humbled him.

Isabelle kissed his cheek. "You're my hero."

He blushed and grinned like a goofball.

After going to bed that night, Danny lay there comparing Isabelle's life to his own. He never knew anyone with such deep hurt before. Despite the extraordinary moments of the day, he returned over and over to his impulsive act of kissing her on the cheek before the storm. Faced with her pain, words had failed him or he would have never done such a thing.

From the moment he first saw her under Purser's Bridge, he felt an irresistible draw toward her he could not explain. He had plenty of friends, all of them boys his own age. His friendship with Isabelle was different of course, but not because she was a girl. Okay, if he were honest, she was downright pretty, and the way she liked him back made him feel special, but there was more that he couldn't define as yet.

Unbelievably, thunder rumbled in the distance, signaling yet another storm.

"Are you awake?" David asked, interrupting his reverie.

"Yep."

"Can I come over?"

He sighed and scooted to the outer edge of his twin bed. "Bring your pillow."

Shadow, Oklahoma
Fall 1965

TWENTY-TWO

Isabelle joined Denise Coulter and their usual gaggle of ninth-grade girlfriends on the gymnasium bleachers at the pep rally for the first football game of the season. So far, this first year of high school was certainly an exciting new world. There were new girlfriends, more boys from surrounding areas to consider, even the classes and a few of the teachers were interesting. Most important for Isabelle were the school chorus and the play the school put on every year.

As usual, the girls in her little group were gushing and giggling over Darren Coulter. Danny's older brother was the quarterback and co-captain of the varsity football team. Along with half the girls in school, Isabelle had a crush on handsome Darren. Of course Denise Coulter didn't quite understand all the fuss over her brother, but generally let the girls blather on with a minimum of eye rolling and sarcasm.

Down the bleachers to the right, Danny and his best friend Jimmy joined their group of friends. Art was still Danny's passion and throughout the school he was admired for his talents. Usually, the artsy kids were a small, tightly knit contingent, but Danny wasn't defined by any one social group in the school. Unlike Darren, who was much quieter and easygoing, Danny's independent nature and spirited disposition made him more popular in general, though Darren had the heartthrob title all to himself.

"I don't know why everyone likes Darren so much," Holly Adams said in her ear, nearly mimicking Isabelle's own thoughts. "Danny's the cute one."

Isabelle found her friend's statement disconcerting. Pretty, popular Holly could have her choice of lots of boys.

"One word you don't want to use with Danny is cute," she cautioned.

Holly frowned at her. "What's wrong with cute?"

"Because he's always been so little, people pat him on the head and tell him how cute he is. He hates it."

Looking past Holly to Danny and his friends, she considered him for a moment in an attempt to be objective. She supposed you could describe Danny's baby face as cute, but the limited adjective greatly minimized what she considered to be his better qualities. If Holly didn't recognize his intelligence and depth of character, she was just another superficial, silly girl, and Isabelle believed her friend to be smarter than that.

Holly sighed. "I just love it when he smiles at me."

Holly had just hit on the exact physical quality Isabelle adored most. When she was having a bad day, Danny could breeze through and change everything with one of his easy smiles.

"Yeah," she said quietly, "that's one of my favorite things about him too."

Holly gave her serious consideration. "Have you ever…I mean do you and Danny…"

Isabelle waved her off. "We're just friends."

Holly looked away, a pink blush highlighting her cheeks. Isabelle gave her a playful nudge. "I didn't know you liked him so much."

"Please don't tell him, okay?"

Isabelle glanced down the bleachers again and caught Danny's eye. His mouth spread into the very smile that gave her so much courage, hope, and left her feeling sheltered from harm. An odd, prickly possessiveness seeped into her thoughts. If she were honest, she didn't want Holly, or anyone else for that matter, to have him.

"I won't say a word," she murmured.

In October, Holly Adams invited her freshman friends and some of the older kids, including Darren, Danny, and their cousin Elliot to a Halloween party at her parents' home.

Isabelle rode to the party in the backseat of Darren's car, squeezed between Denise and the oafish Elliot. Danny sat up front fiddling with the radio dial, trying to tune the station in and tone down the static.

"I wish this was a costume party," Denise said.

"Not me," Elliot responded.

"I like dressing up too," Isabelle said to Denise. She poked Danny in the shoulder. "What about you?"

"If this was a costume party, I wouldn't be going."

"You don't act all that enthused anyway," Denise said. "I hope you're at least nice to Holly, since this is her party and all."

Like Isabelle, Denise knew that Holly had a crush on Danny; unlike her, Denise wanted to nudge her brother toward Holly.

Danny shot Denise a look of irritation. "Why wouldn't I be nice to her?"

He turned back to the radio and finally got a better signal, filling the car with the song "You've Lost That Lovin' Feelin.'" Denise immediately started belting out the chorus and Isabelle joined her. Danny turned around and grinned at them. Darren joined in the singing. Elliot groaned and covered his ears.

Since Holly was one of her best friends, Isabelle had spent hours at the Adams home. The rambling southern colonial-style house was one of the finest in the county with plenty of surrounding pasture for their group of horses.

Isabelle particularly loved Mrs. Adams' huge collection of records, many of them from Broadway shows. She and Holly spent hours in her room, listening to music, sometimes singing along to the records, but mostly talking.

Holly's father was a local attorney everyone respected. Mrs. Adams' family owed a high-end furniture store where she worked as the bookkeeper. Though they had more money than most, Holly and her younger sister weren't spoiled. In fact, they were some of the kindest, most generous people Isabelle ever met.

After a BBQ, the kids gathered in the barn to play music and an impromptu game of spin the bottle at Elliot's urging.

"Come on," Elliot said to Danny. "Spin the damned thing."

Danny grabbed the empty wine bottle and spun it without conviction. It turned three times, slowed then stopped in front of Holly.

Isabelle was beginning to wonder if the bottle wasn't fixed. Each time he took a turn, fate pointed the bottle directly at Holly. Danny leaned over the circle and gave her a third cursory peck on the lips.

Isabelle watched him with interest. Most of the other boys seemed eager to touch and kiss. Sometimes, he was hard to understand.

Isabelle's turn came and she gave the bottle a quick spin. She held her breath as it rolled toward Darren Coulter. For the past few months, her attraction to Darren had reached uncomfortable levels. Whenever he was around she became tongue tied and foolishly giggled for no real reason. Of course, the bottle rolled right past Darren and stopped in front of Elliot. Isabelle released her breath in a disappointed rush. Of all the boys, Elliot was her least favorite. Not that he was hard to look at. Elliot had attractive features. The main problem with Elliot was an unwarranted high opinion of himself.

This was the second time the bottle had stopped in front of Elliot. The first time she had turned her head just in time to redirect his kiss to her cheek. From the way he was grinning at her now, she knew he was on to her tricks.

She looked across the circle and found Danny looking directly at her, his face a deep shade of red, like when he was mad about something. When Elliot rose on his knees and leaned across to kiss her, Danny jumped to his feet.

"I'm not feeling good," he said. "I think I'd better call it a night."

"Oh, Danny don't go," Holly pleaded. "We don't have enough boys as it is."

He turned, walking backwards and patted his abdomen, "Sorry, I must have eaten too much."

When he disappeared outside the barn, some of the other boys followed his lead, then a few of the girls.

Isabelle offered Elliot a thin smile and shrugged. "I guess the game's over," she said.

Outside, she saw Darren had drifted away with Fran Simmons, so she hurried to find Danny. He certainly hadn't wasted any time. He was already near the end of the private drive. Isabelle ran to catch him and tugged on his jacket sleeve as he reached the blacktop.

"Mind if I walk with you?"

He shot her an annoyed look, "Of course not."

Home for Danny was quite a walk, but even farther for her.

"I thought we were supposed to ride home with Darren," she said.

"He's with Fran. You can wait around for him if you want, but you might have a long wait."

The air was chilly and the nearly full moon bathed the countryside in soft blue light. She shivered and crossed her arms over her chest.

"It was so warm earlier I didn't think to bring a sweater."

He removed his jacket and draped it over her shoulders.

"Now you'll be cold," she said.

"I'm fine."

Isabelle bumped him with her shoulder. "I don't know why you're not interested in girls."

He shot her an irritated glance. "Who says I'm not interested in girls?"

"Well, you sure don't like kissing them."

Danny bent to pick up a few stones from the roadside then started pitching them into the field.

"Are you going to answer me?" She asked.

"You didn't ask a question."

"How come you don't like kissing girls?"

"I like kissing girls," he said with a little shrug.

"Holly might not think so." Isabelle laughed. "Was that your idea of a kiss?"

"Well, yeah, under the circumstances."

"What circumstances?"

He rolled his eyes and she gave him another little shove.

"I don't know. I just don't like her, okay?" he said.

She couldn't argue with that. Holly was considered one of the prettiest girls in school and there were lots of boys interested in her, but Danny had every right not to like her. Isabelle hummed and they walked side by side, not speaking for awhile.

"I thought I was going to have to kiss Elliot, but you saved me," she said.

"Glad I could be of assistance."

"I've never kissed a boy," she admitted shyly. "I certainly didn't want him to be the first."

He looked over at her, "Never?"

Embarrassed over her confession, Isabelle felt her cheeks flush with embarrassment. Danny stopped walking, his expression shifting to the tender look she adored. When he looked at her like that, life was less complicated. As he slowly leaned toward her, the thought entered her mind that he intended to kiss her. They had known each other for over three years now, their friendship was strong, but the idea of them kissing seemed so absurd she giggled.

She reached over and touched the end of his nose playfully. "Can I tell you a secret?"

"Sure," he replied softly.

"I was hoping the bottle would stop in front of Darren."

He stared without moving for nearly a full minute. He didn't blink once.

Isabelle waved a hand in front of his face. "Are you there?"

He straightened his back, seemingly shaking off whatever had him transfixed. "Darren?"

There was an odd, unfamiliar edge to his voice. Maybe he thought she wasn't good enough for his brother.

"What's wrong with me liking Darren?" she asked hotly.

"Nothing," he replied in a flat tone.

He started walking again, picking up the pace considerably.

She hurried to catch up. "Why are you acting so weird?"

"I'm not acting weird. You just surprised me."

Isabelle squinted at him. "You're jealous of Darren."

He stopped abruptly. "What?"

"There's no reason to be jealous, Danny. All the girls I know think you're just as cute as a button."

He groaned and started moving toward home once again. Isabelle hooked her arm through his and kept in step.

"Do you think I'm being silly? I know every girl in school likes Darren. Gosh, he's so handsome and wonderful, who wouldn't like him? Do you think I have any chance?"

Danny pulled away from her. "I'm not interested in talking about my brother."

Behind them, the headlights of a car illuminated the road. They moved to the edge as the car slowed beside them. The driver's window slid down with a soft whirring sound.

Aunt Rosalie grinned at them from behind the steering wheel. "Hey there! You kids need a ride?"

Though her divorce from Hal was finalized over two years ago, twenty-one-year-old Rosalie was still adrift. Other than her sister Vera, she had no family to return to and had remained in her little house. With the exception of Elliot's mother (who considered Rosalie "white trash"), Rosalie received plenty of support from all of the Coulters.

Since the night Danny stood up to his uncle and protected Hal Junior, he and Rosalie had bonded on a very personal level.

A few months ago, Rosalie started working at the Piggly Wiggly and grew chummy with one of the checkers, another divorcee. When the two of them got together, they sometimes drank a few too many margaritas, which appeared to be the case this evening.

Danny stepped up to the car and placed a hand on the door. Isabelle spotted Hal Junior asleep on the backseat. The strong odor of alcohol wafted out of the car, reminding her of the night her mother won the singing contest and her life was forever altered. Repulsed, she backed away, hoping Danny wouldn't suggest they accept Rosalie's offer.

Danny leaned down to speak to his aunt. "You know you shouldn't be driving like this, especially with Junior in the car Aunt Rosalie," Danny said. "Let me drive you home."

Rosalie patted his hand and smiled. "That's sweet of you, but there's no need to worry. Everything's under control. You kids go on and climb in. I'll have you home in no time at all."

Isabelle tugged on Danny's shirt and he glanced over his shoulder at her. She shook her head no. He turned back to Rosalie and tried one more time. "Please, Aunt Rosalie, let me drive."

"Get in, or move back," she said pushing his hand off the car.

Danny stepped away and Rosalie gunned the engine, spinning the tires on the asphalt, rubber squealing as the car shot forward like a rocket.

Isabelle wrinkled her nose. "I hate the smell of…"

A loud pop, like gunfire, drowned out the rest of her sentence. They watched in horror as Rosalie's car veered off the edge of the road then bounced down the embankment, landing on the rutted dirt and gravel path leading to the river with the engine still racing. The harmony of Rosalie and Isabelle's screams bounced off the hills as the car headed straight for the water.

Danny started running toward the river. "Get help, Issy!"

Isabelle ran back to the party where she called her father and Cecil Coulter. The Adams' family and everyone from the party piled into several vehicles and hurried back to the river arriving just as Cecil and Marshall flew over the bridge in their trucks. Down below, the top of Rosalie's car was barely visible. Danny, Rosalie, and Junior were nowhere to be seen.

While Cecil waded out in the river toward the car, everyone stood motionless on the bank. Isabelle's heart was beating so hard she could hear the thumping in her ears. She swallowed the urge to scream Danny's name.

Cecil ducked below the surface of the water, but after a minute stood straight again and waded toward the bank. "No one's in there."

They divided into groups and began shining their flashlights on both sides of the river, calling out to Danny and Rosalie.

"Daddy" Darren called, "over here!"

Not far downstream, Rosalie was lying on the river bank with her eyes wide open. Cecil knelt next to her, placing two fingers on her neck for a pulse. He stood again, shaking his head, sending a grim message that made Isabelle's insides twinge.

"We better see if anybody found Danny and Junior," Marshall said.

Isabelle pushed aside her shock at seeing the dead woman and continued searching with everyone else. Grandma Sarah's prediction about Danny and this river rang in her head, but she kept the prophecy to herself. She feared speaking the words aloud might make that prediction a reality.

Downstream from the bridge, Danny crawled from the river clutching Junior in his arms. He lay the toddler down in a patch of soft grass and rolled to his back sucking in air.

In the last few minutes, he had made some hard choices. By the time he dove into the cold river, the water level had reached the top of the doors and the front of the car was sinking quickly. Oddly, the headlights and interior lights of the car were still working. Rosalie's body was slumped over toward the passenger door. He reached through the open window and grabbed her arm, pulling her upright. Her head swung toward him, the dashboard lights casting an eerie, ghastly glow to her skin. Her gaping mouth filled with water and her eyes were open and lifeless. Shocked Danny released her arm and backed away, treading water. Junior's screams drew him back to the task at hand. He grabbed one of Junior's little arms, pulling him from the backseat, past his dead mother, and out the window. Junior clung to his neck, screaming in his ear all the way to the river bank. He sat the toddler on the grass, instructed him to stay put then returned to the nearly submerged car for Rosalie.

When Rosalie's dress snagged on the gear shift, trying to dislodge the dress and drag her limp body to the surface took him way beyond the comfort one breath allowed. Finally, when he managed to surface, he gulped air and floated downstream a bit. After hauling Rosalie's body to the grassy bank, he discovered Junior was missing. He stood and scanned the dark night looking for the little boy, screaming his name in utter panic. He spotted Junior toddling further downstream at the river's edge and started running, calling for Junior to stop. To his horror, Junior tripped then tumbled down the embankment, splashing right back into the river. Without a second thought, Danny went back into the cold water for a third time.

Right now, with Junior safe beside him, he could hear voices calling to him, but was too winded to call out. Fortunately, Junior once again began producing ear-piercing screams that could probably be heard all the way to Shadow. He pulled the child closer and gripped the straps of Junior's overalls to keep him from running off again.

After a few minutes, he managed to sit up. He could see the intermittent flash of lights as the others neared, but they seemed to be moving too slowly. He tried to stand but his legs were weak and he plopped back down with a hard thud. The toddler's wailing had lessened to a pitiful cry and he pulled Junior onto his lap, wrapping his arms around the small body to try and warm him as much as possible.

His father was the first to appear. "Danny!"

His father knelt beside him, pulling him into his arms, hugging Danny and Junior together. Marshall stepped up and took the boy, quickly heading back toward the bridge.

Cecil helped Danny to his feet and embraced him. "I'm so glad you're okay."

His father released him and they walked back to where a crowd had gathered near Rosalie's body. Someone had covered Rosalie with a blanket and he was grateful not to have to see her dead face again.

Danny sat on the tailgate of his father's truck and accepted the mug of hot chocolate his mother pressed into his hands. Despite the blankets wrapped around him, he couldn't stop shaking. Stripping off his wet clothes and slipping into a hot bath sounded like heaven, but he had to stay until the sheriff finished with him. He understood that in part the uncontrollable trembling had nothing to do with being cold and wet. Seeing Rosalie's lifeless eyes wide open and her long hair drifting lazily on the current was an image he would probably never forget.

Isabelle shuffled towards him with another blanket and tucked it around his legs then hugged him tightly. "I'm so glad you're okay. I kind of panicked when we couldn't find you."

"I don't know what you were worried about," he said irritably. "You know I'm a good swimmer."

Isabelle looked away from him, tears spilling down her cheeks. "I was scared."

Danny wasn't in the mood for one more second of drama. "I don't know what you're getting so worked up about. Rosalie's the one who died, not me."

She pulled out a tissue and wiped her eyes, then blew her nose. "Don't you remember Grandma Sarah's premonition about you and this river?"

He groaned loudly. "Stop."

"Losing you would be one of the worst things that could ever happen to me," she said quietly, her voice cracking.

He couldn't bear her histrionics right now. He looked her in the eye, knowing full well what he was about to say would make her mad. And that was the point...he could handle her anger better than this gloom and doom.

"This probably wasn't my night," he said with a shrug. "After all, I'm young, and it is a patient river."

She shoved him so hard he fell off the tailgate.

Danny climbed to the top of the old clubhouse, immediately loosening his tie and unbuttoning the top two buttons of his dress shirt. From this perch, he watched with dread as Uncle Hal crossed the creek down below and started up the hill towards him.

The last three days had been brutal, culminating in Rosalie's funeral today. After returning home this afternoon, he had slipped away from the crowd gathered at his grandparents' house. He had no desire to talk about what happened ever again, especially with his unpredictable uncle.

Following Hal's hasty departure three years ago, he had landed in Oklahoma City where he still lived with Vera. Though he sent child support checks regularly, Hal had only visited his son sporadically, always alone.

Danny's grandfather had immediately contacted Hal with the news of Rosalie's death, but there had been no word from him until he appeared at the funeral today. Hal had explained that Vera believed she would not be well received by the Coulters and had chosen to remain in Oklahoma City, assuring none of Rosalie's family attended the funeral.

Danny cringed as Hal climbed up on the roof of the clubhouse, the plywood bowed as he eased himself down to the surface.

"I told you I wanted to talk to you," Hal said. "Are you hiding from me?"

On those few occasions when Hal had returned to Shadow over the past few years, he had sought Danny out, offering apologies for his behavior the night of his drunken rage. In each instance, Danny rejected the feeble attempts outright. Today he was just too exhausted from the turmoil of the last few days to feed much energy into his dislike of Hal.

Danny shrugged. "I'm hiding in general."

"You're really an odd kid, Runt."

Danny noted Hal's eyes were red rimmed, and since he seemed completely sober, Danny wondered if he was actually experiencing grief for the wife he mistreated then tossed away so easily.

Hal turned his attention to the landscape. Dark circles and bags under his eyes made him look much older than twenty-four. "Sure is a nice view."

Danny nodded. "I want to build my house here when I'm grown."

"You plan on sticking around Shadow? I thought you'd be more adventurous than that."

He had dreams of getting out, seeing the world, like any other fifteen-year-old boy, but he also knew Oklahoma would always be home. Of course, he didn't care to discuss any of this with Hal.

"Will you be taking Junior back to the city with you?"

"I'm not going back." Hal said, stretching out. "I'm going to apply for a GI loan and start a business right here."

Danny digested that statement for a moment. Everyone always said Hal would return for good one day. Though he wasn't particularly thrilled with the notion of Hal being around, the move would probably be best for Junior and that mattered a whole lot more.

"What kind of business?" he asked.

"Car repair is the only thing I was ever any good at."

Hal lit a cigarette and silence reigned for a few minutes. Beyond the river, the sun inched toward the skyline, turning the low blanket of clouds crimson. The air was growing chilly.

Hal flicked his ashes over the edge of the roof and they skittered away on the wind. "Why don't you come to work for me once I get things up and running?"

Danny eyed him suspiciously. "You'd be willing to teach me?"

"Hell, Danny, it's the least I can do."

"Careful, Uncle Hal, you just called me Danny."

"I know what I said." Hal laughed and poked him with a finger. "Don't get your hopes up. You're still a runt."

"Don't I know it," Danny said with a weary sigh.

Hal reached over and patted him on the back, his eyes filling with tears. "You'll always be a giant in my book."

Shadow, Oklahoma
1966 Spring

TWENTY-THREE

No one was surprised (let alone disappointed) when Vera did not return with Hal to Shadow. Hal reluctantly agreed that staying on Coulter property was best for Junior, so he returned to his little house on the hill. The question of just how long Hal could make the situation work in the best interest of his child was on everyone's mind.

After months of considerable effort, Hal finally had the financing in order and purchased an old auto repair shop from an owner/mechanic who had closed the place down five years ago and retired. Since everything about the garage was rundown, Danny's father, grandfather, and Uncle Robert offered to help as much as possible to bring the place into working order.

When his father set out one Saturday morning for a look at Hal's garage, Danny tagged along. Fearing Hal wouldn't follow through on his offer, he hadn't mentioned to anyone that his uncle had offered him a job. He hoped that perhaps his presence in the garage might jog his uncle's memory.

His grades were good, but he wasn't sure his parents would believe he could handle school, ranch work, and a part-time job. Youthful cockiness insisted he would do just fine. All he needed was for Hal to open the door.

The concrete block garage had three large bays and a storage room behind a small office. A set of wooden stairs outside led to a room over the office.

Danny took the tour with Hal and his father, listening idly as they discussed the necessary improvements. Hal focused on the task at hand, like a real adult.

When the two men wrapped up their conversation without any mention of him working there, Danny's spirits fell. As his father headed toward their truck, Danny stepped up to Hal and took a chance.

"Are you going to hire any help?"

Hal shot him an irritated look. "I have to get this place in shape before I consider hiring anyone."

"Let's go, Danny," his father said.

Disappointed, he slumped down on the seat of the truck, vowing never to take Hal at his word again. The dream of earning enough money for a car was fading fast.

Instead of heading toward home, his father turned the truck toward the center of town.

Temporarily distracted from his self-pity, he sat up a little straighter. "Where are we going?"

"I thought we'd get ourselves some lunch."

Private time with his father was a rare occasion. Feeling special, Danny's mood brightened a little.

Ruby's Diner was the most popular restaurant in town. There were daily homemade specials like a meatloaf, fried catfish, chicken and dumplings, cakes and pies, but Danny loved the cheeseburgers. On Saturdays, the place was always hopping. While they waited to be seated, his father chatted with several people and Danny mulled over the idea of confronting his uncle once he got the garage up and running.

Finally, a booth opened up and he slid into a seat opposite his father. They both ordered the number two special, a cheeseburger and fries. Once the waitress delivered Danny's chocolate shake and his father's black coffee, his father focused on him. "I understand Uncle Hal offered you a job."

Stunned, Danny managed only a quiet: "Yes sir."

"Are you considering it?"

Danny shifted around in the booth, trying to keep his enthusiasm under control. "I'd like to try, if you'll let me."

His father took a sip of his coffee then considered him for a moment. "You know his disposition is a bit... irregular. He won't be the best teacher, or boss for that matter."

The drunken abuse was burned into his memory and not something he would likely forget in a lifetime. Still, he wanted the job so badly he had to try. "I think I understand how unpredictable he can be."

His father nodded solemnly. "I guess you would."

"I'll keep up with my chores at home, Daddy. I just want to earn some money so I can get a car."

"Mama and I are most concerned about your schooling."

Here was yet another surprise: his mother knew.

"I won't let my grades slip, I promise."

The waitress approached and placed their food on the table in front of them. Danny shook the ketchup bottle, poured a glob onto his plate for the fries, added mustard to the hamburger bun, and took a big bite.

"I see you've given this job offer a lot of thought," his father.

He had a mouthful of food, so he nodded enthusiastically.

"Well, all right then, you give it a shot." His father looked him in the eye. "But if he mistreats you in any way whatsoever, I will expect you to walk away. Do we understand each other?"

Danny nodded with enthusiasm. He couldn't believe his good fortune.

TWENTY-FOUR

Danny turned the tractor and started up the next row toward the blacktop in deep thought regarding the painting he just started at school yesterday. His previous art teacher had a heart attack just before Christmas and retired after thirty-five years. The new teacher was young and eager to bring fresh possibilities into her students' lives. When she introduced the class to oil paints, Danny found a new medium to love. The possibilities were so stimulating he hated to see Friday come when he was cut off from the art room. With spring break just around the corner, the time away from this newfound passion would be even longer. He worked for Uncle Hal every Saturday now and hoped that soon he would have enough money to buy his own oil paints, brushes, and canvas. The car he dreamed of for so long was not the current priority.

Elliot's friends had just dropped him off at his house and were now headed up the gravel road toward the blacktop. Danny watched as the car stopped and one of the teenage boys inside popped out a window aiming a gun at Denise and David who were riding horses in the pasture on the other side of the road. Suddenly David's horse reared and David fell back in the saddle then down to the ground. Denise pulled her horse up short and quickly dismounted, running to David's aid. The boy with the gun took aim at Denise, popped off a shot, and she grabbed her thigh, grimacing in pain.

Danny lifted the plow blade, shifted the tractor and gave it gas, picking up speed as it bounced across the field. The boys on the road were all out of the car now with their backs to him, and seemed to be in no hurry to leave. Another boy took aim with the gun, sighting one of the goats in a nearby herd. Danny recognized the old Plymouth as belonging to Rob Crenshaw, the biggest bully at school. These three bullies, along with Elliot, frequently made life hell for many people.

As the tractor came closer, they turned, and the humor briefly left their expressions. To get to them he would have to crash through the rail fence. Those boys stood there and began grinning at him, evidently expecting he wouldn't dare tear up the fence. Rob Crenshaw grabbed the gun out of his friend's hands and pointed it at Danny.

When he came right on through the fence they ran for the car. Danny steered the tractor up the embankment to the road right at them. The car started to pull away but he was on top of them now and drove the tractor into the right rear panel, pushing the back of the car off the road.

Rob Crenshaw jumped out as Danny backed the tractor up and shifted into neutral, waiting for Rob's next move. Rob ran over to the tractor shaking his fist at Danny.

"I'm going to kick your ass Coulter!"

They were both in their third year of high school, but Rob was taller and outweighed Danny by a good twenty pounds. Undeterred by his opponent's size, Danny jumped from the seat of the tractor without a second thought. They fell and rolled together on the asphalt, punching and swearing until his father's strong hands jerked Danny up and away.

"Stop this! Both of you!"

The other boy's shirt was torn and his lower lip was bleeding. Danny hadn't pulled any punches. Rob, on the other hand, hadn't landed a single blow worthy of a boy his size.

"They were shooting at Denise and David!" Danny told his father.

"It was just a BB gun," said one of the shooters, holding up the gun as proof.

Cecil stepped forward and jerked the gun from the boy's hands. "You boys go on."

Rob pointed at Danny with open contempt. "He needs to pay for what he did to my car!"

Cecil stepped closer to him. "I have a little boy over there with what looks like a broken arm from what you boys did. I suggest you go on home before I call the sheriff."

The boys started toward their car. As Danny bent to retrieve his ball cap from the road, he saw Rob give his father the finger. He covered the fifteen feet between them without hesitation. For the second time, his father had to separate them. He held Danny by the back of the shirt until the other boys drove away.

His father was breathing hard from the exertion. "While you finish this field, I'll be thinking of a way to convince you not to fight every time somebody makes you mad."

His father started away and Danny slipped his hat on his head, surveying the damaged fence.

"And I'll expect you to repair that fence right after you finish the field," he father said without turning.

There were three barns on the ranch and Danny's parents actually had the largest. Since winter broke, an ongoing project had been to scrape and repaint the barn. His father decided the appropriate punishment for fighting with Rob would be for Danny to spend spring break painting one end by himself.

Three weeks after the BB gun incident, Danny stood with his parents looking up at the finished product, waiting for their judgment. While he was proud of his work, he expected their ruling might not come down in his favor.

His parents squinted up at the barn, eyeing the painting in stunned silence. The first day of his punishment, he stood in the very same place with a plan. At a Christmas flea market last November, he had picked up an old art history book and became particularly captivated by the section devoted to the paintings of Michelangelo. After some research and querying his new art teacher at length, he mapped out a course for a mural. With the assistance and secrecy of Darren and David, the work had been remarkably easy for him. Since this end of the barn faced his grandparents' home, he had enlisted their secrecy as well. Today was the first time his parents had actually seen what he had done.

He shifted his feet impatiently, waiting to see which way his parents thinking would go.

"He says it's a copy of what's on the ceiling of that chapel over there in Rome," his mother murmured, keeping her eyes on the hand of God reaching out to Adam.

"You were supposed to paint the barn as a punishment, not an art project." His father looked down at him, seemingly mystified by his third son. "You're really something, you know it?"

Apparently mesmerized, his mother continued to stare at the barn. "What do you think Cecil?"

"Well," his father said at length, "I guess all that's left for him to do is sign the thing."

Finally forcing her focus away from the barn, she frowned at her husband.

"Don't look at me like that, Caroline," his father said. He waved a hand at the painting. "It's got God and everything."

She turned her eyes back to the painting. "When Calvin Peebles came by this morning to deliver the front loader Robert ordered he must have seen this painting and spread the word around town. People have been calling all afternoon wanting to know can they come out and get a look. Even Preacher Glazier called to say he was thinking we should hold Easter sunrise service right here."

His father returned his attention to the wall, pursing his lips as he considered the idea. "Sort of like the beginning and end rolled into one packaged deal," he said finally.

His mother sighed loudly and pointed to a dark mound a little ways from the barn. "We'd have to move the manure."

His father's face twitched then he burst out laughing. When his mother joined in, Danny breathed easier. Then they started laughing hard, holding onto each other. He didn't quite get the joke, but was relieved they weren't angry with him.

His mother smiled, her eyes sparkling as she looked up at his father. He gave her an affectionate kiss on the cheek. "And you wonder where Danny gets his temperament."

Shadow

Shadow, Oklahoma
1966 Fall/Winter

TWENTY-FIVE

These days Danny, Denise, and David rode to and from school with Darren instead of taking the bus. On the way home on a beautiful October afternoon they saw a group of people gathered on the front porch of old George's house and several cars in the driveway, including the sheriff's car.

Knowing Danny's close relationship with the old man, Darren pulled his car to the shoulder of the road and stopped. All of them got out, but only Danny approached the house. Fearing the worst, his heart pounded loudly as George's little dog came running to him.

Deputy Sheriff Dermott Pomeroy hooked his thumbs in his gun belt and gazed down at him from the porch. "Afternoon Danny."

"Is George all right?"

Pomeroy shook his head. "I'm sorry to say George has passed."

Danny's eyes teared. He sucked in a breath and looked away trying to fight the sorrow rising inside. Over the last four years he had grown very fond of

George and his sudden death was like losing a family member.

"You need to go on home," Pomeroy said gently. "We're getting ready to move George in a few minutes."

Danny started away, but had a sudden thought and turned back. "Does his son know?"

George's only child lived in Phoenix with a paraplegic wife who had a multitude of health concerns. He called often, but seldom visited.

Pomeroy nodded. "He'll be on his way as soon as he can."

He headed back to Darren's car with George's little dog on his heels.

"So what's going on?" Darren asked.

Danny looked at him directly, fighting to hide the sadness welling in him. "George is gone."

"Gone?" Denise asked looking around. "Do we need to start looking for him?"

Danny squinted at her, irritated that he needed to explain. "He died Denise."

Denise's hand flew to her mouth. "Oh, my gosh."

Danny climbed into the backseat with David and George's little dog jumped into his lap. Darren and Denise got in front and they rode home in silence.

Danny, Darren, Dwight, Uncle Robert, Elliot, and Cecil served as pallbearers for George's funeral.

Afterwards, the church had a meal in the fellowship hall where George's son approached Danny and Cecil. There was a deep weariness about him and he walked stooped over as if life weighed heavy on his shoulders.

"I wonder if I might have a word," he said.

"Please do," Cecil said, waving at a chair.

George's son looked at Danny, offering a little smile. "My father thought a lot of you. I wanted you to know how much I appreciate your looking after him." He looked at Cecil now. "Your whole family was so wonderful to Dad. I really appreciate all your help."

"He was a good man."

George's son reached into his pocket and pulled out a key ring which he held out to Danny. "He wanted you to have Mama's car."

Stunned, Danny looked to his father for his opinion. Cecil shrugged his shoulders and Danny accepted the key ring and murmured his thanks.

Danny strolled along to the center of the bridge doing his best to ignore his friend Jimmy's goading. After the sad turn of events this week with George's death and funeral, attending the first school football game earlier tonight and now a bonfire at the river had lifted his spirits.

Like Isabelle, his friend Jimmy's Native American roots ran strong on his mother's side.

Jimmy came from a large, historically rowdy, but good-natured Choctaw clan who had lived in the area long before Oklahoma was a state.

Jimmy wasn't yet accustomed to the rapid growth of his body over the past year. With the exception of the football field, where he played left tackle and protected Darren with consistent perfection, Jimmy was clumsy and uncoordinated.

Still hyper from his team's win tonight, Jimmy was attempting to goad him into climbing to the top of the bridge.

"Come on, Coulter, where are those famous balls of yours?"

Danny laughed, "Why don't you do it? Everybody knows you've got nothing to lose."

Jimmy shoved him from behind and he stumbled forward about three feet. Jimmy might be big, but they had been friends since the first grade and Danny knew his friend's weaknesses. He grabbed Jimmy's shirt, backed him to the rail and bent him backwards so swiftly the much larger boy didn't have an opportunity to defend himself.

Off balance now, with his upper body hanging over the river, Jimmy started sweating. "Damn it, Danny. Let me up!"

He smiled slyly. "Say the words I need to hear."

Jimmy closed his eyes, repeating the phrase they had been using since they were in grade school through clenched teeth. "You are lord and master of my universe."

Danny pulled him back, jumped onto the railing, walking the outer edge more to keep Jimmy from retaliating than anything else.

Tiring of his little stroll on the edge, Danny sat on the rail and dangled his feet over the water, watching the kids gathered around the bonfire with idle curiosity. "I talked to Uncle Hal about that Chevy George gave me. He's going to tow it to his garage and help me fix it up."

Jimmy struck a match and lit a cigarette, the small flame lighting his face like a beacon in the dark night. "What do you want with an old piece of junk? It's probably nothing but rust."

Danny knew the Chevy George kept in the garage could be something special with some work.

"I'm going to sand it down and paint it metal flake blue. Hal knows where I can get a 327 engine." He could see the car clearly in his mind and smiled at the possibilities. "It's going to fly."

Jimmy snorted. "And where do you plan to get the money for all this?"

"Working for Uncle Hal."

"Yeah, until you're forty."

Danny was confident. "I'll get it done."

"My brother's coming home on leave next Friday," Jimmy said. "I can get him to buy us some beer, if you want to chip in."

He'd tried a few sips of beer with Jimmy and his brother last summer and the taste had disgusted him. "I'll pass," he said.

"Danny!" Darren called from below. "Time to go. Come on!"

"I'll walk!"

"No! You know the rules. You came with me..."

"You leave with me," Danny finished in unison with Darren.

Now that he had his own car, Darren seldom walked anywhere. Since Danny had ridden to the ballgame with him, their parents' rules dictated he return home with him.

He swung his legs back to the pavement and jumped down, heading for the end of the bridge. "See you later."

"Hey!" Jimmy called. "Are you busy on Sunday?"

He turned and walked backwards facing Jimmy now. "Why yes, as luck would have it, we're putting up hay. Interested in helping out?"

Jimmy laughed. "Nah, you go on and have fun."

Danny jumped over the end of the bridge to the sloping hillside, landing softly in loose dirt.

"Danny! Come on!" Darren yelled again.

"Geez," he groaned. "I'm coming!"

In his rush, he didn't see a girl sitting in the shadows and stepped on her. She screamed, he lost his balance, stumbled backwards, and fell headfirst into the river. He came out of the cold water sporting a gash in his scalp. Blood, mud, and river water streaked down his face. Darren helped him up the river bank then slapped him on the head.

"Thanks a lot. Now you'll get my car all wet." Darren said, slapping him again. This time Danny struck back.

"Stop hitting me! I've got a cut."

"Why did you jump in the river?"

"I didn't jump. I tripped over some girl and fell in."

Darren looked toward the bridge. "What girl?"

"I don't know. I didn't actually see her. I just stepped on her."

Darren started toward the bridge. "Then how do you know it was a girl?"

Danny trotted along behind Darren. "Because she screamed."

They went to the spot where Danny fell in and found no one. Darren shoved his hands on his hips.

"So where's your mystery girl?"

"How would I know Darren? All I know is she was here, I tripped, and fell in."

"Sure you did," Darren snapped, shoving him then heading back toward the car. "Let's go."

Danny placed his hand to his head. "Wow, I'm bleeding a lot. Let me have your shirt."

"Use your own damned shirt."

"Mine's muddy and wet."

Darren moaned and stopped in front of his car. "You're such a pain. Kneel down so I can see the top of your head."

The moment Danny knelt in front of the headlights Darren immediately peeled off his shirt, pressing it to the wound on Danny's head.

Darren sighed loudly. "Looks like you need stitches."

On Sunday afternoon the temperature rose to the high eighties and the air was thick with humidity. While Denise drove the truck pulling the hay bailer and wagon, Danny, Elliot, and Darren stood on the wagon catching the bales coming out of the chute and stacking them.

When the truck reached the end of the field by the blacktop, Denise cut the engine, signaling a break. Darren spotted his girlfriend Fran's car parked along the road and hurried away while the others took the opportunity to have a cold drink and sit for a while.

Danny and Elliot sat on the edge of the wagon, swinging their legs over the side. Denise grabbed sodas from a cooler in the back of the truck, popped the tops off, and handed a bottle up to both of them. Everyone's attention was drawn to the top of the hill where Darren and Fran were engaged in a kiss.

Elliot wiped the sweat from his forehead with a bandana and grinned. "Looks like Darren's done for."

Danny would have to agree. Since starting to date Fran, Darren thought of little else.

A pretty blonde emerged from the passenger side of Fran's car and leaned against the door. Her blue-jean cutoffs were tighter and shorter than any Danny ever saw. She crossed her long tan legs and stared at Elliot, Danny, and Denise.

Danny whistled. "Who's that?"

"Her name's Sue Ellen." Denise said drily. "She's been trying to buddy up to me at school the past two weeks, but all she really seems interested in are you two."

Danny looked to Denise in surprise. "What?"

Denise twisted up her mouth. "She's not the first girl who tried to be my friend just to get to my brothers."

"I had a date with her last night," Elliot grumbled. "I took her to the movies and everything seemed fine, but when we got to the river she disappeared on me. I don't know what her problem is."

"Maybe she's not into being groped," Danny said.

"Shut up," Elliot growled.

Danny jumped down and strolled toward the pretty girl with the intention of annoying Elliot, but with every step the girl became more stunning and the less confidence he had in this hasty decision. When he stopped on the inside of the fence, she smiled widely.

"Hi Danny."

He usually had no trouble talking to girls, but knowing this beautiful stranger had been buddying up to Denise to get next to him left him feeling both flattered and unsettled. When even the easiest reply failed to come to mind, he stood there grinning like a simpleton.

After receiving no response from him, she took the reins. "I hear you got hurt at the bonfire. How's your head?"

He removed his Braves baseball hat and leaned forward so she could see the wound on the top of his head. He had a bald circle and a row of stitches.

She grimaced. "Does it hurt?"

Danny shrugged. "Not anymore."

She gazed down at him through her eyelashes and smiled playfully. "Want me to kiss it and make it better, seeing as it was my fault and all?"

He grinned and relaxed a little. "Was that you I stepped on?"

A gentle breeze lifted a strand of her blond hair across her face. She pulled the strand away with a little toss, never taking her eyes off him. "I was hiding from Elliott."

"Nobody warned you about him?"

Her blue-eyes grew cold as she looked down to the field where Elliot stood fuming. "Fran said he was a jerk, but he seemed so cute I didn't listen. I've never been with such a rude boy before."

"I guess that pretty much sums him up."

She studied him for a moment then straightened her back and changed the subject.

"I just moved here to live with my grandmother," she said. "Fran's my neighbor."

"That would make you Peach Habersoll's granddaughter."

She rolled her eyes dramatically. "This is such a small town."

"Yep."

"So, you're Darren's younger brother, right? What grade are you in?"

"I'm a junior."

Down below in the field, Denise blew the truck horn signaling their break was officially over.

"Gotta go," he said.

She locked eyes with him. "I'll look forward to seeing you around."

He turned and started down the hill. Halfway down, he turned, walking backward for a last look. She treated him to a bright smile that made his heart race.

TWENTY-SIX

Danny shrugged his shoulders into one of Darren's shirts. Although the shirt was a bit loose across the shoulders, the fit wasn't too bad since he had finally started to grow.

Somehow the school had determined he deserved first place for a painting he spent a total of two hours creating. He had turned the canvas into exactly the kind of abstract piece his teacher found interesting. Now he was being praised for a painting he considered to be junk and today he would be given an award at the student art show.

Downstairs, his mother pounded on the stair railing. "Daniel! Get down here right now or we're going without you!"

No doubt she would carry out the threat. Still, he was the person receiving the award, so it would be silly for the family to go without him.

He glanced in the mirror, hoping the stripes in the borrowed shirt would make him look taller. Despite the five inches in height he had gained, the mirror still reflected the same runt. He slipped on his Sunday shoes and didn't bother to tie them before tackling the stairs and his mother's scrutiny.

As he descended, his mother stuck her hands on her hips and eyed him carefully. "Everyone else is already in the car. What in the world were you doing?"

"Trying on Darren's clothes. Did you ever notice he has incredibly bad taste?"

She clucked her tongue and pushed at his long hair. "You should have gotten a haircut."

Danny dodged her touch. "I thought we were in a hurry."

His mother sighed loudly and followed him outside to the ancient family station wagon, where Denise, David, and his father waited. Darren would be attending, but had already left to pick up his girlfriend, Fran, and her lovely next door neighbor, Sue Ellen. Dwight, now nearly twenty, was assisting Uncle Robert in delivering a calf.

Cecil started the engine as Danny and Caroline opened the car doors. "It's about time," Cecil grumbled.

Danny slid into the seat next to Darren, who glared at him. "Who said you could wear my shirt?"

"All I own are your hand-me-downs." He shrugged his shoulders with an air of feigned indifference. "I'm just wearing this one a little early."

Darren punched him in the arm. "Stay out of my closet."

Their father shot them a warning glance in the rear view mirror. "Hush."

"Jerk," Darren muttered under his breath.

Danny spread his lips into an exaggerated smile showing all his teeth and pushed a pair of sunglasses up the bridge of his nose with a middle finger.

Miss Cray pinned a blue ribbon to his borrowed shirt then handed Danny a framed certificate and check for twenty-five dollars that he accepted with a genuine smile. Despite his feelings with regard to the painting and award, the money would help with the purchase of the new oil paints he needed.

After the ceremony, his father shook his hand and his mother hugged him, just as Isabelle broke through the crowd.

"I'm so proud of you, what a masterpiece" she said, her words dripping with sarcasm.

He couldn't believe her audacity. Just two days ago she stood next to him, took a long look at the painting and declared he should throw it away and start over.

Danny narrowed his eyes, mouthing the word liar at her.

Her hand flew to her mouth as if shocked by his harsh accusation then she turned to his parents. "Hello Mr. and Mrs. Coulter."

His mother gave Isabelle a hug. "Honey, I swear you get more beautiful every time I see you."

In this, Danny wholeheartedly agreed. Isabelle did indeed seem prettier by the day. Her wide grey-green eyes were set above high cheekbones and when she smiled they radiated her lively spirit. Her shiny black hair hung nearly to her small waist. One of his favorite images was watching all that hair sway when she walked in her bouncy way. His attraction to her seemed to have no end. Since the feeling wasn't mutual, being with her these days was delicious torment.

He kept a wary eye on his parents as they moved away to examine his painting up close. Though he would never admit it, his father's approval was the most important. His mother would see the painting through her heart, but he was fairly certain his father would be more practical and wouldn't like the abstract piece anymore than he did. He had fought so hard to gain a little ground with his father, now that stupid painting might just put a dent in what respect he had achieved.

"You look nervous," Isabelle said.

He shrugged, not wanting to admit how much this moment weighed on him. His teacher joined his parents at the painting and waved him over.

"Here we go," he said.

Isabelle looped her arm through his and walked with him. "Your mom and dad may not understand art, but you know they're proud of you."

He stopped a few feet in front of his parents and teacher and took a deep breath. Familiar fear slipped in the back door and, expecting the worst, he squared his shoulders, preparing to defend his passion once again. Isabelle rubbed his back in small, comforting circles.

"I never believed there was much future in this hobby of yours," his father said. He nodded toward Danny's teacher. "Miss Cray insists I'm wrong."

The teacher beamed at Danny. "I was telling your parents about scholarships and grant programs in the arts. You have so much talent Danny. You really should start thinking now about what university you want to attend."

"I don't imagine I qualify for a scholarship with my grades," he said.

"Oh, nonsense, you are one of my brightest students. With a little effort…"

She went on and on, the same speech he heard at least a hundred times from her and several other teachers. Outwardly, he always insisted that going to school forever wasn't for him. While art had become a near obsession, he was a Coulter and therefore expected to be realistic. In the world his family inhabited, artistic endeavors were frivolous, if not downright impractical.

When Miss Cray finally finished her speech, his mother looked to him. "I'm very proud of you, Danny."

"We both are," his father added quickly.

Surprised, Danny blushed deeply. "Thank you," he managed.

Isabelle slipped her hand over his and bumped him with her shoulder. "Told you," she murmured.

Across the room, his friend Jimmy caught his eye and motioned him over to where a few of his friends were gathered. Danny excused himself and joined his friends. As he talked to them, Sue Ellen's voice cut through their conversation.

"Hey, Danny," she drawled in her sexy, southern way.

Danny switched his attention to the fetching Sue Ellen. She had made quite an impression on nearly everyone in the high school. Most of the girls, including his sister and Isabelle, disliked her intensely. Most of the boys were hopelessly taken in by her curvy, well-developed body and nearly palpable sexuality. The teachers found her difficult and Danny had overheard his art teacher, Miss Cray, call her cunning.

He was aware his friends were staring openly, especially Jimmy, but couldn't consider their reaction. Every time she batted her baby blue eyes at him he lost the ability to function on more than a base level. He allowed himself only a quick scan of her voluptuous body, before complete paralysis set in.

"Congratulations on your award," she said.

Danny took in a quick, sudden breath, and nodded, the best he could manage with his libido in overdrive. Sue Ellen moved closer, stroking the satin ribbon pinned to his shirt.

"How does it feel to win first place?" She punctuated her inane question by moving so close he could feel her body heat.

Danny smiled weakly. Every encounter with her was incredible torture, yet he wouldn't have missed one second.

"Can I call you sometime?" he said quickly, surprising himself.

She smiled brightly, "How about tonight?"

Danny managed a nod. Sue Ellen again stroked the ribbon with a fingertip, looked up at him, and smiled coyly before drifting back into the crowd. Jimmy stepped up beside him. Together, they watched Sue Ellen sashay away.

Jimmy whistled softly. "Holy Moly."

"I'm going to ask her out," Danny said, more to himself than to Jimmy.

Jimmy laughed and slapped him on the back. "You're in way over your head."

Danny nodded solemnly, "Oh yeah."

"You've inspired me," Jimmy said. "I'm thinking of taking art next semester."

Danny laughed, regaining some of his normal composure. "Since when do you care about art?"

Jimmy gestured toward his worthless painting. "If some squiggly lines and a few splotches of paint can get a loser like you a date with a girl like Sue Ellen, I'm in."

"I don't have a date yet."

After finding the courage to ask Sue Ellen if he could call sometime, Danny's next hurdle was actually making the call. Sue Ellen, her mother, and stepfather lived with her grandmother, Peach Habersoll, a mean old biddy who behaved as if she was smarter, richer, and generally a cut above everyone in Shadow. None of those beliefs had roots in reality as far as anybody could tell, but few challenged her with the truth since she was nothing but a bully masquerading as southern charm.

Peach Habersoll's real name was Matilda, but she preferred to be called Peach, and everyone assumed the nickname stemmed from her home state of Georgia. Every Sunday morning she strutted down the center aisle of church with an air of authority, stopping occasionally to speak to a chosen few before proceeding to the second pew up front where everyone would be sure to see her. Few had the audacity to sit in Peach's pew uninvited.

She always wore diamond rings on at least four of her fat fingers. For church, she covered her snow white hair with a seemingly endless collection of ugly hats, some of which blocked the view of those unfortunates seated behind her. In chillier weather, she sported a fancy mink stole.

Peach ran the ladies auxiliary at church and sat on the town council. She had also created and was president of the Shadow Beautification Committee.

She was a formidable opponent to anyone who dared challenge her anytime, anywhere. Danny knew that lesson first hand. During vacation Bible school a while back, Peach took it upon herself to chastise his little brother for sneaking a cookie. She grabbed him by the back of his shirt, shook him hard then swatted him on the rear. David, only five at the time, started to cry. Danny was nearby, working on a craft with his age group, but ran to his brother's aide, shoving Peach away.

"Why you little beast," she exclaimed, reaching for David again.

Danny placed himself between her hands and David. "Leave him alone!"

"He was stealing."

"My mother made those cookies. Why don't you take it up with her?"

Peach gasped and raised her hand to slap him just as Preacher Glazier hurried over. "What's going on here?"

Peach lowered her hand and pointed at ringed-finger David. "This one was stealing cookies." She turned her fierce gaze on Danny, her sweaty upper lip lifted in an ugly sneer. "And this one is downright sassy."

Preacher Glazier looked down at David who was still crying.

David held the cookie out to the preacher. "I'm sorry."

Danny pointed at Peach. "She hit him!"

"Children should know their place," Peach shot back.

Preacher Glazier turned to Peach, his cheeks flaming red, his words tightly measured. "We don't hit children."

The mild reproach clearly flabbergasted Peach. She pulled her shoulders back and stuck out her chin. "Spare the rod, spoil the child."

"I think it would be best for you to return to your charitable duties in the kitchen, Mrs. Habersoll."

Peach stormed away and Preacher Glazier knelt in front of David. He pulled a linen handkerchief from his pocket and wiped David's tears away with a gentle hand. "Are you okay?"

David nodded solemnly. The preacher stood again, looking at Danny. "I suppose you were only defending your brother."

Danny glanced across the room to the doorway where Peach had disappeared. "Yes, sir."

"Were you sassy?"

He looked the preacher in the eye, not even a little bit apologetic. "Yes, sir."

The preacher reached forward and patted him on the head. "You boys go on back to your projects."

Danny drifted back to his group with David sticking by his side. They never shared the incident with their parents, but always kept a wary eye on Peach.

Given his history with the hateful old woman, Danny was more than a little apprehensive about calling her home to speak with Sue Ellen. After supper, he sucked up his fear, picked up the receiver, and dialed Sue Ellen's number. Relief flooded him when Sue Ellen answered. Even better, she said yes to his request for a date.

Since Darren's girlfriend lived next door to Sue Ellen and Danny had no car, Darren graciously offered to double date and provide transportation if Danny paid for the gas.

On their first date, they went to a movie. This was Danny's first real date. He paid for her ticket of course, opened doors for her, and was the best gentleman he knew how to be. He made no move to touch her, not even to hold her hand or wrap his arm around her shoulders during the movie the way Darren was doing with Fran.

On the way home in the backseat of Darren's car, Sue Ellen scooted over until they were thigh-to-thigh then casually dropped her hand onto his leg just above the knee, immediately drawing his full attention. As they neared her grandmother's house, she looked up at him and leaned closer. Without any thought at all, he kissed her soft lips, lingering ever so slightly while her hand slipped higher on his thigh.

At her grandmother's house, he walked her to the door.

"I had a great time," she said.

He knew he was grinning like a fool, but couldn't rein in the smile. "Me too."

She rose on her tiptoes, kissing him quickly. "Goodnight."

After working for Uncle Hal all day, Danny took a quick shower in the little apartment Hal had created over the garage, threw on some clean clothes, and found Darren waiting for him in the parking lot. They drove to the lake on the other side of town where they were to meet Sue Ellen and Darren's girlfriend Fran. When they arrived, they found the girls waiting at a lakeside picnic table with a feast spread out before them.

In contrast to Fran's conservative dress, Sue Ellen had on a short shift, several inches above her knees, something she certainly couldn't have worn to school without being sent home.

"Whoa, that girl is just looking for trouble," Darren said as he switched off the engine.

After eating, Danny and Sue Ellen took a stroll around the lake. Sue Ellen slipped her hand in his.

While he marveled at the softness of her hand, he worried his own was too rough. As they rounded the last bend of the lake, an area secluded by tall trees, Sue Ellen paused looking up at him. Reading her signals, he slipped his arms around her waist and leaned in for a long kiss. The soft crush of her body against his own took his breath away.

After a heavy make out session, Danny realized night was falling quickly and they returned to the cars where they discovered Darren and Fran wrapped up in each others' arms in the backseat of Fran's father's car.

Sue Ellen grinned wickedly at Danny and wiggled a finger at him, indicating he should follow her to Darren's car.

Minutes later, the windows of the car were fogged over from their heavy breathing. "Hanky Panky" floated out over the speakers and she seemed to be taking the lyrics to heart. With the exception of Uncle Hal's sister-in-law, Vera, Sue Ellen was the boldest female Danny ever met, taking him places he'd barely imagined.

Just knowing Darren and Fran were only a few feet away kept him shy at first, but Sue Ellen was making control nearly impossible. His experience with girls up to this point was limited. He had expected Sue Ellen to be just as inexperienced, but right now he would have to agree with his friend Jimmy, he was in over his head.

She pushed him back against the door and sat next to him on the seat, leaning forward for a kiss. He slipped a hand under her dress, his fingers sliding up her silky thigh then paused, planning to proceed in increments as she allowed. She unzipped the front of her dress, lifted his other hand, guiding it through the opening to a bare breast. Danny laughed nervously.

Sue Ellen grinned at him. "You like?"

"You're making me crazy," he whispered.

She walked her fingers playfully up his thigh until she located his erection. When she began to stroke him, he closed his eyes.

"Damn," he murmured.

Sue Ellen laughed softly. By this time, Danny didn't care if Fran, Darren, his mother, or Preacher Glazier himself were standing there looking in the window.

She leaned forward, whispering in his ear. "I love you."

He heard, but was incapable of responding to her impassioned declaration.

TWENTY-SEVEN

Isabelle spent most Saturday nights with her girlfriends. Unfortunately, Holly Adams had to cancel their plan to go to the movies at the last minute, and all her other friends were busy.

Her father and Mama Rose invited her to tag along to a church supper, but she declined. Now she was restless and bored. She nibbled on a sandwich, tried to work on a history paper for school, but lost interest quickly. She turned on the television and, finding nothing on except Lawrence Welk and Flipper, quickly turned the television back off again. She drifted to her bedroom, played some records, and tried to read a book, but her mind wandered. She found herself staring at the wall where Danny's drawings hung. A few years ago the edges had started to curl, so she had framed them. She felt privileged to have the drawings and would never replace them with the posters most of her friends had hanging on their walls of popular rock bands.

These thoughts led her to thinking about Danny. Since he started dating Sue Ellen, she hadn't seen much of him. When their paths did cross, he seemed distant and distracted.

In gym class a few weeks ago, she overheard Sue Ellen talking and laughing about the ways boys were so easily manipulated. Isabelle finally understood why Sue Ellen had singled Danny out of her long list of admirers. His independent nature was just the challenge a girl like Sue Ellen thrived on. She wanted control and he was falling in line nicely. Isabelle seriously doubted that any of his better qualities were even attractive to a girl like Sue Ellen.

Most disturbing for Isabelle was the tenderness in his eyes when he looked at that girl. Typical of him, he wasn't holding back, but a girl like Sue Ellen was completely unworthy of his full-blown, straight-from-the hip brand of devotion.

Still, Isabelle knew all too well, if Sue Ellen mistook his kind heart for weakness, she was in for quite a surprise.

As the sun edged toward the horizon, she decided to take a chance and call Danny. Denise picked up on the second ring. After a bit of chit chat, Isabelle got to the point.

"So, where's Danny tonight?"

"Are you kidding? He didn't come in until after one this morning," Denise responded, then laughed. "He's not going anywhere for a month."

"Let me guess. Was he out with Sue Ellen?"

"Since he met her he seems to have lost his mind. Mama's about ready to chain him in his room to keep him away from her."

She took a moment to savor the news that Danny's mother didn't approve of Sue Ellen. She already knew where Denise stood. Denise had complained loudly about Sue Ellen trying to buddy up with her just to get close to her brother. While this was not an unusual circumstance for Denise with all three of her older brothers, Sue Ellen had been the most obvious...and least welcome to date.

"Is he allowed to talk on the phone?"

"To you, sure. Just a minute."

On the other end of the line, Isabelle heard footsteps thumping up and then down the stairs. After a brief exchange of mild insults with his sister, Danny picked up.

"Well, well, if it isn't Miss Issy-Belle Long," he drawled.

"Imagine my surprise to find you at home."

"I'm grounded for coming in late last night."

"Denise told me."

Danny sighed loudly. "So, what's up?"

"Can I come over?"

"Since when do you need an invitation?"

"I wasn't so sure anymore. Since meeting the perky Miss Sue Ellen, you don't seem too interested in old friends."

"Hey, I've called you quite a few times," he snapped. "You're the one who's always busy."

Isabelle smiled, "Oh, poor Danny."

"Come over if you want to."

With that, the line went dead.

Given the near darkness and her fear of the critters roaming the hills between their homes, Isabelle decided to take the blacktop. She grabbed a flashlight and set out on the much longer walk. Luckily, the weather was unseasonably warm for early December with only a slight breeze. She slipped through the fence skirting the Coulter ranch, walking the edge of the empty field toward Danny's house. Drawing closer, she spotted him standing at the edge of the steps. Both porch lights were on and he appeared to be irritated.

Hearing her approach, he turned, facing her. "You took the road?"

"I was afraid to take the shortcut."

"I walked all the way over looking for you."

She bristled at his prickly tone. "Well, if you hadn't hung up on me, we might have worked things out."

She climbed the first two steps, expecting him to step aside. When he held his position, she put her hands on her hips, scowling up at him.

"Are you going to let me on the porch?"

He sighed and stepped back, waving her to the swing with an exaggerated bow.

She kicked off her shoes and curled her legs beneath her, facing him. "So, tell me what's making you so crabby."

He shifted his attention to the night sky, taking his time with a response, as if the question required deep thought. As she studied his silhouette, an uncomfortable foreboding began tingling at the base of her skull. The sense that he had changed in some irrevocable way began to take root.

"I'm in over my head with Sue Ellen," he said finally.

Good grief. Was he saying he thought he loved that awful girl? She hoped for some sign she had misunderstood, but suspected he was never more serious. The reality landed like a solid blow to her heart. She wasn't at all prepared for the moment another female took her place in order of importance, especially Sue Ellen.

Angered by her suspected loss, she tried (and failed) to keep the bitterness out of her voice. "I don't know what you see in her."

He switched his gaze to her. His steady examination made her cringe, but she wouldn't allow him to see the fear pulling at her. He looked away again, speaking softly, as if he were confiding in a trusted friend. She understood, even if he didn't, in this area she was not to be trusted. He was her gift, one she would fight to keep.

"I can't sleep," he began, "I can't eat. I lose track of what I'm doing because all I can think about is Sue

Ellen. Mama's convinced I've had the flu for the past six weeks and keeps giving me major doses of castor oil. Between Mama and Sue Ellen, I'm worn out."

His mother's use of castor oil was a strong deterrent to colds, flu, missing school days, fighting with siblings, general crankiness, and any attempt to get out of chores, but Isabelle doubted the remedy would have much influence on Danny's present condition. Still, the image of his mother force feeding him a gallon jug of the oil to cure his ridiculous infatuation gave her a twinge of guilty pleasure.

"I guess your mother's cure-all can't get to the root of this problem," she said.

Finally, his face relaxed into a little smile, and he looked more like her Danny. He shifted his weight and the swing rocked sideways.

Isabelle attempted to consider the impact this turn of events might have on their relationship. Unfortunately, jealousy had a powerful grip on her at the moment, making logic difficult. To buy some time, she decided to play along, pretending to care about his association with a girl who was clearly all wrong for him.

She sighed and brushed her fingers through his thick hair. "I guess I'd better get to know Sue Ellen a little better."

Danny swatted her hand away from his head. "I wish you would at least try. She doesn't understand how one of my best friends can be a girl without it being anything more."

She felt the sting of him considering her merely one of his best friends, but focused on the fact that Sue Ellen was suspicious. Knowing just how to irritate him, she didn't bother to check her smile.

"Is she jealous?"

Danny grunted at her. "What's there to be jealous of?"

Isabelle bristled and fired right back. "So, she's just one of those insecure types."

"She's no different than a lot of people. They just don't get our friendship."

"What nonsense. Why can't we be friends?"

"Well, you must admit, at our age the opposite sex starts getting more important."

"True," Isabelle conceded, "but not with us. We're like brother and sister, right?"

Danny lifted his legs off the ground stretching them straight out. They began to swing higher and faster.

"Issy, I love my sister," he said, then added softly, "but the way I feel about you is nothing like that."

Like always, he eased the fear she wouldn't admit out loud. He might be changing, Sue Ellen might have tarnished his innocence with her cunning ways, but at his core, he was still the same boy she loved.

Isabelle sighed and laid her head on his shoulder. "My sweet-faced, big-hearted friend, you are my courage and my light."

"Don't get carried away now," he drawled.

"Comet rider had an angel's face and a lion's heart," she murmured waving her hand through the air. "He swept through the night on a flash of lightening and captured my soul."

"Careful," Danny said with a soft chuckle. "If Mama hears you, she'll think you need a dose of the oil to cure these mad ramblings."

"Someday, I'm going to write a song about you. I'll get it so right, you'll weep, Danny Coulter."

"No, Issy," he said quietly. "One of these days you'll just move on and forget all about me."

She moved closer, laying her head on his chest, needing him. "You're wrong. You'll always be part of my life, Danny."

Sighing, he wrapped an arm around her, pulling her closer. Isabelle sang soft and low, while he rocked them.

She did her best to be objective about Sue Ellen, and failed. Even without Danny in the picture, the project would have been doomed. The blonde-haired, blue-eyed, long-legged, busty, all-American beauty was exactly the kind of girl she detested. That girl used every inch of body to generate attention and, when Danny wasn't available, she shamelessly flirted and teased other boys.

Isabelle quickly understood that for Sue Ellen desirability equaled power. While Danny was certainly under her wicked spell, he remained independent enough to keep her attention. If he ever yielded completely, there was no doubt she would quickly lose interest.

Following a school dance, everyone gathered at the river for a bonfire. Danny was occupied with a group of friends and the awful girl stood off to the side watching him with obvious annoyance. Isabelle decided this was the perfect moment to keep her promise to Danny and approached Sue Ellen, though she had no intention of befriending her.

Sue Ellen eyed her suspiciously then nodded to the group of boys. "He's over there."

Isabelle glanced at Danny about twenty-five feet away, the place she would certainly rather be. "I thought it was time you and I got to know each other," she said. "You know, since Danny and I are such good friends and all."

"So I've heard."

Isabelle forced her attention back to the vixen. "We are just friends."

"Sure."

"Look," Isabelle snapped, "I'm only here because he wanted me to get to know you."

"No, you look. He doesn't need you hanging around anymore, so why don't you wiggle your little brown butt back to your own people."

The heat of anger spread up Isabelle's neck to her face. She stepped closer, "My own what?"

Sue Ellen smiled and Isabelle understood that by allowing this stupid girl to get under her skin, she was giving her exactly what she wanted. With considerable effort, she kept her hands to herself and spoke calmly.

"Hurt him and I'll hurt you back, promise."

TWENTY-EIGHT

Isabelle always spent the week between Christmas and New Years Day with Grandma Sarah. Since Christmas Day fell on a Sunday this year, her father intended to take her to Tulsa in the afternoon. Unfortunately, he came down with a case of the flu on Christmas Eve. Rather than disappoint her sweet grandmother, Isabelle came up with the idea that Danny could drive her to Tulsa in her father's truck or Mama Rose's car.

As expected, Mama Rose was squeamish at the idea. "Oh, I don't know if it's proper for you two to go off like that…"

Her father blew his nose, coughed, and held up his hand, stopping Rose's protest. "They will be just fine, Rose." He paused to cough again and turned to Isabelle. "If his parents give their okay, you kids can take my truck."

Early in the afternoon of Christmas Day, she dialed the Coulter home and learned from Denise that Danny was out spreading hay to the cattle, but would be back soon. Denise invited her to come over and join them for their Christmas Day tradition of a board game marathon.

As she topped the hill between their homes, an icy gust of wind took her breath away. Down below, she spotted Danny approaching. She split the quiet of the afternoon with a loud whistle and he raised his head. His mouth slipped into an easy smile, just the way she liked it.

"Well, well," he drawled, "Merry Christmas, Miss Issy-Belle Long."

"Thanks for coming to meet me Comet."

He winced and stopped short. "You know I hate it when you call me that."

"Sorry," she lied smoothly. She still loved the nickname she gave him four years ago. "I need a favor."

As she came up beside him, another gust of cold wind hit them. He stuck his hands in the front pockets of his jacket and hunched his shoulders waiting for her to elaborate.

"Would you to drive me to Tulsa to visit Grandma? Daddy said we can use his truck."

"When did you want to go?"

"She's expecting me tomorrow. We can come back on Friday."

"I have to work on Friday. We'll have to come back Thursday."

She smiled at the ease with which she could count on him. She linked her arm through his and cuddled closer. "Do you think your parents will let you go?"

"It's Sue Ellen that's going to be the problem."

She jerked away from him and stopped in her tracks. "I can't believe what I'm hearing. Are you going to let her tell you what to do?"

"C'mon, Issy, let's go. I'm cold."

Obviously, he didn't intend to address her question.

"I never thought I'd see the day you'd let a girl run your life."

He sighed loudly. "I have to tell her."

"I need to know today."

"Fine! Can we go back to my house now?"

His parents gave their permission for him to drive her to Tulsa. While she sat down at the kitchen table with Darren, Denise, and David, Danny called Sue Ellen, joining them only minutes later, his face flushed.

"Uh-oh," Darren said, "somebody got in trouble."

"Did you get permission to drive Isabelle to Tulsa?" Denise chimed in.

Danny glared at the two of them. "I don't need *permission*."

"Are we still going?" Isabelle asked quietly.

He turned his attention to her. "I said I'd drive you, and I will. Can we please just play the game now?"

Early Monday morning they set out for Tulsa. To her relief, they talked and laughed like old times, and he never mentioned his girlfriend one time.

As usual, Grandma Sarah met them at the curb. In the spirit of the holiday, she wore a red bow on the top of her head, bright red lipstick, red overalls, and the perfect smile. She embraced Isabelle and squeezed tightly.

"Hey-O, Little One."

Danny retrieved their bags from the back of the truck and made his way around to where Isabelle and her grandmother stood.

Sarah clapped her hands. "Oh look, here's Comet!"

Hearing the nickname, Isabelle laughed and he shot an irritated look her way. She smiled sweetly, once again ignoring his annoyance, thoroughly enjoying how her grandmother was so crazy about him. Over the years, he had accompanied her to Sarah's a number of times and they had developed an easy, affectionate relationship.

Sarah didn't give him time to set the bags down. She wrapped her arms around him for a good, long hug then stood on her tiptoes and tossed in a kiss on the cheek for good measure. "You're getting so tall!"

Danny grinned widely. "Maybe you're shrinking."

She laughed and patted his chest. "Maybe so, maybe so."

After calling their respective parents to let them know they had arrived safely, Sarah steered them toward the kitchen.

"I made some breakfast rolls," she said.

Isabelle caught Danny's eye and he rolled his eyes. Sarah was branching out with her cooking experiments and sometimes the end result wasn't all that appealing. Today the fare wasn't half bad. The cinnamon rolls were made with refrigerated biscuit dough, cinnamon, sugar, and plenty of white icing. The downside was the addition of dried fruit.

Isabelle plucked a chunk of orange fruit from her roll and looked across the table to Danny. He in turn shifted his gaze to his plate where a brown lump of unidentifiable fruit lay. She turned to her grandmother, holding up the sticky orange bit.

"What is this?"

"That's an apricot," Sarah said. She nodded at Danny's plate. "Comet has a prune."

Danny eyed the prune then looked to Isabelle. "Trade you."

She popped the apricot in her mouth, smiled, and winked at him. "Yum."

After breakfast, Sarah stood, looking to Danny with a solemn expression. "If you will excuse us for a bit, Isabelle and I have some business."

She followed her grandmother to her small bedroom where Sarah closed the door and went to her dresser. Opening the top drawer, she pulled out a wooden box, placed it on the bed, removed a postcard, and handed it to Isabelle.

"I got this last week, from your mother."

The front of the postcard said: Greetings from Biloxi, Mississippi. On the back her mother had written: Doing fine. Tell Issy-Belle I love her.

Isabelle sat on her grandmother's bed and touched the words with her fingertips, her eyes full of tears. Grandma Sarah sat next to her and patted her back. After four years of silence, eight scribbled words were all her mother had to offer.

Sarah sighed. "I don't know if this little postcard is good or bad for you." She ran a gentle hand over Isabelle's back. "Doesn't seem like much, all things considered."

She seldom cried over the loss of her mother anymore. She hadn't taken out her mother's damaged red heels in over a year. She rarely felt the urge to gaze at her mother's face and the framed photograph of the two of them lay under a pile of socks in her dresser. Though there were still times when the sight of a stranger with her mother's stance, a woman with a long braid hanging down her back or a laugh like a song would take her unawares, the moments were rare. She had moved on.

Isabelle wiped the tears from her face. "I used to miss her so much." She paused for a deep breath, guilt and sorrow rising in equal measure. "Now she doesn't cross my mind most days."

Sarah nodded, her own sadness evident, reminding Isabelle that she wasn't the only one who had lost her mother. She wrapped her arms around her sweet grandmother.

"I'm so glad I have you Grandma."

When her tears were dried, Sarah steered her back to the living room and Isabelle tucked the postcard into her purse. Danny was in the kitchen finishing the breakfast dishes and cast a curious glance her way. She tried on a smile that didn't quite work.

"Come in here, Comet," her grandmother called. "Let's open some presents."

Isabelle brought along several gifts for her grandmother. Over the past year, she had put together a photo album. She also found a Fourth of July hair bow with sparkly stars she thought her grandmother might enjoy wearing on her favorite holiday. Mama Rose had knitted a blue cardigan and hat out of soft merino wool. From Marshall, there were bags of beef jerky and the penny candy he knew Sarah loved, plus an envelope containing a little cash he managed to squirrel away.

Sarah immediately donned her blue sweater and hat then presented Isabelle and Danny their gifts with a smile full of pride. "I made them myself at the community center."

She gave Isabelle a set of handmade white bone and beaded earrings. Danny received a woven oblong basket. He ran his fingertips over the symmetrical and colorful weave as if he were touching woven gold.

"When our girl called and told me you were bringing her up to see me, I knew right away I had just the present for your art supplies," Sarah explained.

"It's beautiful, Miss Sarah. Thank you."

He rose, offered her a kiss on the cheek then went to his bag and pulled out a wrapped package for Sarah. After carefully removing the Christmas paper, she gasped and put her hand to her mouth.

Isabelle couldn't see around the paper and leaned forward. "What is it?"

Sarah lifted a picture frame and turned it around for her to see. Danny had drawn Isabelle standing on a mountain top with her arms thrown open wide, the wind in her hair, her face turned up to a sunny sky, eyes closed. She looked serene and joyful.

Sarah hugged the photo to her chest and looked to Danny. "My favorite girl."

He grinned widely. "Mine too."

Isabelle couldn't believe her ears. "What about Sue Ellen?"

He looked into her eyes. "You're special Issy."

The tears were back. This day was beginning to feel like an out-of-control roller coaster ride: up, down, hard jerk to the right then back to the left. Within the space of a few minutes, a measly little postcard had reopened her deepest wound, and this kind-hearted boy, with his undemanding affection, once again eased that hurt.

Obviously confused by her reaction, Danny frowned. "Why are you crying?"

How do you tell someone they are your gift without sounding dumb? She decided it might be best to keep her answer straightforward, like him.

"You both make me feel so loved," she said.

"Good," he and Grandma answered in unison. Everyone had a laugh and the tension dissolved.

Shadow, Oklahoma
1967 Spring

TWENTY-NINE

Danny noticed a tiny spot of car polish on the hood of his Chevy and wiped it away with a soft cloth before standing back to admire the vision. The metal flake blue sparkled under the florescent garage bay lights. A slow smile spread over his face.

Hal walked around the back bumper chewing on a cigar. "This is one fine-looking automobile, Runt. I'm not sure you're worthy."

Danny smiled even wider. After a lot of hard work and every cent he could scrape together, the car was finished. Hal had been highly instrumental in this success by working right beside him, finding parts, and bargaining with the paint shop for a better deal. Hal expertise as a mechanic and teacher had turned out to be a pleasant surprise. Danny had learned a great deal in a short time. However, figuring out ways to deal with his unpredictable uncle was still a challenge.

"Thanks Uncle Hal. I couldn't have done it without your help."

Hal nodded and lit his cigar. "I enjoyed myself."

"Want to go for a spin with me?"

"Can't." Hal squinted at him through a haze of smoke. "I need to get over to Nadine's and pick up Junior so she can go to work."

Hal was referring to his second wife, whom he met in one of his favorite haunts where she tended bar. After a heated bit of dating, he sweet talked Nadine into marrying him and moved from the ranch to her place in town. With the exception of trying harder to be a better parent, Hal hadn't changed all that much and Nadine turned out to be a practical woman who tolerated little of what she termed "hoo-hah" from anyone, thus Hal's second marriage was just about as short as his first. After only three months, Nadine kicked him to the curb and Hal returned to his little house on the ranch. The upside was Nadine had developed a soft spot for Junior and he still spent a great deal of time with her.

Hal peered inside Danny's car and scratched his head. "I think we might have overlooked something."

Danny had no idea what that might be. Concerned, he leaned forward peering into the car too. "What?"

"Don't you need some blocks to reach the pedals and a pillow to sit on so you can see over the steering wheel?"

Danny bristled at the dig. He stood straighter and glared at Hal. "I guess you didn't notice I've grown some this past year."

Hal Coulter stood right at six-feet tall. The top of Danny's head came to the level of his eyes. "Sorry,

I missed that altogether. What are you now, five-one, five-two?"

Danny eyed him angrily. "Does it make you feel better about yourself to belittle me?"

"Ah, now Runt, I was just joking around."

Danny opened the inner office door and started signing off the work orders of the day. "I'm sick of everybody's jokes."

Hal was right on his heels. "You going out with that little blonde tonight?"

"I'm through talking to you."

"There are some condoms in the top drawer of my desk, take yourself a handful. I've met that little girl and I know you need them."

Danny tossed the clipboard on the desk and reached for his jacket, ignoring Hal. He knew from experience that acknowledging his uncle's crude observations would only lead to further discussion.

Hal dropped into a chair and pointed his cigar at Danny. "You got one of those short men complexes, Runt, just like that fellow Napoleon bone-a-party."

"I'm not a man yet. I'm only sixteen."

Hal snorted. "Trust me, if you're keeping that little blonde satisfied, you're a man."

The string of insults and goading was typical. Danny had learned Hal was more tease than anything and didn't take him too seriously, at least most of the time. While Hal had mellowed some, his mood could vary from day to day, dependent upon the intensity of his hangover or the state of his relationship with a current female companion. There seemed to be a never ending string of women willing to take a chance on handsome Hal, but Danny certainly wasn't interested in taking dating advice from someone like him.

Danny opened the inner garage door and headed for his car. He started the engine and backed the car out of the garage bay. Hal walked to the edge of the doorway and waved at him. Danny tossed back a little wave and headed for an evening he suspected he would regret. He had allowed Sue Ellen to talk him into having supper at her grandmother's house.

Despite his parents' disapproval, he had continued to date Sue Ellen exclusively. After months of Sue Ellen's repeated requests, this was the first time he had allowed her to talk him into coming inside her grandmother's house.

Her grandmother, Peach Habersoll, was an arrogant woman who looked down her nose at nearly everyone in Shadow for reasons that escaped most of them. Danny knew Peach's history, both the embellished version and the truth. There was the Peach Habersoll version: Southern belle from Atlanta falls madly in love with huckster; huckster drags sweet, innocent belle to the backwoods of Oklahoma, away from her wealthy, well-established, blue-blood family in pursuit of a get-rich-quick scheme; huckster uses belle's dowry to finance a deal and when the law comes after him, huckster abandons belle with a baby on the way (Sue Ellen's mother). According to Peach, she looked her situation square in the eye and pulled herself up by her bootstraps to become the fine, upstanding member of their community she was today.

The major difference between Peach's version and the truth was that for ten years she swore the huckster would someday come to his senses and return on hands and knees. In this expectation, she was alone. Despite her disdain for Oklahoma, and Shadow in particular, Peach remained long after the obvious truth descended. She found work as a seamstress at the finest clothier in town and made a life for herself.

A side effect of Peach's profound comedown was the war she waged on all males that continued to this day. Tonight she was zeroing in on Danny.

She eyed him over the top of her half-glasses from her queenly perch at the head of the table. "My, you're a small one, aren't you?" she said. Though she was smiling, her tone belied any good will. "I thought all you Coulter boys were the big, farm-boy type. Which one is your Daddy?"

Since they all attended the same church for years, he was quite sure she knew exactly who his father was, but played along. "He's the postmaster."

"Of course," Peach said, offering him an icy smile. "You have his rounded shoulders, don't you?"

Danny stared at her in disbelief. He would rather eat dirt than to have to sit here with this mean old woman. The single reason he stayed was Sue Ellen. He looked across the dining room table and watched Sue Ellen's stepfather, Linus, chomp open-mouthed on a chunk of roast beef. With his small black eyes, long, pointy nose and chin, he reminded Danny of a big rat.

Sue Ellen's mother wasn't much more agreeable to share a meal with. She pushed at her food and never took a bite. She kept her head down, focusing on her plate, completely in her own world. Sue Ellen had told him her mother took medication for her "nerves." Danny figured if he had to wake up and look at Linus every morning, he might need something for his nerves too.

"Tell us, Danny," Peach began again, speaking in a slow, exaggerated manner, "do you plan to be a postman like your father or something like that after you finish high school?"

"Oh no, ma'am," he said sweet as sugar, "I thought I'd work down at Hansen's and sell hats to the church ladies to go along with the dresses you alter." He paused to smile thinly, imitating her style. "I want to have a respectable career like you."

Peach's mean eyes narrowed even more. "Are you getting smart with me boy?"

"A small, round-shouldered boy like me getting smart with a sophisticated lady of your status? No, ma'am, I wouldn't dare."

Sue Ellen kicked him under the table. Her stepfather laughed, spitting meat onto the lace tablecloth.

Peach threw down her napkin and glared at her son-in-law. "Once again, I've lost my appetite."

Linus grinned at Danny and winked. Danny sat back in his chair and folded his arms over his chest. Like Peach, he had no appetite.

Linus speared another piece of meat and pointed his fork at Danny, the fresh chunk of roast beef dangling from the end. "Maybe you can help me with something Danny Boy. I heard this town's claim to fame is the world's largest cow turd. Supposedly, the city council had the thing bronzed and put on display down at the mayor's office." He paused to swallow a few gulps from a tumbler of gin and tonic. "They say the turd came from your family's ranch. Is that true?"

Danny pushed his chair away from the table and stood.

A slow grin spread over Linus' face, but there was no humor behind it. "You mess with my little girl and I'll bronze your balls just like that turd. Understand?"

"I'm not your little girl," Sue Ellen said.

Linus switched his oily-eyed gaze to her. "Since when Susie Q?"

Danny placed his napkin on the table and headed for the front door with Sue Ellen calling after him. She caught up with him just as he reached his car.

"Where are you going?"

"Don't ever ask me to come inside again."

"Why? What was so horrible?"

The idiotic question set him back for a moment, but he attempted an explanation anyway. "For starters, your Grandmother's downright hateful."

The hurt in Sue Ellen's expression switched to indignation. "I suppose your family is perfect."

"No, but they're not deliberately mean."

"Grandma is just set in her ways. She's had it hard."

He didn't want to argue with her. He may not like this house or the people inside, but this was her family.

He pulled the car door open. "I'll call you later."

Sue Ellen grabbed his hand. "I thought we were going to spend some time together."

Linus opened the front door and stepped out on the porch. He shot Danny a hard look before turning his gaze to Sue Ellen. "Get in here and help with the dishes."

Sue Ellen looked at her stepfather and a vague bitterness drifted into her expression. Suddenly, she didn't look so young or vulnerable anymore.

Peach pushed past Linus and bent to snap a leash on her toy poodle. She stood straight again and looked up at Linus. "Leave the girl alone for once."

Linus pointed a finger at Danny. "Keep your hands to yourself. Understand?"

Sue Ellen tugged on Danny's arm. "Let's go."

Danny seldom took her to the river anymore. Sue Ellen's idea of a date always revolved around sex and there were just too many prying eyes so close to home.

He drove to a small park on the other side of town and parked facing the lake. He cut the engine and turned the radio down low. All the way there, Sue Ellen had cuddled close, rubbing his thigh like always. Now, she leaned close to kiss his mouth and her hand found the tight bulge in his jeans. He groaned in her mouth and pushed her hand away.

"I don't have anything," he said.

"There are other things we can do." She gave him a quick kiss on the lips.

Despite the reaction his body was having, he wasn't in the mood for making out, or anything else for that matter.

He sat away from her. "Don't you ever just want to talk? You know, get to know each other better?"

She smiled wickedly, unzipping his fly. "Sure Danny, what do you want to talk about?"

"I want to do more than just have sex every time we're together."

"We do. Don't be silly."

"Please, Sue, this isn't right. You know?"

She put a finger to his lips. "I know you had a horrible time at Grandma's. Let me make it up to you."

Danny pushed her away and zipped his fly.

Her pretty blue eyes narrowed. "I suppose you'd rather be with your precious Isabelle."

Right now, he would, but kept that knowledge to himself.

"How long has your mother been married to Linus?" he asked.

"Since I was nine."

"Do you like him?"

She moved away and folded her arms over her chest. "Why?"

"Because he gave me the creeps. Was it just a bad first impression?"

"I doubt that. I think you had your mind made up about my family before you stepped in the door."

"Your grandmother was the only one I had an opinion of and that's only because she acts like she's better than everyone else."

"Well, Danny, that's because her great-grandfather owned one of the most successful tobacco farms in Georgia. She comes from old blood."

Danny laughed shortly. "Maybe it's time for a transfusion to freshen things up."

Sue Ellen slapped his face so hard it made his ears ring. "Take me home."

"Maybe you should walk," he came back tightly.

"If you put me out of this car, we're through!"

He started the engine and shifted into reverse. "We're through anyway."

THIRTY

Danny swung his car over to the curb in front of Peach Habersoll's house hoping Sue Ellen wasn't angry with him for being late. This was their first date since their fight two weeks ago and he was running behind because he had been forced to chauffeur Denise and her friends around like some taxi.

Still, a more important issue weighed on his shoulders. Just before leaving the house tonight, he looked his mother in the eye and lied about where he was going. While she was never a gossip, his mother couldn't avoid the never-ending chatter regarding Sue Ellen. From the first moment she learned he was dating Sue Ellen, his mother disapproved. He had only made the situation worse by coming in after curfew so many times. When Denise, the informer, took it upon herself to announce how pleased she was that he and Sue Ellen had broken up at supper last week, his mother couldn't have been happier.

"Finally," she said, "you found a little common sense."

If asked to explain his attraction to Sue Ellen, he realized the honest answer would be her appearance. She was a beautiful girl, shapely in all the right ways, and his shameless body wanted her pretty much all the time, a desire she was more than willing to accommodate.

Sue Ellen was waiting on the porch when he pulled to the curb. She jumped in the car almost before he brought it to a complete stop.

"I'm sorry I'm late," he said. "I had to drop Denise and her friends off at the roller rink."

Sue Ellen slid over close and wrapped her arms around his neck. "It's okay, you're here now."

Danny shivered at her cold touch. "Why were you waiting outside?"

She tilted her face up and fixed him with her blue eyes. "I couldn't wait to see you. I've missed you so much, Danny. I hope we never break up again."

Driven by the need she stirred so easily, Danny kissed her right there in front of her grandmother's house.

Sue Ellen pulled back and smiled at him. "Let's skip the movie."

"I thought we agreed to go somewhere neutral," he argued weakly.

Sue Ellen's leaned closer still, pressing her soft breasts against his arm. "I've missed you. I don't want to be around other people. I just want to be with you."

He sat up straighter and put the car in gear.

She snuggled closer, her hand drifting high on his thigh. "It's almost dark. Let's go out to the lake."

He shifted his hips and pushed her hand away. "Cut it out."

"Come on, Danny." She giggled wickedly. "We'll stop before anything happens."

"Sure. Just like the last time."

Never one to give an inch, she grinned at him. "I know you like it."

"Sue, I can't concentrate. I'll probably hit a tree."

Sue Ellen unzipped his jeans and slid a cool hand around the warmest part of his body.

He turned onto the two-lane highway just as a hard rain started falling, reducing visibility. He reached to flip the wipers on and out of the corner of his eye caught sight of Louise Linde's big Pontiac bearing down on them fast. The big car T-boned his Chevy with such force it was pushed off the road, into a ditch, and the car began rolling in a field.

As he was thrown to the right then lifted forward, Sue Ellen fell away to the floor under the dash. His head slammed against the steering wheel then he was thrown back again and to the left like a rag doll. His body rose, limp now, lifting higher. His head banged into the roof and he came forward one last time, slamming against the steering wheel, fracturing his right forearm, bruising ribs, and snapping the steering wheel in two. The incident became a jumbled mass of flying glass, the road, ditch, and field rolling through. Finally the car slammed into a sturdy oak and rested on the passenger side.

He lay in a contorted heap on the passenger door. Sue Ellen climbed over him then out the driver's window and began screaming for help. Breathing was difficult in his crumpled state, so he attempted to shift his weight. Pain shot through his torso, like one hundred daggers piercing his chest. He groaned and lay back. After taking a few shallow breaths he clenched his teeth and eased his right leg forward, shifted his hips a few inches then stopped to breathe again. There was so much pain it was difficult to discern one injury from another, but his right arm was throbbing. In the dim light he couldn't see much, but he peered at the arm and thought he could see broken bone just beneath the surface of the skin. In reaching out to examine the arm, he realized his zipper was down and he was exposed in the worst possible way. Using his left hand, he attempted to manipulate his delicate exposure, but the zipper got in the way. He managed to flatten the zipper and pulled on the tab, but the zipper was stuck.

Overhead, Harold Palmer, the owner of the dry cleaners poked his head through the driver's window and shined a flashlight in Danny's face. "Hey, Danny, let's get you out of there."

Harold lay down on the driver's door and stretched out, reaching through to Danny. "Grab my hands."

"My right arm is broken," he managed.

"Then let's see what we can do with just the left."

Danny stretched out his arm and Harold leaned in farther, grabbing his arm below the elbow. As Harold pulled him to his feet, Danny did everything he could not to make a sound, and failed. The pain was unbelievable. Standing now, other hands gripped him under the right arm and pulled him up through the driver's window where cold rain slapped his face just before he blacked out.

His face was bruised and swollen in a line above his right ear to the left side of his chin. He had a mild concussion and several loose teeth. His right eye was bloodied and swollen. Blood oozed in a thin trickle from his right ear. His right forearm had a compound fracture and would soon be in a cast. His neck felt like someone had twisted his head all the way around and his bruised chest felt like he had been struck repeatedly with a sledgehammer. His right calf had a deep puncture wound. Worst of all was the knowledge that he had been pulled out of the car with his fly undone. He cringed at the thought of what else those helpful folks had seen.

When his parents learned that he had lied to them and the state of his undress, he had little doubt they would make his life miserable, especially his mother.

As if on cue, his mother pushed back the curtain and stepped up to the bed, her face a mask of concern. She leaned over and kissed his forehead with tears in her eyes. "Are you in pain?"

"It's not bad," he lied. "Is Daddy here?"

"He picked up Denise and her friends from the roller rink. Once he gets everybody home, he'll be down."

"I'm so sorry, Mama," he said desperately.

She scrutinized his battered face and patted his hand. "I'm just happy you're okay."

"Where's Sue Ellen?"

"Peach took her home."

Danny flinched at his mother's harsh tone, but made himself ask the question he most dreaded. "Do you know everything?"

His mother sighed. "I'm very disappointed in you Daniel."

Danny turned his head away from her direct gaze and closed his eyes.

The ER doctor breezed in and offered a quick rundown on Danny's injuries, showed his mother x-rays of his skull, chest, and right forearm.

"We're going to keep him here overnight for observation. He will need to be seen by an audiologist to determine the damage to his hearing," the doctor said. "Other than that, he should recover well in time." The doctor shot him a weary look. "You were very fortunate."

Danny didn't feel properly grateful. Right now, pain and humiliation demanded all of his attention.

After a long, sleepless night, the doctor released him the next morning. A volunteer pushed him in a wheelchair to the hospital entrance with his father walking alongside.

Once they were curbside, his father started toward the parking lot. "I'll just get the truck and bring it around."

Logic cautioned that he sit right there and wait for the truck. The bullheaded, Coulter part of him, urged him to get up and take his lumps. He wanted to be tough, to push through the pain, and stand up like a man...foolish bravado he would soon regret.

"I'll walk," he said to his father.

Every step sent shooting pains from his groin into his abdomen and back. The pain in his chest was unrelenting, making breathing difficult. After a limping, sweating, grunting trip across the parking lot, they finally arrived at the truck where easing up and onto the bench seat put him over the top. He immediately swung his legs back out the door and vomited until he dry heaved.

His forehead was gleaming with perspiration when he forced himself upright again. He closed the door and gritted his teeth.

"Ready?" his father asked.

The best he could do was nod.

The sun was fading on Sunday afternoon when Isabelle climbed the stairs to Danny's bedroom. News of the accident was the talk of Shadow.

She sat on the edge of his bed and gently brushed the dark hair falling over his forehead away. As her fingers drifted over his battered face, she realized how soft and smooth his face was. Both Dwight and Darren had light beards by sixteen. As always, Danny's body was taking a slower course to maturity.

He opened his eyes. "Issy-Belle," he whispered with a little smile.

She popped the cap on a bottle of Dr. Pepper and slipped in a straw. She offered him the bottle and he took three long pulls.

"Why are you here?" he asked.

"John Parks said Sue Ellen looked just like a vampire when he saw her at the accident. He said blood was running down her chin and everything. I've got a string of garlic, a silver crucifix, Daddy's hammer, and three wooden stakes in case she shows up to finish you off."

"Why was she bleeding?"

She had meant to be funny. Instead of getting her joke, he zeroed in on Sue Ellen again. His concern over the girl sickened Isabelle. Would he ever see Sue Ellen for what she really was?

"She just had a busted lip," she said.

"Was Mrs. Linde hurt?"

"She got a couple of bumps and bruises, otherwise she's okay. The cops say it was her fault. She'd been playing bridge and drinking martinis all afternoon and was so snookered she didn't know she ran the light."

"What about Sue Ellen?"

Isabelle tossed her hair over her shoulder. "What about her?"

"Was she hurt anywhere else?"

She shook her head and looked him in the eye. "Not until she sees me."

"Issy..."

She held up a hand to silence him. Her eyes teared up. Her throat was so tight speaking was difficult. "I warned her not to hurt you."

He frowned at her. "Mrs. Linde is the one who hit my car."

"If Sue Ellen hadn't been, um," she paused, choosing her words carefully, "distracting you, you might have been able to avoid the accident."

Danny shifted his weight in the bed and grimaced, reminding her exactly why she was here. This morning after church her father had taken her to see Danny's car on Hal's lot and knew he and Sue Ellen were lucky to have survived.

He closed his eyes. "Mama gave me one of those pain pills," he murmured.

"Do you want me to go?"

When he didn't respond, she sat watching him, realizing they had reversed roles. Weakened and made vulnerable by this car accident, but more so due to Sue Ellen's influence, he needed her assistance.

She heard one time that if a person played foreign language records while they slept they could wake up speaking fluent Italian, Spanish, French, or whatever. That notion gave her an idea. She leaned forward and placed her lips near his ear.

"You don't love Sue Ellen," she whispered. "You must stop seeing her."

She watched him sleep for a few minutes, kissed his forehead, and whispered. "I love you."

On Monday, Danny made his first trip downstairs. He was stiff and sore from head to toe and the long staircase was a challenge.

His brothers and sister had already left for school and he was surprised to find his father sitting at the kitchen table with his mother. They looked up as he entered and, based on their solemn expressions, he knew the moment had arrived for them to hand down his punishment.

He eased his body down into a chair and did his best not to show how much the simple act hurt. His father sipped his coffee and looked across the table to his mother. She inhaled and then exhaled slowly before speaking.

"Your father and I have decided to send you over to Uncle Virgil's for the summer. With your cousin

James away in the Army, he could use some help with the farm."

He looked from his mother to his father in disbelief. "Please don't do this to me."

His mother folded her arms over her chest. "You're going and that's the end of the discussion."

"What about my job with Uncle Hal?"

She shook her head. "Hal will just have to understand. You need some time to cool off with this girl. Uncle Virgil's farm is just the place for a hot-blooded boy like you."

His mother's older brother and wife were his least favorite relatives. Luckily, they lived a couple of hours away in Arkansas and he didn't have to see them too often. An overly-zealous Baptist, Uncle Virgil's predictions of hellfire and damnation terrified Danny so much he had nightmares when he was younger. Virgil's wife was a grim woman who hardly said a word. Danny couldn't remember ever seeing her smile. He expected to be punished, but living with them sounded like a prison sentence.

"Mama, I probably lost part of my hearing, my car is totaled, my arm's broken, and I can hardly walk. Can't you let it go at that?"

"Don't get smart with me Daniel."

"I'm not," he sighed.

"What you did is disgraceful. I'm ashamed of you."

"I know you are and I'm really sorry, but sending me to Uncle Virgil's is more than I can bear."

She leaned closer, drilling him with a ferocious look. "Oh, you'll bear it all right, or you will find yourself another place to live."

His father grunted and sat back in his chair.

His mother shot her husband the same hard gaze. "If he refuses to go, he can just pack his things and move out of here." She slapped her palm on the table. "I will not be lied to, disgraced, and disobeyed anymore!"

Danny stood slowly. He wanted to hurry out of the room in a show of angry defiance, but his body wasn't up to such a display. He eased his way to the door then turned to look at his mother, matching her anger and then some. "If I had another choice, I'd take it Mama."

"Well, you don't, so just wrap your mind around that."

On his first day back at school, Sue Ellen approached him in the hall after third class. They hadn't talked or seen each other since the accident five days ago.

"Why haven't you called me Danny?"

While he sported a bruised and swollen face, loose teeth that ached, and a black eye, her only apparent injury was a swollen lip. He shifted his books between his casted arm and chest and opened his locker door.

"My parents grounded me from everything, that includes the phone," he said mildly.

"Darren said you got in a lot of trouble."

He dropped two books in the locker and pulled out the two he needed for his next class then closed the locker door. "They're sending me away for the summer."

"Why? The accident wasn't your fault."

"This isn't about the accident as much as..." he paused trying to find the right words. "You know, how they found me when they pulled me out of the car."

She looked down the hall, her mouth drawn into the pouty little girl look he had grown to hate.

"So, what am I supposed to do all summer?" She asked using her little girl voice. "Do you expect me to just sit around doing nothing?"

Following her line of vision, he spotted Rob Crenshaw, the bully he fought for shooting BB's at David and Denise last year, approaching with a couple of friends.

Rob grinned, cocky as always. "How's it hangin' Danny Boy?"

Rob's friends snickered at the insinuation. Rob winked at Sue Ellen and her attitude swung from childish to flirty in less than a heartbeat.

She took a step away from Danny and smiled. "Hi Rob."

In a flash of insight, Danny absorbed the truth he had been resisting for months. She was a manipulative, self-centered girl. He couldn't condemn her too much though. He was nearly as bad. He knew all along what she was. He went out with her because he liked her flirty attention and the easy sex. Their relationship was a sham.

The warning bell rang for their next class and Rob and his friends moved along. Danny turned for the stairs, sickened by the certainty that he had been a fool.

Sue Ellen called his name and he paused, looking back, the pendulum of truth cutting wider and deeper with each pass. His state of mind must have been written on his face because her expression slipped from one of expectancy to confusion.

She had regained the pouty little girl expression. "Will you try to call me?"

He didn't bother with an answer. He turned for the stairs, lost in the storm raging inside him. He didn't see her for the rest of the day and by the last bell his resolve was set. How to tell her they were through was the only issue he hadn't worked out.

As it turned out, he needn't have worried about how to break up with her. The knowledge of his impending absence seemed to give Sue Ellen all the incentive she needed to spin off in another direction. Within days, she was hanging on the arm of Rob, the bully.

When he came through the door after school with Darren, David, and Denise right behind him, his mother was waiting with a letter in her hand. She waved the letter at him.

"You and I need to talk," she said.

Denise sighed. "Oh boy, what did you do now?"

"What is it about Mama?" he asked, ignoring Denise.

"Apparently you got a nearly perfect score on your SAT's."

"Well, I'll be damned," Darren said.

Danny reached for the letter and scanned the results. He hadn't really studied all that hard for the tests and was just as surprised as his mother.

"I can't believe this," he murmured.

"Well, I'm very proud of you Daniel," his mother said. She gave him a quick hug. "Daddy will be too."

Shortly before his departure for his uncle's farm, his mother took him for a hearing test where they concluded he had a thirty percent deficit on the right. When he received his hearing aid, he resented the plastic contraption so much that no matter how often or serious his parent's threats, he intended to leave the thing in his pocket. He still heard well on the left side and was already learning ways to mask the impediment.

He was allowed to attend Darren's high school graduation and party, but the following day his father woke him at five in the morning and drove him to Arkansas to begin serving his sentence.

All the pain, humiliation, and loss he had undergone due to the accident didn't come close to the misery he experienced watching his father drive away from his uncle's farm, leaving him behind.

In late June, Isabelle's paternal grandfather passed away after a battle with lung cancer. She travelled with her father and Mama Rose to a small town in southwestern Texas for the funeral. Other than one cousin in Tulsa, Isabelle had never met her father's family, including the grandfather who passed, so for her this was more of a curious event.

Her father's mother died years ago, when he was in his early twenties. Like Isabelle, her father was an only child, but he had an abundance of aunts, uncles, and cousins. Here, Isabelle saw some of the "mix" her father spoke of. There were black, brown, and even lighter skinned folks who seemed more white than anything else. Of course, like her father, there were those whose Cherokee heritage was undeniable.

For her sixteenth birthday in July, her father bought her a car out of an inheritance he received as the sole beneficiary of his father's estate. He didn't buy her just any car. She was now the proud owner of a shiny red 1967 Ford Mustang convertible.

Shadow

Shadow, Oklahoma
1967 Summer/Fall

THIRTY-ONE

As the long, hot summer wound down, Isabelle got the notion to drive across the state line and collect Danny from his banishment in Arkansas. She reasoned with her father and Mama Rose that she had driven to Tulsa by herself to see Grandma Sarah a few times over the summer and the distance from Shadow to Danny's uncle's farm in Arkansas wasn't much farther. At first, her father said he needed to think about the proposal, and Mama Rose of course cringed at the idea, but she wore them down. Danny's parents were just as skeptical, especially Caroline, but they gave in after Marshall convinced them Isabelle could handle herself just fine.

She set out for Arkansas early on Saturday morning with the top down and her favorite radio station playing the weekly top ten.

She did fine until she turned off the state highway in Arkansas at the little town which was supposed to be ten miles from Danny's uncle's farm. She came to a four-way stop unsure which way to go on the rural blacktop. After about fifteen miles, she pulled over to study Cecil's handwritten directions, but at this point they were no help. She turned the car around and headed back to town to find a phone. At a gas station, she slipped a dime into a payphone and dialed the farm. An unfamiliar male voice answered before the first ring was complete.

"Hello," she said. "My name is Isabelle Long. I'm a friend of Danny's. Could I speak to him, please?"

"Come on, Issy. It hasn't been that long since we talked."

"Danny?"

He laughed shortly. "What's the matter with you?"

His laugh was even richer than his voice. It took Isabelle a moment to recover.

"You sound different," she said finally.

"Well, I changed some over the summer."

"The phone didn't even finish the first ring. What were you doing, sitting on top of it?"

"Yeah, as a matter of fact I was. I was hoping it might be Darren calling. He's supposed to take me home today, but he's late."

"He's not coming."

He groaned. "Please tell me you're joking."

"Settle down Comet. I convinced everyone to let me make the trip in his place, but I'm lost. Can you give me directions?"

She brought the Mustang to a halt in front of the two-story farmhouse and stared through the dusty windshield at the guy on the porch steps. No one could ever call Danny Coulter "runt" again and mean it. He was at least three inches taller than the last time she saw him. The white T-shirt stretched over his muscled chest and biceps contrasted with his dark tan.

Shaking off her astonishment, Isabelle climbed out of the car and grinned. "You're looking incredibly healthy, Comet. I guess working your butt off was good for you after all." She pointed to the packed bag sitting next to his hip and laughed. "Ready?"

Danny wrapped his arms around her, lifting her easily. "Take me home, Issy."

Over the years, he had hugged her a few times, but today's embrace was different. The arms around her didn't belong to a boy. He set her back on her feet and turned his attention to her car.

"Where did you get this?"

"Daddy bought it for me."

Danny walked around the car and whistled. "You are so spoiled."

"Not true. I got a job at the Piggly Wiggly to pay for the insurance and gas."

He turned toward the porch for his bag. "Let's get out of here."

"Don't you have to say goodbye to your relatives?" She asked.

"They're at a family reunion in Little Rock."

While he retrieved his suitcase and placed it in the back seat, she forced her attention away from his body to the two-story farmhouse where white lace curtains fluttered in an open second-story window. The image of a soft double bed with feather pillows and Danny's smooth, tanned skin contrasted against some white sheets came to mind and she blushed. She really needed to stop reading Mama Rose's romance novels.

Danny frowned at her. "Are you okay?"

His question pulled her back from the sudden daydream. She looked at his sweet face and tossed him the keys. "Think you can keep it on the road?"

Danny tossed the keys right back. "Daddy kept my license."

"You really were a prisoner for the summer, weren't you?"

"I don't want to talk about it."

For the first thirty minutes of their drive, she told him all about the highlights of her summer: meeting her father's family, getting the car, working at her first real job, and best of all the church revival where she was a featured vocalist. While sharing her joys, she managed to put aside her very confusing attraction to the new Danny.

She glanced his way and smiled. "I stood up there on the stage of that revival tent and felt at home. I know what I want to do with the rest of my life."

He rolled his eyes. "Was there ever any doubt?"

"Yeah," she nodded. "I've given thought to being just a wife and mother a few times."

He frowned at her. "You can do that and be an entertainer too."

"You can't love two things with your whole heart at the same time," she said.

"I'll make note of that," he responded coolly.

Surprised, Isabelle glanced over at him, but Danny had tilted his face up to the sun and was smiling. Boy was he ever handsome.

Isabelle had noted a roadside park on the way to pick him up and pulled over there now.

"What are we doing?" Danny asked.

"Mama Rose made us a picnic lunch."

She spread a blue and white checkered tablecloth on the picnic table and removed ham and cheese sandwiches, potato salad, pickles, and bottled soda from a cooler. For dessert there were homemade chocolate chip cookies.

This morning, as she watched Mama Rose prepare the lunch, she believed there was enough to feed six people, but Mama Rose had insisted Danny was a teenage boy and would be hungry. As Isabelle watched Danny consume his food, she understood how correct Mama Rose had been.

Finished, Danny eyed the empty containers then turned his focus to her cookies.

She drew her food closer to her. "Are you still hungry for crying out loud?"

Danny grinned sheepishly. "I'm always hungry anymore."

She pushed her cookies across the table. "Here."

Sitting opposite him now, without the distraction of driving, Isabelle studied him openly. Most of the girls at school had labeled him "cute" because of his size or "sweet" because of his baby face. The new Danny Coulter may not have changed inside, but without a doubt the changes on the outside were going to turn heads and alter those particular adjectives forever.

Danny caught her studying him and frowned. "Why are you staring at me?"

"I'm sorry," she said. "I'm just so shocked at what is happening to your body."

Danny slowly lowered his head until his chin rested on his chest. His eyes widened in mock surprise. "Ah! What am I going to do with it?"

"Stop it," she laughed. "I just meant you've grown up to be..." she paused, waving a hand at his body, "quite attractive."

Danny's face relaxed into a grin. His gaze locked on hers, holding her gently. "Driving a red Mustang has turned you into a heathen."

Isabelle sighed. "Just stating a fact. The girls at school will be all over you for sure."

Danny's laugh bathed her in comfort. "Mama has a cure for what ails you," he said.

"I found the perfect name for your daughter."

All humor left him. He swallowed hard. "My what?"

"Remember Grandma said she saw your daughter with stars all around?"

Danny put his hand over his heart and exhaled. "Oh, that."

"Namid."

He leaned closer, squinting at her, as if he hadn't heard correctly. "What?"

"Namid, it means Star Dancer."

"Ah," He said with a little nod. "Well, I kind of hoped I'd have all boys, since girls are so complicated and all."

"We're not complicated. We just have more than that one thing on our mind."

He smiled sweetly, teasing her. "I do love cars."

She threw a bottle cap at him. "Stop it. You know exactly what I'm talking about. All boys think about is how far they can go with a girl. Look at you and Sue Ellen."

His attitude shifted again. "You have no idea what you're talking about," he said tightly.

"Maybe not," she said with a little shrug. "But I do know you'll have a daughter. Grandma saw it."

He considered her for a minute, his brown eyes sparkling. "Namid," he said softly.

Isabelle couldn't help but smile. The day seemed so perfect, just the two of them like old times, until he nearly ruined the moment.

"Did you see Sue Ellen this summer?" He asked.

"Yep."

"She doing okay?"

Isabelle sighed loudly. "Why wouldn't she be?"

"I talked to Darren a few weeks ago and he said she might have to move."

"I hope she does then maybe you'll forget about her."

He looked away and sighed. Isabelle found his silence difficult to tolerate.

"I don't know what you see in her."

He stuffed his trash into a baggie and tossed it overhand into the air. It fell neatly into a trash barrel ten feet away. "Well, it's over at any rate."

Relieved, Isabelle laughed. "What? I thought you were crazy about her."

He glanced at her then away. "There was a time."

"Well, you deserve much better, Danny. She's been telling everyone all summer how all you wanted to do on a date was talk, like you were girlfriends or something. She says she was merely trying to encourage you to be a man when you lost control of the car."

The look on his face told her all she needed to know. Her words had struck bone. She was even a tiny bit ashamed that the pain she had just inflicted gave her such satisfaction.

Danny had a big smile on his face as Isabelle swung the car off the blacktop and onto Coulter property. His father's truck was parked behind the station wagon in front of his parents' home. Denise was on the porch reading a book and jumped up and ran inside when she saw the car approaching. By the time they parked, his family was pouring out the front door.

Darren was the first down the steps. He grinned and hugged Danny warmly. "Welcome home.

"Thanks Darren."

Darren eyed him up and down. "I'm glad you finally grew, but did you have to get bigger than me?"

Though he hadn't measured, Danny was certain he was still shorter than Darren and would never have Darren's muscular physique, but he understood his brother's exaggeration. Typical of Darren, his intention was to acknowledge their equality.

He smiled at his brother and played along. "Maybe I won't have to wear your hand-me-downs anymore," he said.

Darren laughed. "I can only hope you stop raiding my closet."

His father was next. He patted Danny on the shoulder. "Good to have you back. How were things over there?"

"Pretty much what I expected," he responded with a little shrug. "Work, eat, work, church, work, sleep, pray, pray, pray, and then work."

"Did you get any art done?"

That his father even considered his passion took Danny back for a moment. He shook his head. "A little, but I was usually too tired from the work part."

Danny didn't know what to expect from his mother. She had only made it as far as the bottom step. As he approached, she watched him with wet eyes and a strained expression.

"Hi Mama."

"Lord, Danny, I wouldn't have known you on the street."

She wrapped him in her arms and hugged him tightly. Nothing, not even an embrace from Isabelle, was ever better than one of his mother's whole-hearted hugs.

"I missed you so much," he whispered. "I'm so sorry for the way I acted before I left."

"We're not going to talk about that today. Come on inside, Denise and I made a big supper with all your favorites."

THIRTY-TWO

On the Friday before Labor Day weekend, Danny finished feeding the horses and started toward the house when he spotted Isabelle coming down the hill. She whistled like he taught her and gave him a big wave. He waved back and watched her approach, her hair swinging in a bouncy ponytail. She had on blue jean shorts, a white peasant blouse, and no makeup. Her natural beauty took his breath away.

She stopped in front of him, slipping her hands into the back pockets of her shorts. "Did you get your driver's license back?"

"Last week. Why?"

"I need a favor."

He slipped off his work gloves and waited patiently.

"This will completely ruin your weekend," she began hesitantly. "So, I'll understand if you say no."

While she babbled on, he focused on the details of her face, thinking how best to draw what he was seeing, and feeling.

"Your parents probably won't let you, but it wouldn't hurt to ask," she said, snapping him back to

~ 319 ~

the moment. "I wouldn't want you to do anything to get in trouble."

"For crying out loud, Isabelle, what do you need?"

"I talked to Grandma last night and she told me she knows where my mother is," she said, then took a deep breath. "I was supposed to go with Daddy and Mama Rose to a rodeo in Dallas, but they said if I could get you to go with me to see my mother it would be okay. Will you?"

He understood completely how important this was to her. "Where is she?"

"A little south of Des Moines."

His eyebrows shot up in surprise. "Iowa?"

"I know this means spending a lot of time on the road, but if we both drive, we can do it. We have the extra day this weekend and..."

He held up a hand, interrupting her sales pitch. "I'll talk to Mama and Daddy, but I'm sure it will be okay with them."

Danny leaned against the hood of Isabelle's Mustang, sipping strong coffee, hoping to create a little energy. Despite her proposed plan to share the driving, he had driven most of the night while she slept or sat in the passenger seat jabbering nervously.

He watched as she knocked on the door of the apartment manager. A rough-looking woman opened the door and glared at her. Danny couldn't hear what they said, but saw the woman motion toward a row of bungalows. Isabelle quickly stepped closer to the woman and they had a sharp exchange he couldn't quite hear. The manager stepped back inside her apartment and slammed the door in Isabelle's face. Isabelle offered the door her middle finger and walked back to him.

"What was that about?" he asked.

"She said the drunk back in bungalow fifteen uses the name Carrie Forrester, but she's an old squaw and couldn't possibly be the mother of a little picaninny like me."

Isabelle looked back at the manager's closed door, her eyes narrowing to slits. "Bitch!"

Danny studied her for a minute then glanced toward bungalow fifteen. The closer they came to this moment, the more he wanted to make Isabelle get back the car and take her home. If he hadn't known her so well, he might have tried.

He sighed and crushed his empty paper cup and threw it onto the floor of the car. "Let's go see for ourselves."

Isabelle switched teary eyes to him. "I'm scared."

Danny put an arm around her shoulders and hugged her close as they approached the bungalow.

A small, thin woman answered the door. Her skin had a jaundiced pallor and her eyes were lusterless black pools. A heavy braid lay over one shoulder. She wore an old housecoat, loose orange socks, and smelled of cigarettes.

She squinted at Isabelle for a second then started to shut the door, "Wrong place, Kid."

"Mama wait. It's me, Isabelle."

"Who are you calling Mama? I haven't been anybody's Mama for a long time. "

"Please, I just want to talk."

Isabelle's mother rubbed the tip of her nose and squinted at Isabelle again. "What is it you think we have to talk about? Do you think we need to discuss them good old days in Okie-homa?"

"I wanted to see you again. I've missed you so much. Please, can we just talk?"

Danny stood to the side, waiting for Isabelle to scale the summit of this pain, ready when she needed him. Hearing her plead was almost more than he could bear.

Isabelle's mother smiled, spread her arms, and turned in a ghoulish imitation of a model. "I imagine I'm quite an inspiration."

Isabelle reached out to touch her mother. "Come with me. Let me help you."

Her mother recoiled from Isabelle's hand and shot a look at Danny, "You with her, Boy?"

"Yes, ma'am."

"Take her out of here and don't let her come back."

With that, Isabelle's mother pushed her out of the way and slammed the door. There was a loud "click" as she bolted Isabelle to the other side of the world.

Isabelle kicked the door with her foot then started pounding on the door with her fist. "You owe me an explanation!"

Danny tried to pull her away, but she pushed him backward and continued to beat on the door.

The manager opened her door and stepped out, waving a telephone receiver at Isabelle. "You've got two seconds to move on or I'm calling the police."

Isabelle turned her fury on the manager. "Go on and call them you old..."

Danny stepped up, took Isabelle's hand, and did his best to pull her away. "Issy, come on. I don't want to go to jail."

Isabelle twisted her hand from his grip. "Your family is perfect! I don't expect you to understand this. Go on back to the car and stay out of the way."

"No."

"Then shut up!"

Danny scooped her up into his arms and carried her to the car. Isabelle kicked and screamed, but his grip was firm. He sat down on the hood of the car and held her against him until she stopped struggling.

"Sometimes you have to let people be," he whispered.

"I don't want to."

"I know, but you've got to let her have her pride."

"Pride? Did you see what she's become?" she moaned. She covered her face and began to cry. "She was so special, so beautiful."

Danny didn't talk. Holding her more gently now, he stroked her hair. When she was calm enough, he placed her in the passenger seat and drove them out of there.

Eight hours later, Danny stood on Grandma Sarah's porch with Isabelle sleeping soundly in his arms and tapped the front door with his foot. He thought she might wake as he lifted her from the car and carried her to the door, but crying for the first half of their journey must have exhausted her.

Sarah opened the door and squinted in the bright afternoon sun. Without speaking, she directed him to the spare bedroom where he gently placed Isabelle on the bed and covered her with a blanket.

Sarah motioned for him to follow her to the kitchen and pointed to a chair. "Have a seat. Want some coffee, Comet?"

Danny smiled wearily and leaned back in the chair. "Yes, ma'am."

Sarah placed an aqua cup on a yellow saucer in front of him and filled the cup with thick, red-brown liquid.

She grinned proudly. "It's got a touch of cinnamon."

Danny lifted the cup and took a cautious sip. The foul, sluggish concoction lay on his tongue like molasses. He grimaced and choked the bit down.

Sarah laughed and rubbed the top of his head affectionately. "Might need to thin it out with a little water, I guess. Add some sugar while I boil some water."

Danny pushed the cup away and cleared his throat. "I need to talk to you before Isabelle wakes up."

"What's going on? Have you married my sweet girl?"

Startled, Danny shook his head quickly. "Oh, no, it's nothing like that. She's been to see her mama."

Sarah closed her eyes. "I shouldn't have told her."

"I think she had a right to try, don't you?"

Sarah's expression hardened. "You should have stopped her."

Danny met her gaze directly. "I think I'd have more luck trying to stop a train with my telekinetic powers, Ma'am."

"You stop that ma'am stuff, Comet. My name's Sarah."

"And my name is Danny."

Sarah chuckled. "We'll discuss this name business another time. Tell me what went on."

"She wouldn't even talk to Isabelle. She shut the door in her face. That hurt her so much." He paused, sighing. "I didn't know what to do. Her father told her she could go, but he and Mama Rose went down to a rodeo in Dallas. Since I thought Isabelle needed to be with her family right now, I brought her here."

Sarah studied him for a moment then reached across the table and patted his hand. "My granddaughter has all she needs."

Isabelle woke as the sun was starting to set and looked around the room. Realizing where she was, she sat up and looked out the open door of the bedroom. Danny was lying on Sarah's old sofa, staring at the ancient black and white TV.

Hearing her stir, he looked away from an Abbott and Costello movie to the bedroom. A little smile softened his tired face and she never loved him more.

"Where's Grandma?" she asked as she approached.

He pointed toward the kitchen. "In the lab, experimenting."

"Have you gotten any sleep?"

"Nope. You're talking to the first victim of your grandmother's gourmet coffee blend. I'm wired for sight and sound, but all other brain activity has pretty much ceased."

Isabelle sat next to him on the edge of the sofa. Reaching out, she ran a hand through his soft dark hair.

He looked up at her. "Do you feel better?"

She nodded slowly, her mind not on conversation. Since the day she picked him up from his uncle's farm, a curious attraction to him had sprung to life. And, after what happened with her mother, she never appreciated his gentle heart more.

"Thank you for today," she said, daring to meet his eyes.

He shivered and brushed her hand away from his head. "Stop it. You're making my ear ring."

She wasn't through indulging her need to touch him and ran her hand over his soft cheek with a smile.

Danny pushed her hand away again. "What's the matter with you?"

"I was thinking you owe me a kiss."

Danny stared at her, his expression unreadable. She had to touch him, whether he liked it or not. She ran the tip of her index finger over his slender-fingered hand resting on his chest.

"Remember the night Rosalie drove into the river? You were going to kiss me," she said.

His mouth spread into a sly grin. "What makes you think that?"

Isabelle couldn't wait another minute. She leaned forward and kissed him. He tasted like sweet cinnamon. After a moment, Danny responded with subtle enthusiasm. She pressed harder, enjoying the comfort of his soft lips. He wrapped his arms around her and drew her to him. A wave of heat swept through her body. She had kissed a few boys, but his kiss was passionate and delicious.

"You kids stop doing that on my couch," Sarah called from the doorway of the kitchen.

Startled, Isabelle sat up, casting a sheepish glance at her grandmother. "Sorry."

When her grandmother disappeared into the kitchen again, Isabelle giggled nervously then looked down at Danny. Layers of emotion flickered through his expression, not all of them easy to interpret.

"What's wrong?" she asked.

He eyed her for a minute then took a deep breath. "Look, I've been awake a long time and my brain isn't firing quite right. I'd appreciate it if you'd let me off the hook for now. I promise we'll talk about this later."

She bristled at being put off. "Talk about it now or forget it."

"You're bouncing me around like a rubber ball, Issy," he began softly. "Up until this moment you made it clear I was just a friend, now you want to make out on your grandmother's couch?"

Her mouth curled into a little smile. "If I'd known you could kiss like that I would have kissed you sooner."

He closed his eyes and sighed audibly. "Not today."

"Don't you want to at least try?"

"What is it exactly that you want to try?"

"Dating."

"I can't believe what I'm about to say," he began, his voice weary. "For as long as I have known you, I have hoped you would see me as more than a friend, the way I see you, but not now. This is just the wrong time."

Annoyed, she leaned away from him. "What's wrong with right now?"

He studied her for a moment. Her hand rested on his chest and she could feel the gentle rise and fall of his breathing.

"What you just went through with your mom," he said softly. "I can't fill that space for you."

He was right of course. While he was her gift and made her life easier, he did not have the power to mend her wounded heart, but she wasn't ready to concede that point at the moment. Instead, she chose anger over truth.

"I guess you think Sue Ellen was a better choice?"

"Oh hell," he came back fiercely. "All you talk about is leaving Shadow behind, then of course there's the BS about how you can't love two things at once, blah, blah, blah."

"Maybe, I've changed my mind," she snapped. She took a deep breath and as the next thought came into her head she smiled widely. "When it comes time for me to leave, I'll take you with me."

Danny's expression shifted from disbelief to narrow-eyed anger. He swung his feet to the floor and headed for the front door. When the screen door slammed behind him, Isabelle followed, but there was no point in hurrying after him, he was already halfway down the block.

Sarah joined her at the door. "You kids need to settle down."

"I don't understand him Grandma."

"I may be old, but I got good ears. You'd better stop treating that boy like he's your property."

Isabelle put her face in her hands and started to cry. "I can't lose Danny too."

Sarah wrapped an arm around her waist. "His heart won't let him go far."

THIRTY-THREE

He and Isabelle hadn't discussed what happened at her grandmother's house. On the ride home, they kept to their usual style of conversation, back to being friends again. Mostly, he had no regrets over what he said or did that day. He knew he loved her and certainly wished for more, but he wanted her to see him as more than a shoulder to cry on or a sounding board for her troubles.

In addition to beginning his last year of high school, there was a lot of work to do around the ranch this time of year and he had resumed his job with Uncle Hal, so he had plenty to occupy his time. Unfortunately, the more mundane tasks gave him time to think and his mind returned time and again to Isabelle and their single perfect kiss.

She had her job, her friends, her cute little car, and their paths didn't cross too often. When they did see each other, the moments felt increasingly awkward, the conversation forced.

Isabelle was right about one thing: lots of other girls were paying attention to him, and once he had a car again, he intended to date as many as possible. Maybe one of them could help him forget all about her.

Danny's friends repeated what Isabelle told him regarding Sue Ellen's behavior over the summer. Of course, no one knew his relationship with her was over; he wasn't even sure Sue Ellen knew, since there really hadn't been an official end. When people attempted to caution him with their stories, he shrugged his shoulders in complete disinterest and told them he no longer cared what she did.

After the first Friday night football game of the season, Danny rode to the river with his friend Jimmy. Sue Ellen was already there. He walked past her without saying a word and joined his friends who were building a bonfire. Moments later, she tapped him on the shoulder.

"Can I talk to you for a second?"

Danny turned, eyeing her coolly. "Sure."

She looked around at his friends, then back to him. "Privately."

He shrugged. "This is as private as it's gonna get."

The other boys snickered. Sue Ellen stepped closer to him.

"I guess it makes you feel like a man to belittle me like this in front of your friends."

He had nothing to say to her, and stood there, patiently waiting for her to finish.

After a minute, she understood he wasn't going to respond. "All right have it your way," she said. "I'll tell you what's on my mind. Everybody's talking about the little trip you took with Isabelle. Most people say it's time the two of you got it out of your system. I say Isabelle Long finally got her way and came between us."

"Aw come on, Sue Ellen, there is no *us* anymore."

"Did you sleep with her?"

"What we did is none of your business."

Sue Ellen cocked her head to the side and smiled sweetly. "Aw, Danny, do you still prefer to just talk?"

Danny stepped closer, not bothering to hide his contempt, "To anyone but you."

She gasped and stepped back. "Leave me alone!"

"Gladly."

Darren dropped Danny off in front of Hal's garage at seven-thirty the next morning on his way to his own job working as a welder for a company that made cargo trailers.

Hal eyed him angrily as he entered the office. "You're supposed to be here at seven."

"I had to wait for Darren to give me a ride. I'll work until five, okay?"

"Damn it," Hal barked. "Either get your ass here on time, or you don't work for me. Got it, Runt?"

Danny nodded before starting toward the garage. Uncle Hal could be irritable if he had been drinking; from the look of him this morning, it had been a rough night.

Hal's surliness didn't improve much over the morning. He shouted at him for situations Danny had no control over and was even rude to a few customers. By late morning, and a few shots from a pint of Jim Beam, Hal's mood was finally improving.

Just as they were about to stop for lunch, a call came in for a tow truck to the scene of an accident. Hal had purchased the tow truck over the summer while Danny had been slaving away on his uncle's farm over in Arkansas. Adding the truck had given the business a boost Hal couldn't quite handle alone. On a better day, Hal had even said he was glad to have Danny back at work.

Hal tossed Danny the keys. "You drive."

Though he had never driven the tow truck or been to the scene of an accident, Danny was eager to get behind the wheel. Though the car was totaled and the injured hauled away in an ambulance, there were fortunately no fatalities at the accident. Clearing the wreck took over an hour and, with the car finally in tow, they set off for the junk yard. After depositing the wrecked car, Danny steered the truck back toward the garage and his sack lunch. When they reached the edge of town, Hal pointed in the direction of his favorite diner. "Go on down to Ruby's, I'll treat you to a burger," Hal said.

As they neared their turn onto Main Street, Danny heard what he thought sounded like the high school band then saw girls up ahead twirling batons down the middle of the street. The girls were followed closely by the high school banner and marching band.

Hal scrunched up his face as he peered through the windshield. "Ah, damn it! What the hell is this?"

"Rodeo starts today," Danny said. He shifted into neutral and kept his foot on the brake.

Hal shook his head and waved a hand toward Main Street. "Go on."

Dumbfounded, Danny attempted to reason with him. "We can't get in the middle of a parade," he said then added patiently, as if speaking to a child, "We have to wait."

Hal looked at him, as serious as Danny had ever seen him, and spoke slowly, enunciating each word with precision. "Put your blinker on and edge out into the parade."

When Danny shook his head in disbelief, Hal threw up his hands, flung open his door and came around to the driver's side, pulling open the driver's door.

"Move over."

Danny slid over as Hal put the truck in gear and flipped on the blinker.

Millie Tinsdale pulled her two Shetland ponies to an abrupt halt from the seat of her little surrey and stared open-mouthed as Hal edged the tow truck out in front of her.

Folks lining either side of the street gawked, some laughed and pointed, and a few yelled at Hal to get out. Danny flushed a deep crimson, slid down on the seat, and pulled his baseball hat down low. Hal blew the truck horn, took his hat off and waved it out the window, laughing like a fool. He nudged Danny in the shoulder.

"Wave at the folks Runt."

Five excruciating minutes later, they finally arrived at Ruby's diner. Hal jumped out and headed for the liquor store located next door.

"I need some cigarettes," he called to Danny. "Order me a cheeseburger deluxe."

Danny spotted his cousin Elliot in the big booth at the back of the diner with Sue Ellen cuddled up next to him and his usual crowd of friends all around. Elliot grinned when he saw Danny.

"Oh, look," he called. "It's Chatty-Danny."

Everyone at Elliot's table snickered. Danny's assigned nickname was a reference to a popular doll named Chatty Cathy. The nickname stemmed from

Sue Ellen telling everyone all he wanted to do on a date was talk, like they were girlfriends.

Danny took a seat at the counter and placed his order. Elliot sauntered over and leaned casually against the counter, chuckling as if amused by some private joke.

Danny sat back and looked up at Elliot. "Is there something on your mind?"

"We haven't had a chance to catch up. How was your stay over in Arkansas? Did you get religion?"

Before Danny could respond, Hal wandered in. Though there were available seats on either side of Danny, Hal elbowed his way to the very stool where Elliot lounged against the counter, forcing Elliot to step back.

Hal tapped a pack of cigarettes on the counter and shot Elliot a hard look. "Go away, Pus Ball."

"I will in a minute. Right now, I'm asking Danny how his summer went."

Hal lit a cigarette, drew deeply, exhaled, and squinted at Elliot through the smoke. "Ain't it obvious how his summer went? Have you taken no notice there's something different about him yet?"

Danny knew that tone. Hal was baiting Elliot. He picked up his glass of water and took a healthy swallow, waiting for Hal to reel Elliot in. All he wanted was to escape the company of his less attractive relatives and finish this workday.

"He's bigger," Elliot said with a shrug.

"No, no, no," Hal said, waving off that answer. "That's obvious. Try to think for once, will you?"

"Come on, Uncle Hal, what are you talking about?"

Hal grinned widely. "Why Runt here finally grew a pair and told that little girl you're so fond of they were finished."

Hal slapped Elliot's cheek in the pretense of good-natured fun. "You, my boy, are the consolation prize."

Elliot's smile dissolved.

Hal's mock congeniality dissipated quickly. "Now go away, Pus Ball."

Shadow, Oklahoma
Spring 1968

THIRTY-FOUR

Danny spotted the envelope addressed to him lying on the hall table the moment he came through the front door after school on Friday afternoon. For weeks he had been waiting for this very letter.

He lifted the envelope and smiled at the weight. The thick contents meant good news. He took the envelope to his room where he opened it carefully and read the letter several times, making certain he hadn't mistaken the meaning. Since his father wouldn't be home for another hour and a half, he decided to wait to share the news over dinner. He changed into his work clothes and went about his daily chores with a smile.

At dinnertime, he carried the letter in his pocket to the table. Tonight every one of his siblings seemed to have news to share. Denise discussed the plans for her trip with the church youth group, Dwight tossed out the latest decisions for his upcoming wedding, and David wanted money for a class trip, on and on. When David finally finished his spiel, Danny couldn't wait another minute and jumped in before Darren had a chance to start talking. He pulled the letter from his pocket and waved it in the air.

"I have some news."

His mother looked down the table to him. "What do you have there?"

"I've been granted a full scholarship to the University of Tulsa."

Everyone stared in shock as he rose and handed the letter to his mother. His father joined her and they read together.

Darren grinned at Danny. "Wow, way to go."

His mother started crying and, after patting her on the back, his father came around the table and gave him an uncustomary hug. "Mama and I are so proud of you."

"Thanks Daddy."

"How come you didn't mention anything about your plans?"

Danny shrugged. "I didn't want you to be disappointed in me if it didn't work out."

"No matter what you do, we won't be disappointed in you, Danny. You've turned out just fine."

He smiled widely, enjoying the moment.

"It was probably all the castor oil," Denise said.

"And hikes to the barn," Darren added.

His father laughed. "You could be right."

After talking with his family, Danny stepped into the hall to call Isabelle.

"I'm very proud of you," she said tightly.

"What's wrong? I thought you'd be happy."

"I am. It's just that this is a reminder that life as we know it is about to end."

Danny laughed. "Gee, what a cheerful way of putting it Issy."

He arrived at work early the next morning, eager to share the good news with his uncle and saw that the lights were on in the little apartment over the office. Hal used the place for lunch, an occasional nap, and then of course there were the affairs with a string of women, some of them married. He looked around the parking lot for cars that didn't belong. Finding none, he decided to go up to the apartment.

Most days, he would have waited until Hal came down to the garage, but he was too excited to share his news. He climbed the stairs two at a time. At the top, he paused to catch his breath then knocked on the door.

He could hear country music wailing from a radio, and waited patiently, hoping Hal heard. The volume of the music went down and Hal opened the door.

"Danny," Hal said loudly then stepped out and closed the door.

"I wanted to tell you some good news. I got..." he began.

"I'm sure it can wait," Hal interrupted impatiently. "Go on downstairs. I'll be there in a minute."

Danny glanced back up the stairs before turning the corner. Oddly, Hal was still at the top of the stairs watching. Danny opened the door to the office and flipped on the lights. The florescent lights in the garage flickered to life. Since he was early, he headed to his favorite project and didn't give Uncle Hal another thought.

Driving the tow truck had given him a distinct advantage in finding a new car to restore. He had purchased a wrecked 1958 Thunderbird convertible for a few hundred dollars and invested nearly all of his pay in restoring the car. Thankfully the project was nearly complete. He was anxious to have his own transportation again.

THIRTY-FIVE

Isabelle stepped away from the other actors and took her bow. Her cheeks flushed from the applause that greeted her. Tears sprang to her eyes when she heard Danny's distinct whistle. Tonight was the last high school performance he would probably attend. These days would soon be sweet memories.

Danny came backstage after the show and embraced her. "Wow! That performance scores a ten, Miss Issy-Belle."

"I heard you whistling, Comet. Thanks for the courage, as always."

"Are you going to Fran's birthday party?"

"I sure am."

"Can I give you a ride in the Thunderbird?"

Isabelle smiled widely. "You got it done?"

"Yes, ma'am. It runs like a top."

"Sorry, I'd love to, but I'm going with Jimmy."

"You have nothing in common with him. I don't know what you two are doing together," he came back irritably.

Isabelle patted his cheek. "I happen to like good-looking boys."

He pushed her hand away with uncustomary roughness and left.

Danny's friend Jimmy had a light-hearted, take-nothing-serious approach to life, exactly what Isabelle wanted. No commitment was necessary. Still, the breezy relationship couldn't last much longer. One of Jimmy's serious flaws was an overzealous sexual appetite. Unlike her, he didn't have a problem with the notion of casual sex. Isabelle wanted the act to mean something special. So far, she had been able to fend off his advances, but she was certain a confrontation was coming.

Fran's backyard glowed from Christmas lights strung on poles around the patio. A warm, southerly breeze tickled the new leaves and gave the night an airy feel. Soon after arriving, Jimmy drifted away with some buddies to have a beer. Other than the sex issue, Jimmy's other serious flaw looked like it just might be alcohol. She was certainly glad she had insisted on driving.

Isabelle joined in a conversation with Fran and a couple of other girls, intentionally ignoring Sue Ellen who stood right next to Fran.

Unchained Melody started up on the stereo and she stood alone while the other girls paired up with their steady boyfriends and began to dance. She watched Darren's hand caress the small of Fran's back as their bodies swayed in familiar harmony. Elliot and

Sue Ellen's dance was far less romantic. Elliot's hands freely roamed her body as they rubbed together in rhythm to the music. A few other kids shuffled their feet around, nuzzling and making out more than anything else.

Part of her ached for the kind of familiarity a few of the couples shared, especially the tenderness of Fran and Darren, but she couldn't allow herself to get that close to a boy. That kind of intimacy had a price tag. Only when she had given her dream her best effort would she consider giving her heart away.

As if prodded by some cosmic cue, Danny appeared at her side. "So, where's Jimmy?"

"Drinking."

She looked up at him and though she had probably looked at his face a million times, he was never more appealing. Her heart whispered yes, you fool, this is the one. Her brain countered with a less sentimental rebuttal, no, not yet.

His gaze took in the couples on the dance floor. "Want to dance?"

She gave him a sideways look. "It's a slow dance," she said carefully.

He took her hand and guided her before him until they were among the group of young couples.

She smiled at him. "This is nice. Thank you."

He looked down at her, his face relaxing into a smile. The strong desire to lay her head on his chest, to feel his heart beating against her cheek nearly overwhelmed her. She no sooner pushed the thought aside than Danny pulled her closer. They swayed in silence and she closed her eyes, enjoying the clean smell of his shirt, the warmth of his skin beneath the cotton, the strength of his arms.

He sighed. "I'm really going to miss you when I go away."

"Are you getting sentimental on me Comet?"

As the last notes of the song faded, he placed a soft kiss on her cheek, "Yeah."

"Hey, Coulter," Jimmy said. "I turn my back for one minute and you move in. Let's take this outside."

Danny bowed to him. "One dance, Chief Horn-Up-His-Butt, nothing more."

Standing behind her, Jimmy wrapped an arm around her shoulders and pulled her to him in an unusually possessive stance. Danny stared, unblinking and immobile, before turning abruptly and leaving the party. He didn't turn for one last look. He just kept walking, dragging her heart behind him.

After dropping Jimmy off, she parked in her driveway at a little after midnight. As she approached the back steps, she heard footsteps behind her and swung around in alarm.

"Issy?" Danny called from the shadows.

Anger quickly displaced fear. "What are you doing sneaking around my back door?"

"I need to talk to you."

"It's late."

"I know, but I'm afraid if I wait I'll lose my nerve again."

"All right, come inside, but be quiet."

"Let's talk here. I don't want to wake your parents."

Sighing loudly, Isabelle stepped away from the door. "What in the world is so important it can't wait until tomorrow?"

Danny looked up at her, soft moonlight lighting his face. She heard him release a sigh.

"I need to know how you feel about me," he said.

"For heaven's sake, you know how I feel about you."

He tapped the stair rail with the tips of his fingers and looked across the yard.

Isabelle summoned patience and waited for him to continue. Curiously, her heart had begun to pound so loudly it was difficult to hear. With uncanny clarity, she feared they had reached a fork in the road. The decision she made right now would likely affect their relationship for a long time, maybe forever. She silently begged him to stop.

He picked up her hand, rubbing the fingers lightly. "Promise not to laugh at me."

"Promise," she whispered.

"Seeing you with Jimmy tonight tore me up," he looked up at her, a boy on the edge of becoming a man. "You know how I feel about you."

She pulled her hand away and folded her arms over her chest. "There's nothing really going on…"

He held up his hand stopping her explanation. "I know you're not serious about Jimmy."

"Oh," she said, buying time. "Then what's bothering you?"

His shoulders rose and fell as he took a deep breath then exhaled slowly. "I'm pretty sure I've been in love with you since the first time I heard you sing under the bridge."

Just those words would have been enough to push her over the edge, but he had the nerve to look her in the eye when he said it.

Isabelle breath caught in her throat. "Don't do this."

"Why not?"

"Because I'm only sixteen!" she said her frustration overflowing. "I have dreams…"

"I don't want to interfere with your dreams."

"You're so annoying!" She took a breath, lowered her voice. "What do you want from me?"

This of course was a question wrapped around a lie. She knew exactly what he wanted.

"It would be nice to hear you say just this once where I stack up in your *plans*," he came back dryly, the word plans dripping with sarcasm.

She stomped her foot. "You're not being fair!"

"Stop being so dramatic for crying out loud."

"How many times do I have to say it? I just can't be committed to anyone and focus on the career I

~ 349 ~

want at the same time! She paused and softened her tone, speaking her darkest truth. "I saw what my mother's ambition did. I don't want to be like her."

Danny nodded and looked away, disappointment lining his face. Hurting him twisted her insides into knots.

"You need to focus on your own future now," she said gently. "We're not little kids anymore."

He grunted. "Believe me, I know that."

"Then stop trying to make me feel guilty. You're going to college in the fall and I'm leaving next year when I graduate. Grow up, will you? Our childhood is over."

He stepped away quickly. "Thanks for clearing things up."

"Oh, come on, don't go. Let's talk this out."

He swung around facing her. Walking backwards, he tapped his fist on his chest twice, right over his heart, then turned and faded into the shadows of the night.

Her body ached to chase after him, to give in, to beg, plead, and do whatever was necessary to mend the rift between them.

Somehow her feet had taken her to the bottom of the stairs. They were itching to run, but she willed them not to take the next step, if that happened she knew she would not stop until she caught up with him.

She shoved the panic aside, reassuring herself that she and Danny would be all right. Tomorrow he would see she was the one thinking clearly and forgive her.

She should have known him better.

THIRTY-SIX

In late April, Dwight was marrying his high school sweetheart. Surprisingly, Danny's big brother asked Danny and Darren to be among his groomsmen. By Coulter standards, this wedding was an elaborate affair, one his grandmother had labeled "showy."

At the reception, Isabelle walked in with his best friend Jimmy in tow. Of course, the pair immediately came toward him.

He hadn't spoken to Isabelle since the night they had their talk at her back porch. She had called a few times, but he was actually gone each time and couldn't bring himself to call her back. At school he made sure to look the other way if he saw her, or pretended to be too busy to talk.

His desire for her had reached the boiling point that night. He had gone to her house thinking all he wanted was for her to finally tell him how she felt about him. In hindsight, he now knew what he really wanted was for her to dance with him, to ride in his car, to kiss him instead of Jimmy, ultimately to love him back the way he loved her.

He understood her sensible approach to the future and knew she was right. They were much too young and absolutely shouldn't get tangled up in a relationship now. She had her dreams to chase and his were equally important to him.

The truth cutting him the deepest was the sense that his passion for Isabelle was in no way mutual.

"Hey! You in the monkey suit," Jimmy said, showing off his good-old-boy grin.

"Hush Jimmy," Isabelle admonished lightly. "He looks nice."

Jimmy looked longingly at the bar. "Think they'll let us have a beer?"

"Sure," Danny said, "just as long as you let Mama lace it with a little castor oil."

"You still mad at me?" Isabelle asked.

He turned from Jimmy and looked her in the eye, not about to give her the satisfaction of knowing he was in fact still hurt and angry.

"All in the past," he lied with a big smile, an act as phony as Uncle Hal's pledge to never touch alcohol or other men's wives again.

"Good. I was hoping you two would put your war to rest," Jimmy said.

Jimmy may have bought the act, but Isabelle glared at Danny.

"You are such a liar," she hissed.

The wedding party was gathering at their long table and Darren was waving Danny over.

"See y'all later," he said.

From his place at the table with the bride and groom, in an attempt to ignore Isabelle, Danny surveyed the other guests filling the room and spotted Holly Adams sitting with her parents. Holly had always been a pretty girl, even back in ninth grade when she wore braces and had such an obvious crush on him, but now she was downright beautiful.

These days she wore her caramel-colored hair long and straight, as was the popular style. Bangs framed her big brown eyes. Holly was neither petite like Isabelle, nor voluptuous like Sue Ellen, but somewhere in between. Looking at her today, he wondered why he hadn't been interested. Of course, the answer to that riddle lay in his longing for Isabelle. As he swallowed that bitter pill one more time, he reminded himself to move on. Then again, maybe he should just forget all about girls until he left Shadow for University of Tulsa in the fall where he was sure to meet many new girls.

After the toasts were finished, the buffet meal consumed, and all assorted wedding party dances completed, the band struck up a fast song to get the general crowd involved. Danny was the only member of his family without a partner to dance with. Even twelve-year-old David took to the floor with a cousin of the bride.

After mingling for a bit and accepting his grandmother's request for a dance, he watched Jimmy take Isabelle in his arms for slow dance. He stood watching, bathed in misery, as she tilted her head to look up at Jimmy, smiling like she was having the time of her life.

He forced his attention elsewhere, drifting back to Holly who was still sitting with her parents. She offered a little smile when she caught him looking her way. The braces were long gone and she had a beautiful smile. He crossed the crowded room to her table. After making small talk with Holly and her parents for a few minutes, he asked her to dance.

She smiled warmly. "Sure."

Running into Holly at the wedding reception turned out to be exactly what he needed. They spent the rest of the reception together and he drove her home. She invited him to sit with her on the front porch and they talked until midnight.

When he reluctantly rose to leave, Holly followed him to the edge of the steps.

"I've really enjoyed being with you tonight, Danny."

He smiled, feeling better than he had in weeks. "Me too."

A few heartbeats passed while he considered what he wanted to say next. He knew she had been dating a few guys and didn't know how serious she was with any of them, whether he should take a chance and ask her out.

She leaned toward him, as if straining to hear the words he wasn't saying.

He took a breath and plunged ahead. "Would you like to go to the movies sometime?"

She glided closer still, until they were almost touching. "How about Friday?"

He smiled, relieved that she was making this so easy. "That would be great."

Without giving his next move too much thought, he leaned forward and kissed her. When he stood back, Holly seemed a little stunned and he thought perhaps he had been too forward, though she had certainly kissed him back.

"Okay," he said softly, dragging the word out as he exhaled. "I guess I'll see you on Friday."

As he started to drive away, he saw her still standing in the very same pose, frozen like a statue staring after him. He backed up, put the car in park, and addressed her through the window.

"Are you okay?"

She held up an index finger, indicating for him to wait as she approached the car. She leaned down, took his face in her hands, and kissed him with enthusiasm.

Danny was breathing harder when she let him go. "Wow."

"Friday," she said and with a giggle ran up the steps and disappeared into her house.

Senior prom was approaching quickly and he had no date. Most of the people he knew, had lined up dates long before now. Jimmy mentioned that he was taking Isabelle. Darren would of course be escorting Fran. Denise was going with another of Danny's friends.

Holly mentioned the prom often and seemed to be looking forward to the event. He knew she had been seeing a few boys throughout the school year, but she never mentioned actually having a date for the prom. Since they just began dating, he didn't think he had the right to expect her to go with him, but figured he had nothing to lose by asking. At the end of their third date, when he finally got the courage to ask her, he fumbled around like a fool.

"I figure you probably have lots of offers..." he coughed, cleared his throat, and shoved his hands into his front pockets. "I know I'm late asking this and all...you'll probably say no..." he paused again to take a breath.

Holly laughed at him. "What are you trying to say?"

"I wonder if you would consider going to the prom with me."

She made a little tsk-tsk sound through her teeth and shook her head. "You're right, I have been asked."

"Oh," he said trying not to let his disappointment show.

She laughed and threw up her hands. "Oh, Danny, you are something else! I've been dropping enough hints on your head to give you a concussion."

Now it was his turn to smile. "Are you saying I'm slow on the uptake?"

She held up her thumb and forefinger just millimeters apart, "Maybe just a little."

In contrast to his difficult relationship with Sue Ellen and lopsided desire for Isabelle Long, being with Holly was amazingly easy and uncomplicated. She seemed to genuinely like him. Given that she was one of the smartest students in their school, he sometimes wondered how it was that she did not see him for the flawed person he really was.

Holly was involved in plenty of activities at school, her mother's family furniture business, and her church. She was very feminine but, like his sister Denise, had a tomboyish side as well. She had been riding horses all her of life and competed in barrel racing events. She often fished with her father at the surrounding lakes and joined him on hunting trips as far as Montana. She drove her father's old Jeep up the steepest rocky hills and through the mud with bold delight. In fact, she was the most spirited girl he ever met.

Though her singing voice wasn't anywhere near Isabelle's, Holly loved to sing and even let loose with a bit of yodeling on occasion (which always made him smile).

She had an easy laugh and sharp wit. She was probably firmer in her religious beliefs than him, but not rigid. As his mother would say, Holly Adams was a well-balanced girl.

The one aspect of her interests he could have skipped was a love of Shakespeare. She sometimes quoted entire sonnets to him or wrote them out in calligraphy on fancy paper and left them taped to Purser's bridge where he would find them on his way to work in the morning.

So far, the only true flaw he had discovered was her inability to judge distance. Holly insisted Purser's Bridge was dead center between their homes, a fact he disputed and measured out by odometer with her in the car to prove his point. When Holly informed him she didn't care about the piddling difference (it was actually half a mile further to his house from the bridge), he gave up.

He did everything he could to keep their relationship light, a goal Holly unintentionally made very difficult. She kissed him with such unadulterated passion it left him weak-kneed and wanting more.

THIRTY-SEVEN

Isabelle took a seat between Hal Coulter and David in the high school auditorium to watch Danny, Elliot, and her steady boyfriend Jimmy receive their high school diplomas.

Isabelle and Danny hadn't talked much since the night of Fran's party, though she had tried many times by phone, tracking him down at school, even stopping by the garage a few times, he would not make time for her.

"That's a mighty pretty dress, Isabelle," Hal said.

Like everyone else in Shadow, she knew Hal's reputation with women. He always teased her, but thankfully was appropriate.

"Thank you," she said quietly.

"Our boy is about to move on."

Surprised at the implied affection, she looked to him now. "He'll come back."

Hal grunted. "I don't know Sweetheart. Once he's out of Shadow and gets himself educated all that could change."

As she pondered Hal's statement, Holly Adams arrived and asked David to move down a seat so she could sit next to Isabelle. She and Holly had been good friends since Isabelle first started school in Shadow. She knew probably better than anyone that Holly's infatuation with Danny never wavered over the years. And though she had always insisted that she and Danny were just good friends, Holly's recent connection with him felt like betrayal.

When she saw him at prom with Holly, she felt a stab of jealousy that still pained her. She knew they were dating of course, but after seeing them together she saw their relationship was deeper than she had imagined.

After the ceremony, the school principal sought Danny's parents out to praise Danny for scoring in the top ten percent on his college entrance exams.

"Well, I'll be damned," Hal said.

Isabelle looked around and realized that she and Hal were the only two for whom this was news. Even Holly grinned like the proud girlfriend she was. Isabelle barely restrained the desire to give her a sharp poke in the ribs.

At his parents' home for a modest celebration, Danny accepted Isabelle's embrace, but the emotional barrier he placed between them was wide and deep. After the brief exchange, he excused himself and started away, but she caught his sleeve and held on tight.

"I was really surprised when Principal Haggerty told everyone how smart you are."

"Yeah, who would have suspected I had a brain," he said coolly.

"Did Holly know?"

He tilted his head a little to the right and his eyes narrowed in an angry squint. "Why do you care?"

The uncharacteristically sharp-edged question hurt. Apparently, he had no intention of resuming their easy relationship.

"Are you going to be mad at me forever?"

He looked her in the eye, blasting her with his maddening honesty. "I'm always going to love you Issy. I just won't chase you anymore."

"So, we're still friends then?"

He laughed shortly. "Sure."

THIRTY-EIGHT

Danny started working six days a week for Uncle Hal immediately after graduation. He was out of bed before five, did chores at the ranch, and was at the garage every day including Saturday from seven until after five or later. His scholarship would cover tuition, room and board, but the necessities such as insurance and gas for his car were his responsibility. He needed to make as much money as possible to last through the school year. The grind was tough, but he figured the easy summers of childhood were all behind him now.

He was grateful that his relationship with Hal was better these days. Now that he was almost eighteen, the nine years between them made Hal seem more like an older brother. As they worked together, he continued to stand his ground, earning Hal's respect in the process.

Hal also seemed to appreciate the time and effort he gave to learning the trade of being a mechanic, even asking his opinion on certain projects lately. These days, customers sought Danny out, which was just fine with Hal, as long as the customer wasn't a pretty woman then of course Hal elbowed his way into the conversation. While Hal could light up a bar with his colorful personality, his interest in other people ranged from dislike to downright nonexistent when sober.

At twenty-seven years old, Hal's wild ways were by no means over. He still drank too much and had a steady lineup of women following him up to the apartment over the garage. Still, he had settled down enough to build a profitable business and for that Danny respected his uncle. When it came to being a father, Hal fell a bit short of the Coulter standards since he still went carousing often, leaving Junior in the care of his family or ex-wife Nadine. Otherwise, Hal was good to his son and obviously cared deeply for him.

Between the long hours of work and the great connection Danny had stumbled into with Holly, summer flew by quickly. He seldom saw Isabelle, and summer just didn't seem the same without sharing it with her. She crossed his mind frequently, but he wouldn't allow himself to dwell on the loss.

On his last day at home, he attended Sunday church services and the usual family dinner at his grandparents' house before picking up Holly for a date. She wanted to go to the movies and insisted they sit in the back of the theater where there weren't as many people. She took his hand in hers and kissed his fingers when the movie began.

"I'm really going to miss you," she whispered.

He had been dreading telling everyone goodbye all week. Holly wasn't typically an overly sentimental or outwardly emotional girl, but he heard the catch in her voice.

"Oh, I'll be back," he said lightly.

"Will you write to me?"

He wrapped his arm around her shoulders. "Of course."

She laid her head on his shoulder and he was pretty sure she was crying. He had no idea what to say, so he pulled her closer.

After the movie, he intended to take her home, but she asked to go to the river. They strolled along the river bank for awhile, holding hands, talking about nothing in particular. Upriver from the bridge in a shaded little spot, she stopped and looked up at him. He cringed, fearing the tears were about to begin again.

Holly slid her arms around his waist, stood on her toes and kissed him with enthusiasm. This was full-contact kissing and he responded in kind to the urgent press of her body against his own. When they broke apart, she looked up at him with the dreaded tears in her eyes.

"I hope you don't forget me," she said.

He swallowed hard. "That's not possible," he managed.

~ 365 ~

He wiped a tear from her cheek and kissed her again. They walked hand in hand back to the car and he took her home. He walked her to the door, where they kissed one last time. Holly looked up at him and patted his chest.

"Please go before I start crying again."

He turned to look back when he got to his car, but she was already inside.

He was the first of his siblings to leave Shadow. Dwight and his new bride lived in an apartment in town and were in the process of building their own home on the ranch. Darren still lived at home and worked as a welder.

After supper, he spent some time talking with his father and brothers on the front porch before going up to his room to finish packing. His car was already loaded with everything but this last bag.

He intended to get an early start in the morning and be in Tulsa by nine. He was eager to begin the next phase of his life, to really study art and learn new techniques without all the distractions of life in Shadow.

David wandered in and sat on his own bed, watching him. "I'm really going to miss you."

"But you'll finally have a room all to yourself."

"I liked sharing a room with you Danny."

David was thirteen now and not the frightened little boy he once was. He hadn't climbed into

Danny's bed in over four years. He was still the most sensitive of Danny's brothers and Danny knew he would always have a soft spot for his little brother.

"I'll come home here and there and you'll be sorry you said that."

David grinned. "Probably."

Their mother entered the bedroom and watched as he folded a T-shirt. "Isabelle is downstairs."

He groaned and she put her hands on her hips. "I know saying goodbye to everybody is hard, but you best suck it up and take care of business."

She took the shirt from his hands, flipped it this way and that, then rolled it into a tight little tube, and held it out to him. "If you do it like this they won't get wrinkled."

"Well, it is just a T-shirt…"

She wagged a finger at him. "Respect yourself Daniel. I don't want you walking around looking like those hippies I see on the TV."

He couldn't help but smile at her. "I'm going to miss you Mama."

Her eyes watered and her face flushed. "I'll wager not half as much as I'll miss you."

She patted his face and gave him a little nudge. "I'll finish packing these things on your bed. Go on downstairs and say goodbye to Isabelle."

Danny dropped the shirt in his suitcase and headed downstairs, steeling himself for the discomfort of facing Isabelle.

After a long summer with very little contact, Isabelle had hoped all week that Danny would call and say he wanted to get together before leaving for Tulsa. When the hours of his last day at home wound down and he still hadn't contacted her, she grew desperate and drove over to the Coulter ranch.

While Caroline went to get Danny, Isabelle waited impatiently in the kitchen with Denise, attempting to make small talk and behave casually. Inside, her thoughts flip-flopped from hurt to anger to fear. When he finally came through the swinging kitchen door, she found she had to fight back tears.

"Miss Issy-Belle," he said lightly.

"I hope you don't mind that I came to say goodbye."

He leaned against the kitchen sink and crossed his arms over his chest. "Of course not."

She pushed a container of cookies across the table. "Mama Rose made you some of those chocolate chip cookies you like."

He actually smiled. "Please tell her thank you."

An awkward silence filled the room and Denise rose from her chair. "I'll leave you two to talk. See you later Isabelle."

When the swinging door closed behind Denise, Isabelle stood. "Will you take a walk with me?"

"Sure," he said with a shrug.

Once they were out of the house, walking in the warm night air, Isabelle felt easier. "Are you leaving early tomorrow?"

"I plan on getting on the road by six-thirty. Why?"

"I was just curious," she said. "I told Grandma you were going to school up there. She hopes that you will come by and see her sometime."

"I'll definitely go see her when I can. I like your grandmother."

"I'm going to miss you so much Danny," she said quietly.

"I'll be back."

She couldn't bear what was going unsaid anymore. She stopped short. "I don't want you to leave like this!"

He drew back, and sighed loudly. "Like what?"

"As if you and I were never friends, like there isn't any room for me in your life anymore."

"We're still friends," he countered.

"Not like we were."

"Nope."

She slapped his arm. "Stop it."

"You stop it!" he came back hotly.

"You're so mean," she said, her voice cracking.

He sighed again. "I just can't be that little boy giving you what you need anymore Issy."

Sobbing, she ran back to her car, jumped in, and started the engine. Switching on the headlights she swung the car out of his parents drive and found him still standing in the middle of the road.

Isabelle mashed down on the brake and the Mustang slid to a halt. She stuck her head out the window. "Move!"

He stepped to the side and she raced past him leaving a trail of dust for him to choke on.

After a very restless night, Danny showered, dressed, ate breakfast with his parents, shook his father's hand, hugged his crying mother, and climbed into his car at a little after six.

At the end of the ranch road, he sat idling at the blacktop with his conscience nagging him. Instead of turning left toward the bridge, he turned the car around and went back to the house for one more thing.

Hearing him come through the front door, his mother came out of the kitchen as he headed upstairs to his room.

"What are you doing back?"

"I forgot something."

Minutes later, he pulled up in front of Isabelle's home. Her father was headed toward the stables, but approached the car as Danny stepped out.

"Isabelle's still sleeping," Marshall said.

"Yes, sir, I figured she would be." He turned to the interior of his car and lifted a small painting. "I just wanted to give her something before I took off."

Marshall accepted the painting from his hands and gave it a long look. Raising his head again, there were tears in his eyes.

"This will mean a lot to her Danny."

"Please tell her…" he paused, astonished to find the words *I love her* balanced on his tongue.

Marshall's chin jutted forward a bit as he peered at Danny, waiting.

"Tell her I'll see her at Thanksgiving," Danny said finally.

Marshall nodded solemnly and held out his hand. "Good luck up there."

As he approached Purser's Bridge, he spotted a white envelope attached to an end support, right where Holly always left them. He plucked the envelope from the beam, but the brilliance of the sunrise drew his attention.

He climbed onto the side of the bridge to view the splendor. The morning sun illuminated the rolling, low-ceiled clouds with glorious shades of purple, red, and gold.

"Hallelujah," he whispered.

He would miss his family, this land, and his life here, but the possibilities before him were electrifying. He was going to be an artist. He jumped back to the surface of the bridge and climbed into his car, opening the envelope with a bit of trepidation. To his relief, Holly hadn't left another sonnet. Better yet, this was no mushy love letter, which would have been entirely atypical of her anyway. Instead, she had inscribed a quote on her fanciest paper:

> I was born upon thy bank river
> My blood flows in thy stream
> And thou meanderest forever
> At the bottom of my dream
> ~ Henry David Thoreau ~

The river and I will be waiting for you to come back to us.

Love,
Holly

He folded the letter, slipped it back into the envelope, and left Shadow with a big smile.

ACKNOWLEDGEMENTS

A HEARTFELT THANK YOU TO MIKE TIBBS AND COURTNEY WINKLER FOR THEIR TIME READING, EDITING, AND INSIGHTFUL SUGGESTIONS TO ENHANCE THE QUALITY AND CHARACTER OF THIS BOOK.

SPECIAL THANKS TO MIKE FOR THE GREAT TRIP TO BEAUTIFUL KIAMICHI COUNTRY FOR RESEARCH AND FOR ALWAYS BEING SO SUPPORTIVE AND PATIENT.
YOU ARE A TRUE PARTNER AND MY GIFT.

ABOUT THE AUTHOR

Rhonda Tibbs has lived throughout the United States, Japan, and Malaysia. She now lives in Illinois with her husband.